SECRETS OF THE
WEIRD

A NOVEL OF TRANSFORMATIONAL HORROR

CHAD STROUP

GREY MATTER
P R E S S

CHICAGO

SECRETS OF THE WEIRD
ISBN-13: 978-1-940658-80-3
ISBN-10: 1-940658-80-2
Grey Matter Press First Trade Paperback Edition - July 2017

Copyright © 2017 Chad Stroup
Book Design Copyright © 2017 Grey Matter Press
Cover Design Copyright © 2017 Grey Matter Press
Interior Illustrations © 2017 John Kenzie

GREY MATTER
P R E S S

CHICAGO

Novel Website
secretsoftheweird.com

Grey Matter Press
greymatterpress.com

Grey Matter Press on Facebook
facebook.com/greymatterpress

To all the freaks, queers and misfits of the world.
Stay strong. Keep fighting.
When times are dark, never forget there are those
who will stand alongside you and join the battle
when you need them most.

SECRETS OF THE
WEIRD

EMBRACE THE TRANSFORMATION

CHAPTER ONE

TRIXIE LOATHED HER PENIS.

Vile epidermal licorice that dangled between her stick-figure legs.

Painful to look at, alien compared to the rest of her body, an unfortunate and unavoidable sight whenever she was naked.

No matter how much she skewed her vision, the aberration remained.

Taunting.

Tormenting.

She despised this piece of herself with such intensity she wished it could be banished from her body. Even better, if she could crawl back into the womb and somehow have it retroactively removed. Revisionist Reassignment Surgery. She'd have to look into that.

For lonely months on end, she had kept a dull box cutter in the top drawer of her dresser, hidden between the unorganized piles of underwear and socks. Now her slightly overlarge, unalterable hands clutched the hilt at a crooked angle, applying pressure to her shaft. The blade left a temporary and near-painless indentation. No blood was yet to be drawn. Though she had been tempted many times, Trixie could never summon the courage—or stupidity—to follow through with her threats against her own body.

She was only successful at convincing herself it was just useless meat.

And meat is temporary.

Meat is malleable. Edible. Organic matter on the road to eventual rot.

Trixie stole the blade away from her sex, let it drop to the ancient linoleum floor with an echoing clang. She caught her fractured reflection in the full-length mirror and tried her best to ignore it. A reflection was a keeper of secrets. It could either be one's most trusted confidant or most venomous enemy. Tonight this distorted version of herself was a fair-weather friend at best.

Still, the tiniest bit of positivity poked its way into her thoughts. Between the taped-up cracks, and around the edges of spotted glass, she was able to force the traces of her true self to come out of hiding. If she shifted her body just right, one of the largest cracks in the mirror obscured her view of the awful appendage. And Trixie felt picture perfect.

As a girl, her male genitals were just a technicality, a sick practical joke played by that bitch Mother Nature. A beautiful contradiction, Trixie had become an expert in the art of lying to herself.

Self-critical as she could be, Trixie still tried to convince herself that, on her best days, she looked rather fetching despite all the hell-in-heels she had been through. Pale, velvety flesh without an ounce of sun damage. A hairless, smooth form like an unfinished marble statue, just a few chips away from impeccable completion. Almond eyes and auburn hair with awkward bangs. Her pillow lips assured no men ever batted their eyes in disbelief when they gazed in her direction. Even without her mastery of hair and makeup, there was very little about her that was noticeably male anymore. She was quite passable as a woman.

Not stunning necessarily.

Not supermodel gorgeous.

Definitely attractive enough to be someone's third-place trophy.

She honestly didn't turn heads on a daily basis, but blending in as just another woman in the crowd wasn't the worst thing in the world. Closer to a blessing, really.

Trixie plucked two heart-shaped pills from a plastic baggie. Sweet Candy. The convenient, affordable solution for avoiding one's problems. She pinched the pills between her fingers and came close to tossing them into her mouth, but decided at the last second that she would skip the high tonight, save them for when she *really* needed them. Money was tight and she couldn't afford even a weekly dose of this artificial heaven. She placed the Sweet Candy back in the baggie and shoved it into the cabinet beneath the sink, in the dank space behind the toilet paper and drain cleaner.

She put on a top and some jeans and decided watching TV was a better option than wallowing in self-pity. As she entered the living room, the familiar bleating of car alarms and screams from intoxicated thrill seekers trickled in through the open window. Federico, her near-gaunt calico cat, was perched on the sill, facing outdoors. Same as most nights. He mewed a primal tune, calling to the rodents of the deceptively vapid city of Sweetville. Tacky fluorescent lights from the clubs, all-night delis and convenience stores below—streams of which could be seen even from the third floor—added to the low budget feline music video.

"Rico, baby," Trixie whispered. "What's got you so riled up tonight, huh?" She stroked the coarse fur behind his ears and he relaxed, letting the weight of his head lean lovingly into her hand. She gently nudged the cat, he hopped to the floor and Trixie closed the window. "Sorry, hon. I know that's your favorite spot, but I *really* don't want to listen to all that business out there. It's depressing."

Federico offered a strange, long purr, as if in agreement. He squeezed between and around her legs in his patented figure eight.

Now with the cacophonous sounds of the city muted, Trixie became acutely aware of how loud the television was. A rerun of Bill Clinton's inaugural address from the night before. *Boring.* She searched for the remote control, found it wedged between the couch cushions and changed the channel. A helmet of feathered newscaster hair filled the screen. Somewhere in the vicinity of that coiffure was a mouth, a voice following along with the teleprompter.

"*...today marks the two-year anniversary of his passing. Since then, disciples of the late Dr. Dorian Wylde have been roaming the streets of Sweetville in an attempt to convert the general public to their peculiar cause. Wylde, a former plastic surgeon, later became the widely acclaimed creator of the miracle diet drug Witherix. With strict rules regarding weekly fasting...*"

Trixie changed the channel again. More news. This time the newscaster was a woman whose makeup was so thick her face was nearly devoid of honest expression.

"...yet another victim of a violent crime referred to as 'curb stomping' has been discovered in downtown. The victim, whose name has not been released, is currently in critical condition at Sweetville Mercy. A local fascist skinhead youth gang is suspected of..."

Trixie shook her head and clicked the television off, opting for the bedroom and the more soothing sounds of the Cocteau Twins instead. She grabbed the *Heaven or Las Vegas* CD off the top of the speaker and inserted it into her disc changer. She plopped onto her bed, just a mattress and box spring with no frame. The ethereal dream world of "Cherry-Coloured Funk" immediately calmed her.

Federico now tiptoed along the edges of an antique vanity table, the only piece of furniture she owned that was worth more than a garage sale haggle. She had fallen in love with it when she spotted it in the window of Auntie Teek's Furniture and Curiosities and spent an entire week's pay on it. She went a little hungrier than usual that month, but she did not regret it in the least.

The CD had been playing for God knows how long when a crash echoed from the living room.

"Rico, sweetie? Where are you?" she called out in a groggy voice. She whistled, made clicking sounds with her tongue and teeth. Still no answer.

The apartment was only a hair above 500 square feet, so it wouldn't take long to track him down, unless he had managed to discover yet another hiding spot. Under the couch, inside a cupboard, curled in a shoebox in the closet. She wasn't really in the mood for feline games, but would humor him for a few moments if that's what it took.

Trixie entered the living room and felt a wintry breeze that caused her to shiver. She glanced over to the window and saw it was again wide open, the curtains writhing. The noise outside had died down considerably, most likely having moved inside the nightclubs, and Federico was gone.

She glanced out the window and could only see the clusterfuck of nightlife traffic below. Federico always returned faithfully if he managed to escape, but Trixie still couldn't help but worry. A street cat by birth but house cat at heart, he at least still had his claws and could hold his own in a fight. Federico mauled mice like an abstract artist attacked a canvas. Sometimes his homecoming included the broken body of an unfortunate rodent. Not exactly a pleasant work of art.

Trixie closed the window three-quarters of the way, leaving just enough room for him to squeeze through when he returned. She spun around on one foot, felt for the light switch and flipped it on. One of the old bulbs in the ceiling fan made a brief *POP* as it perished—the third one this month—and she made a mental note to have her landlord call an electrician.

She heard a scratching sound coming from somewhere in the center of the room. Once she focused her eyes, the fan's remaining dull bulb illuminated something that made her skin crawl.

Someone was sitting on her couch.

October 20, 1988

Hi, Miss Diary. It's me Trixie. Miss me much?

So I'm fifteen now. Wow, right? Well, almost sixteen I guess. More than halfway there. Whatever. Close enough. I've decided that the name ~~Thomas~~ pretty much needs to be obliterated from my thoughts. Only prob is that it's forced upon me on a daily basis. Just a falsely birthed boy code that needs to be cracked and discarded so I can flourish as a woman. Eventually.

So I've been hanging out with this boy Aron. He's a senior over at Sweetville West. He's kind of a babe, minus the "kind of." Has these baby blue eyes that make me melt into a puddle of goo. Drives a hot red Camaro. He's almost like a jock type, except he doesn't play any sports as far as I know. Does that even make sense? I guess I like that. Maybe. I dunno. I'll only see him when I'm dressed up, natch.

He knows the scoop, I guess. I think. I didn't actually *tell* him The Truth. But I know he knows. He's not blind. I'm not super passable yet, but as long as no one's really paying attention to us he doesn't mind hanging out with me in public. Grabbing some lunch or whatever. Not at the places his friends hang out, though. That's the kicker. He'll hold hands and make out with me if we're hidden down in some deep forgotten crevice of Graves Park. That place is a little on the gross side, minus the "little" part, but it's not like we can go to either of our houses.

I suppose it's a start. Better than being lonely. Plus, he seems to be okay with...everything? I won't really know until things really happen between us. Like, all the way happen. I want to do so many bad, bad things with this boy. Sue me.

Speaking of Graves Park, I keep sneaking away from home on the weekends whenever I get the chance, braving the sticky seats and urine smells of Bus 13 so I can scope out the uncharted streets of downtown Sweetville on my own. It's like another universe from the 'burbs. Well, calling my neighborhood "the 'burbs" is being pretty generous. More like the public restroom of the 'burbs. If you've got a solid four walls and a working roof then you're like royalty around here. Our house is a little newer than most. Guess that makes me the Princess Di of East Sweetville. I really need a place to call my own, a little chunk of the world that's willing to accept me for who I am and let me have my space. I deserve that, don't I?

Still dealing with Mom's illness. Not getting any better. Hank, or Dad—whatever the hell you want to call him—has been pretty much useless. Don't really feel like talking about that stuff right now. Maybe next time, Miss Diary. Don't put money on that, though.

CHAPTER TWO

TRIXIE WAS A FRAIL, TERRIFIED GLACIER. She clamped her eyes shut for two seconds, then unglued them again, hoping the illusion would fade. It didn't. The stranger still sat on her couch, his back to her. There was an odd, hunched shape about him. Presumably the figure was a man, but she of all people knew better than to make these sorts of judgments. Gender coding without damned good proof tended to be problematic.

The intruder didn't move.

Trixie was so gripped with fear that she dared not utter a peep, even though she felt like she could be a major candidate for Scream Queen of the Year if she were allowed to give the audition right this second.

Maybe he was asleep. Maybe he hadn't noticed the light. Maybe she could creep by him unseen.

She decided these were birdbrained assumptions, as what sort of an intruder worth his salt would take the initiative to break into someone's apartment only to take a nap? She could see the headline now: NAP-PING BURGLAR STRIKES DOWNTOWN SWEETVILLE. LOCK UP YOUR PILLOWS AND BLANKIES. She supposed it was possible. She'd certainly encountered stranger things in Sweetville.

However, the man hadn't moved, so maybe the odds were still on her side. Time for Trixie to tiptoe to the kitchen, grab the biggest, sharpest, scariest knife. Maybe even dash back to the bedroom to dial 911, lock her door and prepare for the worst. Her building lacked a properly working fire escape, so it would not be in the best interest of her bones to attempt to flee via the window. The front door was still padlocked as she had left it, but that also wasn't an option because she would have to pass right in front of the intruder. It was clear she didn't have many options. The knife idea seemed most useful. She took a deep breath and made two cautious steps toward the kitchen.

"I'd rather you not attempt anything rash, sweetness," the man said, his back still turned to her.

Trixie released the scream that had been tickling at her throat.

Tears formed at the corners of her eyes and her body quivered. Her bare toes dug into the shag carpet and brushed against long-lost crumbs and fingernail clippings. She nibbled at the corner of her lip, trying to maintain her composure.

"Let's sit and have a little chat," he said, patting the open seat next to him. "Do you have any Chardonnay, perchance? I'm parched beyond belief. I'll certainly accept some Sauvignon Blanc if that's all you have, but really I'm hoping for something more, er, *voluptuous*."

Trixie couldn't trace the accent in his voice. It was generically Eastern European, if Poland was south of Hades. Gruff and deep. There was a rasp to his words that chilled her far more than the wind that still crept through the window. It was a sound somewhere between a whistle and a gargle.

"Uh...I don't have any..."

He turned and cocked his head. His profile was a Picasso.

Trixie's body shook, her eyes darting, legs scooting. She inched toward the kitchen, wishing she had the telekinetic abilities of a tragic prom queen so she could send a knife flying from the kitchen into her hand.

"Please don't move. I'm not planning to harm you. I absolutely loathe unnecessary violence." He paused as if he had forgotten a crucial sequence in the middle of a public speech. "Conversely, I do have an affinity for violence that *is* necessary. Though, realistically, I have enough people in my employ to take care of that for me. Why exert such effort when it's not required?"

He finally got up from his stolen seat, revealing he was barely taller than the back of the second-hand sofa. Not much more than a menacing midget, really. Half a threat.

Trixie involuntarily let loose an inappropriate laugh that had been welling up inside her.

His body was too wide for such a small frame—like a low-rent Augustus Gloop who had never grown out of his awkward phase. He wore a thick, olive pea coat and a dusty pork pie hat that kept his facial features somewhat hidden, as well as a pair of leather elevator shoes that offered him an extra inch or two. After a momentary stare-off, he waddled around the arm of the couch to stand in front of her, his face now visible beneath the remaining dim bulb and the patches of neon light floating into the apartment.

His eyes glowed with a purple hue, and his face was marred by symmetrical scarification that looked like it might have been professionally done. An epidermal road map? But to where? The flickering light from the ceiling highlighted the wicked pockmarks that were as grotesque as they were fascinating.

He extended a gnarled, bloated hand. The tips of his never-groomed nails glistened at the end of each scaly, bulbous finger. His hand was bejeweled with a copper bracelet containing comically large turquoise stones, a watch with a face the size of a small planet, and rings with sparkling sapphires and spikes.

"Pardon my manners. You can call me Kast," he said. "That's with a K, mind you. I don't want you thinking you can sign 'Get Well Soon' on my forehead." He chortled at his own funny.

Trixie was silent. Her brain screamed, but her voice was dry and refused to cooperate.

"Well, I saw your foul feline on the way in. I'm confident that it hasn't done anything with your tongue. Detestable creature. You'll be better off if it never returns. I truly hope you had him fixed. Too many feral beasts in this city. Poison them all and let an Egyptian god sort them out, if you want my honest opinion."

She stared at Kast in shock, unable to believe any of this was real.

"Please," Kast said, extending his hand to invite her to her own couch, "come sit with me. Let us chat."

"What the hell do you want? Why are you in my apartment? How did you—" Trixie balled her fists, struggling to appear tough. "I don't have anything worth any money here. Go rob someone up in the Sweethills."

"Don't fret, pet. I know who you are. I'm relatively aware of your finances. You didn't choose this apartment for its amenities and fabulous view. Audrey's a nice old gal, and she makes a superb rhubarb pie, but I know she can't afford to pay her employees the big bucks."

Trixie gulped, realizing she had been watched, but for how long? And why?

"And I'm surely polite enough to ask before I take anyone's property, always promptly returned," he said. "Try not to take this personally, but I consider my tastes to be a smidge more highbrow. I doubt you'd have anything I'd be interested in. I'm merely here for a proposition."

Trixie felt like she had taken a sip from milk that was a week past its due date.

"I don't... I'm not sure who you've been talking to, but I don't do that anymore," she said. "It's been well over a year since... I'm a totally different girl now. God, I bet Greyson and Orin put you up to this. They did, didn't they? Don't believe anything the Zane brothers have been—"

The dwarf squealed and held one deformed finger to his weather-beaten lips.

"—telling you." Her voice dropped to a murmur.

"Oh, dear. Nonononono. You misunderstand me. Pardon my ambiguity. I did not intend for *that* sort of interpretation. Plus, as it stands, you are not my, *ahem*, type."

She swallowed what little saliva remained in her throat. She could have sworn Kast had nodded his head in the direction of her crotch. He *knew*. Somehow he knew. That pesky penis, always getting in the damned way of nearly every moment of her life. Constantly haunting her. A daily reminder that she was still in her pupal stage.

Trixie felt she deserved to have the facts about her birth remain unknown unless the words came from her very own lips. Even then, she preferred The Truth remain locked away. The combination misplaced, buried in a long-forgotten time capsule. It was her right as a woman, even if it had taken her an enormous amount of work to get to this point—or, perhaps, *because* of this very fact. She wondered who could have—who *would* have—violated her secret. She was now certain that the Zane brothers were behind this invasion of her privacy. They had been disappointed when she ended their little agreement. Even though this part of her past was more recent than she cared to admit, after Ms. Jessica had helped her get that first real, respectable job at MOXY, Trixie felt her old, less desirable ways of moneymaking had become obsolete. Her old life was a first draft that had been so revised and fine-tuned that the memories may as well have belonged to someone else.

"I don't under—"

"Oh, and by the way, I apologize for polishing off your spaghetti leftovers," Kast said. "But I was positively famished. I hope you don't mind. I guess that's the exception that proves my ask-before-borrow rule. However, I *do* still need something dry to wash out my gullet if you wouldn't mind. Quite good pasta, I must say, even straight from the refrigerator. Was that from Mad Mario's? What an exquisite little Italian deli."

Trixie ignored his question and suppressed a contemptuous frown. She had been saving the spaghetti for tomorrow's lunch.

"Well, wherever it was from," Kast continued, "I could have easily consumed twice as much. Of course, *they* wouldn't even have a taste."

Trixie's face twisted into a scowl. She was through being scared. Now she was just plain pissed.

"Diets. My, oh my," Kast said, tapping at his belly. "Not for me at all. I'm a man who loves a hearty meal. But, I digress. I come to represent some business partners from Lower Sweetville. We are at liberty to offer you something you so desperately want."

Kast's use of "they" and "we" was causing Trixie a great deal of confusion, and he noticed the befuddlement on her face.

"Oh, my etiquette is all out of sync tonight. Allow me to introduce you to my associates. Security!" Kast made a quick golf clap and, before Trixie had time to respond, two thin forms slithered from the shadows. Chimerical camouflage that had kept them hidden among the curtains no longer applied.

At first, Trixie thought her mind was playing tricks. But she remembered she had not dropped any Sweet Candy that evening, so there was nothing preventing the apparitions from being real. She figured out quickly, though, who the freakish beings were.

The Withering Wyldes.

Or, at least, a couple of them.

Not that anyone could tell one from the other. Not that they were even considered individuals anymore. Not that there was really a convenient singular form for referencing them.

Trixie wondered what they could possibly want with her. She had never signed one of their many petitions. She had never even made eye contact with them on the street, much less given them any donations for their cause.

They whispered and hissed syllables in a tongue she didn't recognize. The sounds that passed through their pale, chapped lips made her giddy. And she was unable to resist the caress of their clammy, vampirish fingers as they formed gentle cuffs around her wrists.

Like the others of their kind, these Withering Wyldes were six feet tall and some change, one hundred pounds, give or take. Their emaciated frames gave them the appearance of phasmids with delusions of humanity. Flesh a near translucent blue, highlighting their skeletal forms. Black, beady button eyes glimmered on their faces, just above barely-existent noses. Impossibly wide clownish grins revealed teeth caked with plaque. Long, patchy tufts of matted hair adorned a few spots on their long, thin heads and other random body parts. They were vivid, phantasmic dreams that could be touched. Anti-Adonises, yet somehow still attractive.

Of course, that may have been one of their many little tricks.

Trixie turned away from the Withering Wyldes. Though she could no longer see their bastardized bodies, she could still smell them. A distinct cinnamon-meets-vanilla aroma floated through the apartment.

Not at all unpleasant.

Soothing.

Drugging.

Lovely.

Almost euphoric, it was the safest Trixie had ever felt. Like Sweet Candy laced with dopamine. She tried to shake off these thoughts but then released her inhibitions and welcomed the loss of control. She felt the tips of dreams slowly forming.

The Withering Wyldes removed their sinewy hands, leaving faint marks around her wrists like dollar-store friendship bracelets. Trixie returned to reality but with less resistance to her predicament.

"There now," Kast said. "All nice and calm. Nothing like a little pick-me-up, especially when it's all-natural. I may not be Monty Hall, but let's make a deal, shall we?" More impish laughter. Again, he seemed to find himself far more entertaining than Trixie did. But the way Trixie was feeling, how relaxed she had become as a result of being touched by the Withering Wyldes, she almost wanted to humor him.

Almost, but not quite.

She tried to regain control of her senses. Her rational mind begged for her to fight the high and she kicked awkwardly in Kast's general direction.

"Don't force me to get saucy with you, now, love," he said. "I may be small and portly, but I still have ways to cause you grief, if need be. Or to pay someone else to do my dirty work for me." As much as he attempted the contrary, his voice became more nefarious with every word.

Trixie took a deep, meditative breath and locked eyes with Kast. "I don't really have a choice, do I?"

"Well, now, of course you do. Don't be silly. I think you'll be pleased with what we have to offer." He fiddled around with the pockets in the inner lining of his pea coat. "Now where did I put that godforsaken note?"

One of the Withering Wyldes whispered in his ear. Trixie tried to decipher the gibberish. No luck. No English subtitles available. Kast nodded and grumbled back to his lackey.

"Ah, yes, of course. Thank you." Kast removed his hat, revealing a lumpy, balding head topped with protrusions that resembled a miniature Stonehenge. Liver spots dotted his scalp. A folded piece of paper fell from his hat and floated to the floor. He picked it up, unfolded it and squinted with irritated eyes. He pulled a pair of reading glasses from another of the seemingly endless pockets in his coat, put them on and read the paper again with considerably less frustration. Finally turning the paper right-side up, he smiled and held it out to Trixie, whose hands stayed glued to her sides.

"Really, dear Trixie. Don't you trust me?"

October 27, 1988

Oh. My. God. Guess what, Diary? Me and Aron, we totally had...

♥♥♥

Yeah, that.

I don't know if I can even write about this.

I think I might be in love.

A + T. Yum.

I know what I'm talking about, so you just need to read my mind. I'm not going to write it, Miss Diary, so get over it. I've gotta have some sort of privacy, even around you.

It's rare I can shut my yap for this long, but this is so personal I don't even think I care to share it with you. Some things probably need to stay secret.

November 4, 1988

Aron is the shittiest scum-sucking piggiest prick in all of Sweet-ville! No, the whole damned world!

Miss Diary, I'm so glad you're here to listen to me. You're not going to believe what happened! I ditched class today to go surprise him over at Sweetville West. I looked so fucking cute for once, too! A black halter, grey cardigan, baby-blue ruffled skater skirt, black leggings—yes, it fucking matters what I was wearing! I was really trying to make him love me today! I even showed up with a can of Jolt Cola for him, since I know that's his favorite.

And what did that asshole do?

Ugh. I can barely bring myself to tell you.

I timed it perfectly for their lunchtime, and I found Aron hanging out with his buddies on the bleachers. I waved to him and I know he saw me. I guess in retrospect it would have been better if all he did was ignore me. But no, it was so much worse than I ever could have imagined.

This is so hard for me, Miss Diary.

I got up to where they were sitting and said, "Hey babe," or something equally dumb. It's all kind of blurry now. One of the guys he was with, some goober lunkhead in one of those preppie Izod shirts—fuck you, you stupid little alligator—pointed at me and laughed, then did the same to Aron. Then one of the other jerks said, "Who's this homo?"

If Aron had been a real stand-up guy, and the kind of boyfriend a girl like me deserves, he would have defended me. Wouldn't have necessarily required socking his pals in the gut, but that would have been mega bonus points. I would have made it worth his while. You know what I mean?

Anyway, he pretty much did the opposite.

He told them I was some fucking sissy that keeps following him around.

I really didn't know what to do. Maybe I'm a complete idiot, but I really wasn't expecting that! I think I was strong for a few seconds. My eyes weren't quite wet yet, but the dam was ready to break.

I looked right at Aron and said something he already knew, that he told me he loved me last week when we were at Graves Park. Then I whispered, "You took my virginity." Even though it was a whisper, I think his friends heard me. God, I hope they fucking did! I think I may have intentionally made that whisper a little louder just so Aron could suffer some humiliation, too. I couldn't hold back the waterworks after that.

His monkey goon crew turned into a pack of hyenas. Their laughs were demonic!

Aron looked like he was either going to puke or Hulk out. He called me a psycho faggot, told me to leave him alone.

I could see it in his eyes. He hated me with raw passion. The laughs were forced and mocking.

Izod Guy said, "Yeah, beat it, queer."

Real original, fucknuts.

I stood my ground for a few more seconds until Aron started jabbing his finger into my chest. It felt like rubber bullets. I was about to turn around and get the hell out of there but then he shoved me! It was raining a little today and I fell right in a fucking puddle. Before I could get up, he kicked me in the stomach. Hard. Then he put all of his weight on me and pressed my face into the mud. I could barely breathe. He leaned in close and said something I'll never forget, "If I ever see you again, if you ever spread lies about me like that again, I will beat the fucking shit out of you. And that's if you're lucky!"

I don't think I've ever been so mortified before, and I hope nothing in life ever feels lower than this moment. I don't know how it even could. It's got to get better than this, right?

When are people going to understand that I'm not gay? I don't want anyone to be attracted to my boy parts. I HATE THEM! I'd cut them off myself if I knew I wouldn't bleed to death. I'm a girl. I'm supposed to be a girl.

How can I ever trust someone with my heart again?

Life's pretty much over.

CHAPTER THREE

CIVILIZED CANNIBALS RAGED in a living room in Doomston, a small town an hour southeast of Sweetville. Couches, recliners and end tables were stacked against the walls like Legos that didn't quite fit. Mace Akers savaged his guitar with inept grace, his fingers bleeding, the broken high E string dangling and whipping through the air. Between three-chord faux-wanking, awkward posturing and making Popeye faces, Mace managed to squeak out some raw vocals into the dented microphone of the practice room-sized Public Address System. A half-full beer can soared through the air, barely missing his head. Droplets freckled his face and merged with his sweat.

"Do that again and I'll chew your ear off. I prefer my booze in the bottle anyway," Mace said. "Aluminum'll give you Alzheimer's. This is the last song, you fuckos. It's about the hypocrisies of our American legal system. Yeah, you over there by the coffee table, with the crappy home-made circle-A tattoo. You know what the fuck I'm talking about. Back up your beliefs with actions. This song's called 'False Jurisprudence.' ONE-TWO-THREE. GO!"

Steve London shot Mace a confused look, clicked his sticks four times, thrashed his kit in rapid fire 4/4 time like a shirtless man possessed. He made Animal from *The Muppet Show* look professionally trained. His arms blurred so quickly across the toms that they appeared to be softly coasting.

Christopher Faith barely kept the bass guitar portion of the song from falling apart. The notes he hit rang true due to sheer muscle memory. He was lost in a musical vortex, playing with his back to the audience. All anyone in the crowd could see of him was the image on his t-shirt—a blurry photo of children near water, smokestacks looming behind, sandwiched by the words "All the Waste I See, All the Waste I'll Never Be." Remnants of a black X, weathered away by sweat and fury, marked the tops of each of his hands. He did not need the audience, only the ferocity of the sound.

The sparse crowd ate up Civilized Cannibals' short set like a five-course meal. The living room could only handle so much, but still allowed for a modest circle pit. The final song ended abruptly. For a few obnoxious seconds, unintentional feedback seared through the space. Mace kicked the side of his amp with his combat boots and the feedback ceased. Civilized Cannibals packed up their gear without missing a beat, and the toothy kid who set up the show handed Mace twenty-five bucks that had been collected in a hat—five of which turned out to be Monopoly money. Outside, from the back of their van, the band sold five home-dubbed demo tapes and eight patches for a dollar apiece.

"Hey guys," Mace said, counting their stash. "We made out like gangbusters. Let's fill up the tank and grab some grub before we head home."

"Sounds good to me," Christopher said, wiping his sweaty hair out of his face.

"Okay," Steve said. "I gotta piss first, though."

The house party pressed on long after they hit the highway.

* * *

Audrey's Diner. Not the flashiest joint in Sweetville. Located on the outskirts of town, the first sign of any civilization when arriving from the comparatively rural Doomston, and mostly patronized by the odd trucker and wayward traveler. The pastel-pink tiled walls were usually distracting enough to mask the sub-par daily specials. The '50s décor was kitschy enough that most patrons were willing to ignore the occasional cockroach that might skitter across the floor, searching for its next sugary crumb. The floor was a black-and-white checkerboard in need of a solid mopping. And the walls were adorned with photographs of movie stars from the era, complete with forged autographs.

The band entered the diner, high from the gig and on the brink of more conventional intoxication—aside from Christopher, who was sober as a preacher on Sunday. A plump woman with clownish proportions of makeup greeted them with a practiced smile, grabbed three peeling laminated menus and led them to an open booth—of which there were many. Though Audrey's was open twenty-four hours, 1:30 in the morning was not exactly the time to be expecting a pocketful of tips.

"Take your seats, fellas," she said. "Just a warning, don't bother ordering the soup of the day. We're fresh out of bouillon."

The vinyl seats made jarring raspberry noises as Christopher slid into the booth. Steve's chain wallet snagged on the badly taped tears in the upholstery, preventing Mace from taking his seat.

"C'mon, you momohead," Mace said as he shoved him. "Move it or lose it."

"Shut it, assface. I'm stuck." Steve shook himself loose after minimal effort.

A lithe waitress trotted over to their table to take orders. The hue of her pink uniform matched the walls so closely that she looked like a floating, disembodied set of legs, arms and head.

Christopher shook his head in embarrassment, tried not to make eye contact with her. It seemed his bandmates increased their mortification capabilities whenever they were within 500 feet of a female. Thankfully, she was busy setting the table. When Christopher finally looked over at her, she darted her eyes in his direction and offered him a sly smile.

"Hiya, boys," the waitress said. "Today's special is pigs in a blanket with a side of scrambled eggs." Christopher had never heard such an alluring voice exit a woman's mouth. Tone, octaves, cadence—all beautifully original.

"I'm confused," Steve said. "Does that mean it's actually yesterday's special carried over? Or did it just start at midnight and is going for the rest of the day?"

"I'll let you in on a little secret," the waitress whispered. "We don't really rotate our specials all that often." Steve seemed satisfied by this response.

In his head, Christopher became Mr. Smooth. *Hey, I don't really know these jerks. Why are they even at my table? How about you take a ten-minute break and we get to know each other over a chocolate shake? My treat.* Externally, he just shrugged. When it came to the right things to say, his mind was a perfectly scripted film, his reality a tad lackluster.

"So, Trixie, huh? That's a funny name." This was Mace, noting the nametag pinned to her uniform, right above her breast. Mace was physically imposing—six foot four, two hundred forty pounds, with a face chiseled like a freshly laid brick. Even when he was being friendly he was in danger of coming off as a brute. Wearing a shirt with a giant FUCK written on it didn't help his case much, even if the word directly below it was RACISM.

"Um…my parents were big *Honeymooners* fans," she replied.

"Bang, zoom!" Steve, who was normally silent, had become more charismatically animated post-gig. A little booze went a long way with him. Christopher wondered why his strange friend had brought his skateboard inside the diner even though he had not set foot on it that entire night. He was like Linus with his security blanket. He nervously spun the wheels with his hand. The bearings sounded shot. Steve was a gaunt young man. Some might argue he considered skeletons to be the ideal body type. When Civilized Cannibals were playing, it was often difficult to tell the difference between his arms and the drumsticks. This was not for the lack of trying, though. Steve was like a human garbage disposal. He ate anything and everything, including the occasional not-meant-to-be-edible item—paste, buttons, string and, once, a live goldfish.

"Well, I think it's a cool name." Christopher was obviously smitten within seconds of seeing her. He tried catching Trixie's eye again, but she was locked in shy mode. "It's different. Suits you well."

Trixie fiddled with a loose thread on the shoulder of her outfit, smiled at him with the side of her lips and muttered a meek thank you. A brief, awkward silence followed.

"You all ready to order?" she asked. The three boys grunted positively. "What can I get for you tonight?"

Pancake full stack with strawberry syrup, eggs over easy, a side of bacon. Reuben sandwich, extra dressing, sub potato salad for tomato soup. Veggie burger with extra cheese, hold the onion, a side of seasoned curly fries. Two coffees, one black, one with double creamer and one cherry cola.

Trixie scrawled down the order like a seasoned veteran, took the ticket to the kitchen and returned with three glasses of ice water. She placed her fist against her hip, turned to Christopher and squinted.

"Are you like their designated driver or something?"

"Uh, something like that."

"Nah," Mace broke in. "He's a person just like you, but he's got better things to do."

"Shut up, Mace," Christopher said. "She doesn't know what you're talking about."

"Hey, well it's a good song, lyrics aside." Mace was firm in his opinion.

"Are you guys in a band or something?" Trixie asked.

Christopher lit up. This was his "in." History had proven that pretty much any girl would be interested in a guy who played in a band, no matter how terrible the band was. But after careful consideration, he had determined that concept might not apply to him. Bass players were the redheaded stepchildren of the music world. He figured it was worth a shot regardless.

"Yeah," he said. "We're called Civilized Cannibals."

"Cool. Polka music, I assume?" Christopher did not catch that Trixie's tongue was planted firmly in cheek when she asked this. He scrunched up his face, not really knowing how to respond. She shrugged, winked at the boys—the gesture seemed mostly directed at Christopher in particular—and sashayed toward the kitchen.

With failed subtlety, Christopher watched Trixie's feet slide across the checkered linoleum floor. Her walk was just shy of graceful. Clumsily endearing.

"Hey, man. I think she likes you." Steve, the wizard of wisdom.

"Yeah, maybe. She seems kinda cool. Just different, you know? But in a good way."

"Ask her out, man," Mace said. "She's kinda cute. When the hell was the last time you got laid, anyway? The Cretaceous Period?"

"Nah, Mace. Remember? It was that Nazi chick. Cypress," Steve said, chuckling as he swished ice cubes in his mouth.

Christopher cringed when he heard that name. "Guys, can we omit that one from the history books please? That was just a huge mistake. I don't know what the fuck I was thinking even touching her."

"So you're not still seeing her?" Steve asked.

"Uh…nah. No. No way. That's totally done."

"Couldn't blame you if you still were, my man," Mace said. "Could only blame your helpless hormones. Cypress Glades. With a name and body like that, you'd think she was a stripper, not the poser princess of the Hitlerjugend, Sweetville Faction. Hey, 'Dork the Enemy' is as good a slogan as any. Plus, she *is* pretty hot, so that alone gets you off the hook. Did you ever make her call you Adolph in bed?"

"Dude, just shut up."

"You think she'd ever want to hate fuck a Jew?" Mace said. "I could use some violent lovin'."

Christopher knocked his knuckles on Mace's upper arm.

"What the hell?" Mace made a face like a toddler who just had his Tonka truck taken from him. "I'm half. That still counts."

Trixie returned with their food just before a wrestling match broke out. She balanced the trays with balletic precision. Her poise shined when the time clock was ticking.

"Enjoy, boys. Let me know if you need anything else." After distributing the goods, she handed Christopher a small bowl of ranch dressing. "Try this with the curly fries. On the house. I promise it's really yummy. Homemade recipe courtesy of our cook Jonesy." She motioned behind her to the kitchen. Jonesy was huffing and puffing back there, his prominent underbite practically swallowing the rest of his face. He wiped down the counter below the order tickets with a red bandana, then wiped his forehead with it immediately after.

"Oh, thanks." Christopher was quietly stunned by this minute act of generosity.

Trixie left them to their after-midnight meal.

Mace turned to Christopher and said, "Dude, if that doesn't mean

'I want to swallow your sausage,' then I officially know nothing about women."

"Oh, so that would finally make it 'official,' then." Steve's wit was sharp as a shark's tooth tonight.

"Mace…" Christopher tried to think of a profound insult, but Steve had stolen his glory. He ultimately decided on, "Just eat your fucking sandwich."

They tore into their food like starving POWs that had just been released to their homeland.

The meal was consumed, the check was delivered and arguments were made over how much to leave for a tip. Christopher covered the difference to make sure it was satisfactory, and Mace unleashed a respectable belch that smelled like a mixture of beer and corned beef.

Christopher had a sudden burst of brave inspiration. He remembered his Sharpie marker still sitting in his pocket after using it on his hands before their show. He grabbed the last clean napkin from the table, scribbled his name and phone number on it as legibly as he could, then placed it within the folds of the plastic check holder.

* * *

Trixie saw the guys in the band leaving just as a squat trucker type came in to be seated. The guy she gave the ranch dressing to—dammit, she had never even bothered to ask his name—offered her a slight goodbye wave and her heart performed amateur aerobics. She wondered if this boy was actually showing an interest in her or just being cordial. She had noticed him immediately and was pretty much crushed at first sight. He wore his sandy-blonde hair in a skater style, with long, straight bangs. Innocent, untainted hazel eyes. An unblemished face. Average height, weight, general size. Average was good. He was no male supermodel by any stretch, but Trixie had unconventional tastes in men. Imperfection was a bonus, something she could relate to. Despite her full blossom into womanhood, Trixie still felt she had no room to be picky. She knew it would take a special guy to truly accept her past—and her present, for that matter—which was not something she felt comfortable talking to just anyone about.

She chewed her tongue, smiled back at him and watched as he passed through the doors, figuring she would never have the chance to run into him again. Her timid nature gripped her, and she let him slip out of her life. It was probably for the best.

She walked back to their booth, removed the dirty dishes, came back to wipe down the table, took the check to the register and opened the check holder. A napkin fell out and floated in zigzag motions. She clumsily caught it, in fear that it might have to be burned like an American flag if it touched the ground. Her eyes widened when she saw what was written on it. She glanced side to side as if she might be arrested for withholding evidence and shoved it into her money apron.

The napkin changed everything.

CHAPTER FOUR

"I CAN'T DO THIS ANYMORE, CYPRESS. I don't know why I keep falling back into this trap—"

"But—"

"—of hooking up with you. I *hate* everything you stand for, and you've always known that. It's like…"

"It's like what, Chris? Just say what's on your fucking mind already."

Cypress Glades lit a cigarette. It sat wedged between her fingers, which rarely came within an inch of her lips. The burning tip was a red, evil eye.

"It's like I'm sticking my dick in Eva Braun."

"I'll take that as a fucking compliment. You sure weren't complaining a few minutes ago when I was going down on you. Asshole!"

"Well, I'm sorry, but I just— No, I'm *not* sorry. I'm sick of bullshitting myself. Being with you goes against everything I stand for."

Christopher Faith began his move toward the front door. He looked hesitant, as if the soles of his shoes and Cypress's floor were glued together. He fiddled with his bangs, parted them like curtains.

"You know better than that," Cypress said. "All bets are off when the lights go out. Everyone's a hypocrite in bed."

He turned his head just enough that she could only see his face in her peripheral vision. "I'll never convince you to change, but *I've* got to…"

Cypress squinted her jealous emerald eyes, twirled the left side of her Chelsea cut, dug her white-laced 14-hole Doc's into her filthy floor. She did not have to put much effort into holding back tears, remaining cool and calm. She would never, under any circumstance, cry about a fucking *guy*. That would have been so far beneath her it might as well have been in China.

"You'd better watch your back," she said. "Toro's been itching for a good curb stomping."

Christopher snorted. "So typical…"

"Typical what?"

"Braggin' 'bout curb stomps with no pearly-white proof."

"Oh yeah? Yeah? We'll see about that you…you…race traitor!"

Christopher laughed again, still inching away from her.

Cypress rummaged through the top drawer of her dresser, searching for a photograph of a recent victim she had personally stomped. Shards of teeth and chips of concrete decorating the gutter like confetti. Blood splattered across the sidewalk in some bastardized form of street art. A caved-in head that now looked closer to a partially inverted rubber Halloween mask.

Of course, this photograph did not actually exist. But Christopher didn't need to know that.

"There's somebody else," he said. "So that's that. I'm done. I met someone else."

Cypress knew he was lying, but she didn't feel like calling him out. Wasn't even worth the breath she would take.

"You were a lousy fuck anyway," she said. "Goddamn limp-prick pussy. What was I thinking?" Her temper and vocal decibel level temporarily under control. Then: "Get the hell out of here! Ugh!" She pointed to the door, her arm straight like an arrow with true aim.

Christopher's body was now hanging halfway out the door. He paused, as if he had something more profound to add to the conversation, then flashed her a sarcastic peace sign with his fingers and left without another word. The door slammed, vibrating the jamb. A frame slipped from the wall and fell to the floor. Cypress picked it up, dusted it off, and set it on her dresser, briefly glancing at her favorite photograph: a live shot of Ian Stuart, vocalist of Skrewdriver, torn from the pages of *Skinned Alive* issue Number One.

She glanced around her room in a puffy haze, grabbed the next inanimate object she saw—a Goebbels and Göring salt and pepper shaker combo—and threw it against the wall as hard as she could. It shattered into porcelain snow and sprinkled across her bed. Cypress immediately regretted destroying this one-of-a-kind item she had found after some intense digging at the Doomston Flea Market only two months ago. Too late. She'd roll around in the debris later and let the small of her back get nice and sliced. Maybe find the sharpest shard and use it to carve a swastika into her thigh. Bleeding reminded her how alive she was. Made her forget about stupid boys and their liberal politics. Oftentimes, it was even better than sex.

She turned to the frayed red swastika banner on her wall, offered it a brief, halfhearted *Sieg Heil*, brushed strands of her Chelsea out of her face, then grabbed her Mickey Mouse phone and started punching numbers as if determined to break the little squares right off. After a few rings, a groggy voice muttered a hello on the other end.

"Samuel? I need some Candy. *Now.*" Samuel began to answer, but Cypress hung up before he could finish. She had a sudden urge to pee.

On the toilet, she finally shed a few token tears. She counted the red X's on her menstrual calendar tacked next to the sink.

Figures, she thought. *Even I'm not tough enough to defeat the mighty power of hormones. Fucking fuck! This would never have happened to Ilse Koch.*

It was so hard to find a decent hetero white guy in this nowhere town, much less one who had at least a few attractive physical characteristics, even much less one who would put up with her unwavering views. Whatever happened to American freedom? It seemed like everyone in Sweetville was mulatto-this, bi-that, pro-everything, and everyone was so goddamned touchy about every little word she spoke.

Cypress extended her tongue and made a faux gagging sound. *Oh, excuse me. "Racially disabled" or "gender impaired" might be more politically correct. Blech!*

It didn't help much that the few Nazi skinheads in Sweetville were about as desirable as blobfish wearing red suspenders. Probably less intelligent, too. Still, she fucked them when she was extra horny and needed to escape her day-to-day existence—only when there were no preferable options available. Masturbation only held her interest for so long. Working as a receptionist at the Gunther, Gunther and Hayes law firm had taken its toll on her soul. A girl had needs beyond the professional world, though. Prurient needs. Cypress figured that as long as she was in charge of the when and where of said booty calls, these lunkhead Nazis wouldn't have a chance to latch onto any delusions of romance. And she hadn't really wanted something serious and long lasting with Christopher, either. But *she* wanted to be the one who was in control of ending things when they had run their natural course. It was supposed to be *her* decision. She needed to remain in power.

Cypress completed the expelling of her impurities and decided she would need to go hunt for a new temporary boy-toy in the fertile feeding ground of the clubs tonight. Or, more specifically, Club Club, as the only decent spot for underground social gathering in Sweetville was so cleverly named. Samuel might do in a pinch, but he was often a tad…mucky, to say the least. Trying to find a clean spot on his body was about as easy as searching for Waldo at a candy cane convention. Was it too much to ask of a guy to shower on a regular basis? *Eau de toilette* took on a whole new meaning with that scummy punk. At least he was an Aryan male. That had to be good for something. His darkness and grime could be rinsed off with generous soap and water to reveal the shining whiteness beneath.

Cypress fingered through her magazine rack and pulled out a recent issue of *White Woman's Witchcraft*. She flipped straight to a page with a folded corner and the article titled "Human Pheromones: Myth or Untapped Potential?" by Professor Winifred Savant. In recent months, she had become obsessed with this article that made reference to several sections of Dr. Dorian Wylde's final medical essay. Dr. Wylde, along with a man named Dr. Julius Kast and a group of uncredited psychology graduate students, had been conducting controlled experiments intended to tap into corridors of the human mind that would otherwise remain dormant. Wylde's theory was that a person with the right genetic makeup could, if a certain meditative level were reached, take full charge of his or her own flesh. Shape, color, complexion, texture—the limits seemed endless. The process was referred to as Positive Mental Shape-shifting, but it had never been fully tested or proven before Wylde's passing.

Cypress stood up, still clutching the magazine, and became absorbed by her mirror image. She pinched her eyelids and puffed her face until she felt her features looked perfect. But her pure white illusion only lasted so long before her true colors were in danger of being exposed. There was only so much makeup she could cake on her face before she looked like she had been accepted into Clown College.

Professor Savant's article had been a revelation to Cypress. Could Wylde's theory become a part of her reality? She supposed it was possible that it amounted to little more than a parlor trick or attempt at mass hypnotism, but just the idea of it made her nipples hard. She chose to put her faith in science, even if this particular science seemed to contain peculiarities not so easily explained.

Savant had taken some of Dr. Wylde's notes and improved upon them, making them accessible to the public and creating a discipline from the medical mess. There were three rules that Savant claimed would lead to the gift of Positive Mental Shape-shifting: taut posture, technique and practice, and tantric persuasion.

Cypress knew it was possible. She was a firm believer that her dreams were premonitions. Savant's rules became her scripture.

Once, in a particularly vivid nightmare, she had focused too tightly on shifting and swore her nose had expanded a good half inch, taking her directly into what she considered Jewish territory. She hadn't been able to force the effect to revert immediately. Once she woke up, she refused to leave the house for two days straight. She spent hours in front of the mirror, attempting to contour her nose with makeup. This only made it thin and pointy, making her look like the Wicked Witch of the West. An incident like that could never be allowed to happen in real life. She would have to study and practice. Stay focused. Stay positive. Stay white.

Cypress preferred not to work so hard to maintain what she considered a genuine appearance, but she still found the concept of Positive Mental Shape-shifting promising. It seemed her devotion had also led to some powerful side effects. Increased pheromones. There was nothing in Savant's article that explicitly stated why these side effects might occur, but there they were. She wasn't about to start complaining. Her physical presence was already such a powerful tool, working wonders with trapping men in her clutches. But these additional secretions could act as even tighter vices to keep these men in her grip. At least temporarily. Depending on the guy, she could usually keep someone interested for a few weeks. Christopher was a perfect example of this. The combination of the Positive Mental Shape-shifting and pheromones must have worked its magic on him. He was so innocent. An almost-dullard, not the brightest crayon in the box, the definition of oblivious. Like most young men in their early twenties, he was filled with naïveté and excess seed. He never saw the effects coming.

Cypress wished she had legitimate proof of Aryan blood flowing through her veins. Her birth father had bailed on her family—if their grouping of man, woman and child ever had the option of being graced with such formal terms—when she was still in diapers, never to return. It made her ill to think she would likely never know his side of her racial heritage. She was convinced her whiteness would never be complete. These days, Cypress had depressing suspicions that her racial purity was severely lacking. It all depended on how she angled herself in the mirror—or "Angloed," as she liked to jokingly think of it. She shuddered at the thought of being some sort of half-breed. She was better off not knowing the truth if that's what the answer would end up being. She felt being a full-blown Jew would have been a better option.

Her mother was no help in trimming down the family tree. She kept herself so doped up she could barely even remember the guy's name, much less his nationality. There was no family photo album with pictures of Deadbeat Daddy cutting the birthday cake. Only worthless, nonexistent memories. Cypress had found one photo tucked away deep in her mother's underwear drawer, a slightly blurred image of a man who was likely her father, though her mother would never admit it. The man in the photograph looked suspiciously Jewish, perhaps even Hispanic. Difficult to tell based on the quality of the image. She wasn't sure which one would be worse.

Cypress couldn't tear herself away from the mirror. She frowned at the disgraceful reflection and proceeded to apply a lightly caustic bleaching product to her face with a scrub sponge. The sting only tickled for a few seconds as she had adapted her pain threshold long ago. If the tissue tore a little bit, well that was just a bonus. The fresh flesh might begin as pink, but the surface below would eventually be far whiter than before.

There was no color more right than white.

* * *

After Samuel had come over for a quick romp and left her apartment, Cypress still felt a substantial jones for sex. Her desires were often twisted and insatiable, and even a small dose of Sweet Candy gave her a ravenous libido. Club Club could still be a viable option for an entertaining evening.

In her mind, she conjured up a carnal grocery list for a prowling night on the town: hearts for breakfast, pride for leftovers and cocks for a midnight snack. Check, check and check.

With coitus the weapon, her body the luscious bullet, she yearned to dance with demons that walked as men, to discuss the future of White America with people who waged fewer wars than those they mimicked. Usually, though, no one wanted to talk much about racial purity while loud industrial music was blaring through the speakers. They were more about wearing fashionable armbands to shock their parents and teachers than being actually committed to the cause. The politics were just sketchy enough for the crowd there, but a tad too serious for the club environment unless she happened to find the right conversationalist. Most of them would rather dance and fuck the night away, reserving the pseudo-intellectual discussions for post-coital coffee the next morning.

When she arrived at the club that night, she was dressed for the predatory occasion, preparation for cavorting with the denizens of what was often referred to as "Lower" Sweetville by the upper classes. She was a modest Mephistopheles clad in skintight black patent-leather pants, fuzzy leopard platform creepers, and a Brutal Attack t-shirt with the sleeves and neck cut out to expose her shapely torso. Her breasts heaved and defied gravity. They seemed to say, "Come and get 'em, boys. The milk's whole, fresh and plentiful!"

She rolled her eyes at the cracked neon lights on the sign that had been in dire need of repair for months now. The defect made it look like the name was Clu_ C_ub. Toro was working the front door, as always. He was a bald beast of a man, as well as one of Cypress's faithful skinhead crew, so she knew she would never have to pay a cover charge as long as it was his shift. He nodded at her, grunted a few mush-mouth words she couldn't quite understand and allowed her to pass. Rumor had it that Toro had earned his nickname by scaring off a bull with only his voice. Booming as Toro's larynx could be, Cypress figured this was, well, bullshit. Where the hell was anyone ever going to see any bulls roaming around Sweetville? No cows in this town. The nearest farm was probably 200 miles away in Plain Grove. Cypress had it on pretty good authority—from Stacey King, one of her bitchy wannabe skinbyrd "friends"—that Toro was referred to as such due to the impressive size of his joystick and accompanying testicles. She'd find out the real truth for herself if she got desperate or drunk enough, but not tonight.

Probably not.

She sure as hell hoped not. The last thing she needed was another dead fuck. A girl had to have *some* level of taste.

Cypress entered the floor. Ministry's "Burning Inside" rattled the speakers, making them sound like a ticked off nest of hornets. It always took a few seconds to adjust to the epileptic strobe lights that shocked and awed within the walls of Club Club, but they proved effective at masking any potential racial ambiguity. They worked better than any brand of makeup she had ever tried. She glanced at the familiar Wheat Paste Wall, where posters for upcoming shows and DJ nights stuck together like old porno mags. Beneath them were the browning flyers from years long past.

She floated through the crowd, a sex-starved specter. The first faces she saw in the dim light were those of the Zane brothers. They appeared to be chatting up a Goth fatty with a passably cute face who might or might not have squeezed her way into the club with a fake ID. Cypress wondered if the Zanes ever stopped trolling for snatch, if those douchebags even had any standards. Just sliding themselves into anything, as if their dicks were quarters and the random orifices were slot machines about to hit the jackpot.

She did not make eye contact with the brothers or their potential conquest. She had done the deed with the twins a few times, both separately *and* together, but had determined they were too freaky even for her. Too bad, since they were ghost-white and filthy rich. A girl could maybe get used to the deviance with those sorts of benefits, but Cypress preferred a stronger sense of loyalty in her mates. They needed to be closer to senseless little puppy dogs that would lick her boots and like it. Still, a successful white man really lubed her labia.

A pack of Junkie Creeps hung around the edges of the bar. Most of them had long, greasy hair and twigs for bodies. They all wore navy blue jumpsuits. Unless there was obvious facial hair, it was almost impossible to tell from afar which were male or female. Their clothing and entire appearance was vaguely free of gender.

She was fairly certain, though, that she recognized a girl named Sara who she had been acquainted with back in high school. Their friendship had failed to blossom once Cypress discovered the wonders of white supremacy in her sophomore year. Sara was too deeply attracted to R & B music for Cypress to have taken her seriously at that point. Skinheads didn't dabble in silly love songs, especially those written and sung by the lesser races. Cypress questioned what could have happened to Sara over the years. She had everything going for her and still managed to screw it up. A disgrace to her heritage.

A couple of the Withering Wyldes lurked at a booth in the far corner, whispering their inaudible secrets to each other. It wasn't like them to frequent a club like this one, but she knew from experience how difficult it was to find new recruits for a cause, so she shrugged it off. Probably scoping out the Junkie Creeps since they were already about the right size for their needs. Wouldn't take much of a leap to get some of them into their fold. Cypress was certainly strong enough to ignore their temptations. Anyone who chose otherwise pretty much deserved what they got when it came to those cultists.

She noticed a peculiar looking man chatting with the Withering Wyldes at their table. Short, wearing a funny hat. His face looked scarred as if badly beaten. It almost appeared as if his eyes were glowing. Perhaps the result of some wild type of contact lenses. Wouldn't be the weirdest fashion choice that had passed through the doors of Club Club. This guy was definitely not someone she'd noticed on the scene before, though. He looked a little older than the average clubgoer and very out of place. Cypress shook her head in disgust. *Fucking hell,* she thought. *Is this place turning into the cantina from* Star Wars *or something?*

Seemingly out of nowhere, Samuel strolled up to the table where this strange man and the Withering Wyldes sat. *What the fuck,* Cypress thought. Had Samuel mentioned he was coming, they could have carpooled and saved on gas. How did he know these freaks anyway? Probably just dealing some Candy or something. *Whatever.* She wasn't interested enough to find out. Time to ignore stupid Samuel and move on to find some actual fun for the night.

Lithe, wishfully vampiric dancers glided across the floor to Skinny Puppy's "Assimilate." Some waved their hands in front of their faces as if trying to escape a nasty, never-ending cobweb. Others made overly exaggerated steps like they were attempting to avoid a fresh pile of dog shit, while a small group swayed in place like decrepit trees on a windy day. And all of their faces were oh so serious.

Cypress stood in the corner twirling her *Schutzstaffel Totenkopf* pendant in her fingers. Her first boyfriend, Sven—at that time the Big Daddy of the skinhead scene—had given it to her for her sixteenth birthday. Even though it was more than half a decade later and Sven wasn't getting out of prison anytime soon, Cypress still cherished this trinket. She had painted the edges of it with pink nail polish and thought it looked particularly cute.

Cypress spotted her next conquest: an emaciated Goth boy doing some sort of dramatic Peanuts dance all by himself. Not that all of the other dancers weren't flying solo as well. For a scene that seemed so sensual on the surface, the dancing distinctly lacked any erotic qualities. His whiteness may have been mostly pancake makeup, but that was good enough for a night like this one.

His name was Bastian, and she found out later that night he was fond of cutting himself too.

and now a word from
OUR SPONSOR

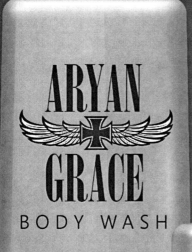

CHAPTER FIVE

A HEALTHY HEAP OF KNOX GELATIN kept Samuel's towering blue mohawk molded atop his head—an eggish noggin attached to an underfed frame. He scratched at the emerging stubble that surrounded his appropriated hairstyle. He'd have to give it a nice fresh shave soon, keep it baby-bottom smooth. His attire was perfectly postured punk: a sleeveless, black-gone-grey Dead Kennedys shirt, a Crass patch—despite never actually listening to the band—meticulously sewn to the knee of his frayed jeans and a matching studded-leather bracelet and belt purchased from Fresh Affair—an "alt" store in the Sweetville Mall. A self-aware fashion victim, using his disguise as a weapon of infiltration. He reveled in the art of authenticity.

Music howled in the background of Samuel's sparse bedroom, just loud enough to be heard in the bathroom. He had already forgotten the name of the band he was listening to. The record skipped incessantly, which sent him into an intense trance that became difficult to break.

He hocked a loogie—tinted pink from Sweet Candy—into the sink and walked over to the turntable to remove the needle, decided he wanted to enjoy the accidentally remixed music a moment longer, swayed with the rapid rhythm, then finally ended it, placed the record into the dust sleeve and tossed it onto a pile of dirty laundry—neglecting to protect it any further. He glanced at his pristine Exploited poster—also purchased at Fresh Affair—taped to the wall. The band's iconic mohawked skull logo foreshadowed what Samuel might resemble once he was placed six feet under, were he to stick with this particular style. He decided he needed to muck the poster up a bit, so he shot a small spear of snot on it and smeared the globule around. He tore two of the corners and decided this was enough to make it authentic. Anyone who came to buy Sweet Candy from him would be none the wiser. He was just another dirty punk trying to make an extra buck.

Samuel's current personal directives applied to his recently discovered fad as follows. First, use the cacophony of hardcore punk as a cloak in an attempt to assimilate with the underground. Earn the respect of the local music scene and move freely within it while searching for new Taste Subjects, for there were many lost souls looking for a cure to their psychological ailments. Discarded children who would never be missed. This was not wrong. It would be a near-charitable service.

Second, keep Cypress Glades in check with sex like vaginal Vicodin. She could not be allowed to eclipse his greatness. Though it might be distasteful, a man still had urges beyond even the deific.

As if haunted by serendipity, the phone rang. It was Cypress. She sounded desperate. Not like her normal self at all.

"Samuel? I need some Candy. *Now.*"

"Okay, I'll be there in a—" was all he managed to get out as a reply before she hung up. He supposed he should have been used to this sort of behavior by now, but it still irked him every time she pulled this shit.

He dragged himself back to the bathroom mirror and practiced his sneer a few more times. The trick was to make it seem natural, like the whole world was beneath his decadent attitude. His image was not as effortless as he would have liked. Not yet. But it would have to do for now. Most of the people he interacted with would not be clear-minded enough to notice.

His charismatic ways worked wonders on the typical gutter punk, but Cypress Glades was a greater challenge. She was on an elevated level, often too sharp for her own good. If anyone were savvy enough to see through his costume it would be her, so Samuel had to take his approach a step beyond method acting. He had to convince even *himself* that he was no poser punk.

Samuel sometimes fantasized about persuading Cypress to partake in the act of Eating with him. He would even make sure to offer her only the whitest of meats. He thought she might relish in the experience if she gave it a chance. It would be pleasant to have a partner of equal stature sharing divine meals with him, like a marriage of messiahs spreading the gospel of what was once known as Consumption Enlightenment. But he couldn't jeopardize his identity. For now, he needed to focus on making her believe in his appearance. Thankfully, she had requested a special delivery of Sweet Candy that she would likely devour immediately, so Samuel wouldn't have to strain himself to uphold his false persona.

He wondered if it was even false anymore. He was beginning to enjoy this new lifestyle, if enjoyment could even be thought of as a word in his vocabulary. The Sweet Candy customers were plentiful. The women were often willing, if not exactly supermodels. The music was even starting to grow on him. Raw, reckless abandon channeled through sound. This was an approach he could support. He thought, perhaps one day, he could even become a vessel for this music from elsewhere. He could finally be reborn as The Angelghoul and receive the recognition he deserved. In the meantime, however, he enjoyed telling the younger crowd in Sweet-ville that he had "moved here from Los Angeles." They would grill him for hours about the punk shows in such a big, thriving city. "Did you ever get to see Suicidal Tendencies with Louiche Mayorga on bass? What about T.S.O.L. before they sucked?" He answered nearly all of their excited queries with an emphatic yes, only offering up an occasional no to make the lie more believable. It was worth going through the trouble of such a balancing act just to see the looks of awe on their faces as he recounted tales that never actually occurred.

Punk really was no worse than any other subculture. Or no better, he supposed, but that was beside the point. Samuel needed to go where he would remain accepted, to whatever degree that might be. Stay at the top of the food chain. Better to be the ruler of scum than to bow down to an unworthy adversary.

He donned a weather-beaten, studded-leather jacket, "borrowed" from one of his more recent Taste Subjects, and headed for the door.

* * *

An hour later, he was huddled in Cypress's bed, sweating profusely and struggling to ejaculate.

In the last few years, he had upgraded his body to an almost average size and weight, but not enough to strip him of the physicality that was synonymous with his former title as The Angelghoul. Despite this, he was still the antithesis of "in shape."

Finding new Taste Subjects had become more and more difficult lately, despite the general apathy of the Sweetville Police Department. Samuel had seen too many public service announcements warning the naïve about the dangers of Eaters, and thus he had resorted to his current situation of going incognito. While this drought did not affect his libido in the slightest, it certainly had an impact on his performance.

He had been Cypress's go-to sex man for several months now, even though she had technically been dating that drug-free dunce Christopher Faith. Normally, Samuel's prowess was more than enough to make her purr. Today, however, he could tell she was definitely less than satisfied.

"Mmmm… Sammy baby. That was fucking hot." As bitchy as Cypress could be, she at least had enough of a kind streak to protect his ego. Perhaps she had missed her calling as an actress. She wrapped her naked body in the only remaining cover—a wool comforter with a gigantic Iron Cross placed directly in the center. Samuel wondered if it had been special-ordered or knitted by her grandmother.

"Yes. Very." Samuel was a stoic man of many deep and intelligent thoughts, yet of little verbalization. He also felt he might blow his cover if he spoke too much. Many of the young men he had encountered within the confines of the punk scene had too much to say with too little substance. Samuel felt he might stand out if he attempted to spread his wisdom too much amongst the peons. Through Consumption Enlightenment, he had learned that none of their armchair politics were worth a damn, though the emotions behind them were often useful passions that fueled their flavorful flesh.

"You know," Cypress said, "you should come to one of our Hitlerjugend rallies one of these days. We could always use another good white man showing his support." This was stated as casually as if she were a housewife inviting her neighbor to a weekly book club.

Samuel picked up a doll that was squeezed between Cypress's bed and nightstand. It wore a home-sewn Klansman outfit, but the sheets were closer to off-white or cream. He removed the hood, only to discover it was a suspiciously tan Cabbage Patch Kid. Cypress snatched the doll from him, shoved the hood on and chucked it to the far corner of the bedroom.

"Hmm. Probably not. But I'll think about it." Samuel appreciated clandestine activities and understood the attraction to Cypress's cause, that purity was something worth striving for. He also knew that such a concept could never exist. All people were bonded by blood and, though that blood may have tasted slightly different from race to race, it was always just a variation of the same theme. Like the difference between bananas and plantains. Or long pig and hairless goat. Not enough to claim one sample was superior to the next. "I thought about it," he said. "Again, probably not."

People were all just potential excrement anyway, fertilizer for the soil. For the soul.

Samuel offered Cypress a small handful of the Sweet Candy. "New formula. I think you'll enjoy it."

She took the pills, threw them in her mouth, barely paused to chew—just enough to attain a quick high—then washed them down with a half can of lukewarm beer that had been festering on her nightstand. Samuel treated himself to a dose as well.

He asked Cypress to insert the pill as a suppository, but she ignored him. He did not let that stop him from pursuing his preferred method by means of his own hands. Three pills this time as he had built up too much of a tolerance.

"I'd like to take a shower," he said. Cypress looked at him questioningly. "Don't take it personal. I just feel a little extra sweaty today. It's... humid out."

"Yeah, sure. Whatever. God knows you could use one. Have a blast." Cypress was clearly trying to restrain the Sweet Candy quivers already taking control of her body. She curled herself into a ball, faced the filthy white wall and made gurgling noises.

Samuel, like always, had still been more or less fully dressed when he mounted Cypress. He was ashamed of his undefined, cadaverous body and never felt comfortable letting anyone see the two insignificant nubs growing on his back, just beneath his shoulder blades. He only wanted to reveal them when they reached their full glory. Then, and only then, he would display them with pride. Until that time, the nubs were a hideous embarrassment.

His pants around his ankles, Samuel waddled to Cypress's bathroom. He nearly tripped on a detached tile in front of the toilet. Once the door was shut, he kicked off his loosely-laced work boots, wiggled off his jeans, removed his leather jacket and tattered shirt, turned the water knob all the way over to the red zone, pulled back the Rainbow Brite shower curtain and stepped into the tub.

The scalding water immediately melted his perfectly coiffed mohawk. The blue hair mopped around his head, transforming him into a reject from Jim Henson's workshop. Urine trickled from his penis and formed into tiny lemon needles as it rode the shower's stream. Loose strands of hair wedged into the drain, resembling mysterious aquatic worms. Backed-up brackish water mixed with his own fluids and feculence and tickled at his toes, so he soaped and lathered his body, scrubbed it roughly until it grew raw and irritated, then rinsed. Then repeated. Rinsed. Repeated.

The water soothed him. He felt the Sweet Candy kicking in. He hiccuped twice, then spit out something black and glutinous, which repeated countless times like a looping videotape. Physical manifestations of musical notes twisted and strutted from between his parted lips, spinning around him in a wet whirlwind. They formed a fanciful merry-go-round. It was a Disney moment. The notes grew bored with their madcap dance and their intentions became decidedly more adult.

They nipped at his nipples and cupped his junk and caressed his buttocks, which was unwelcome, though not lacking a sense of arousal. A large portion of the living, breathing, playful sounds launched themselves down the drain, filling the tub further, while others narrowed their figures and wedged their way into his urethra, which should have been excruciating but was strangely orgasmic.

The tub was now half full, the gap between the water's edge and the tub's lip quickly closing, so he eased himself down to submerge his body, ignoring the discomfort in his groin as best he could. He tricked his lungs, allowing himself to approach a state of drowning, knowing he would not perish within the filthy baptism. It would be a temporary death. A modern version of *la petit mort*. He stroked his shaft in rapid rhythms and emptied what was left in his artesian semen well until it ran dry, and the ejaculate streamed endlessly until the bathwater more closely resembled cheap hand soap. A few moments of private ecstasy, visions of mermaids with liberty spikes, and he opened his eyes and the water had gone down the drain

He pulled himself up and grabbed the first clean-looking towel from the rack and dried himself off, completely neglecting his dripping back. He reached back and stroked his nubs and found that they had grown exponentially. His wings would soon sprout, puffy pillow-white feathered wings. And, oh, how high he would fly.

*"There is a time to let things happen,
and a time to make things happen."* — Hugh Prather

"My name is Legion: for we are many." — The Gospel of Mark 5:9

Rows of swaying, stunned bodies stand wilted like corn stalks well past their harvest. Incessant humming fills the building. Almost insectile, but with the harmony of an orchestra's string section.

The clapperboard reads:

PRODUCTION: WITHERING WYLDES INFOMERCIAL
DIRECTOR: GARTH CHILDS
DATE: 01/28/93

A quick snap of commercial-grade solid resin, and then a caption flickers across the viewing screen:

* Translated pro bono by dedicated followers of The Institute for the Pursuit of Linguistic Fetishism (IPLF)*

Heavily synthesized music seeps from monolithic speakers hooked to each corner of the warehouse, the volume adjusted so it is not disruptive to the filming.

A deceptively elaborate machine clicks, ticks, beeps and bops.

TRANSLATION DATA: *We seek your support. Sign below on the dotted line. Do not think this is a selling of desperate souls, that this is signing your life away.* Au contraire, mon frère. *Small efforts combined with diligent planning bring satisfactory results. Please make a donation. If you can spare it. Any penny helps. Or dollar. Or generous blank personal check made out to the Wylde Preservation Association. We also accept traveler's cheques, francs, pesos and kronor. Just pass on your donation to any of our friendly representatives. You may—you will—see us wandering the desolate streets. Fighting the good fight. We do not rest. Rest is waste. Rest equals moments lost to the sands of time.*

Garth Childs pulls away from his viewing screen, removes his headphones, whistles with his tongue behind his teeth and slashes two fingers across his throat. The portly cameraman in front of him ceases filming. The strange speaking halts. Papers containing the translated speech launch from a laser printer. Garth grabs them, scans the text, turns to the man next to him and says, "This is some great stuff. Nobody's going to bother waiting past two a.m. to watch that old cunt with the turquoise jewelry after they see this. I mean, what's the point?"

"Well, they are very persuasive," says the head supervisor of the IPLF—a man known to Garth only as Harris. His voice is slightly muffled behind a fleece balaclava.

"So who's that scrawny weirdo you've got working that thingamajig over there?" Garth asks.

"William Ekkert," Harris says. "He's the Institute's newest intern. A very special boy, youngest we've ever taken on. Finished high school two years early. I've been very impressed with his work. I gather he'll go far with this career. I'm almost worried that he'll be good enough to make my position obsolete. *Almost.* He has a natural knack for languages. Speaks three fluently, not including, well, whatever it is you'd call *that.* No one's been able to come up with an acceptable name for their language yet."

William Ekkert sits Indian style near the boom operator whose cheap microphone droops like the limb of a heavily weighted citrus tree. William huddles tightly into his own body, as if he wants to invert himself and expose his slight musculature and the slickened sinews surrounding it. He is a captive audience of one, immersed in the obscurity of the words that drift from the ever-stretching reptilian mouths of the Withering Wyldes.

TRANSLATION DATA: *We are simultaneously autonomous and amalgamated. We are synergy incarnate. We serve no one.*

William arbitrarily twists some knobs on the translation machine, adjusts the miniscule wireless microphone clamped to his lapel, attacks some keys on a crude keyboard. The frequencies of the voices in the warehouse are in constant flux. The machine at his fingertips only captures so much. The gears of his ears must take charge and become the technology.

He notices out of the corner of his eye that one of the Withering Wyldes has replaced another in the foreground and has begun to speak, its voice seamlessly blending into the speech from the last one. There is nothing to physically distinguish one from the next and the next and the next, so the first one soon becomes lost in the shifting crowd.

William sneaks a subtle glance at the next one's crotch. As with every other time William has attempted to check, the genitals are shriveled away and hidden behind a bramble of pubic vines. Deflated balloon breasts dangle from almost all of their frames, so that has never been a helpful indicator of gender either. Some of the other Withering Wyldes prance and bounce in the background, moving in loose oval formations as if playing musical chairs. They continue to hum along to the electronic soundtrack. It is like watching a bastardized, sexless version of that Robert Palmer video William remembers being popular a few years back.

TRANSLATION DATA: *Wait. This is incorrect. Information out of date. Please pardon any and all of our discrepancies. The hive is forever changing. Merging. Cross-pollinating. As activists, we often become too busy to keep our records current.*

"Hold on, hold on, hold on," Garth says as he reads the printout. "This sounds like they're deviating from the script. What's going on over there?"

From the other side of the warehouse a crew member yells, "There's a script?"

The cameraman turns to face Garth, shrugs, tries to shove his excess belly back beneath his belt.

"William," Harris says, motioning to his protégé, "can you please take care of this minor digression?"

"Of course, sir." William emits bestial, garbled sounds toward one of the Withering Wyldes near the front. Two of them drift next to the boy, lift him gently by his armpits, pull him aside and whisper soft, enigmatic syllables into his ears that send tickles across his bones. The flesh on their torsos is like vellum paper. William can see the outlines of their ribs, but also believes he can see the ribs themselves as well as the organs behind them. "I'll be back soon," he says to Harris. "I think they have something private to talk to me about. They seem to trust me."

"Perfect," Harris says. "Do try to hurry back." William offers him a nondescript nod.

"Okay, everyone. Take five," Garth says as he waddles to the catering table. He asks the server, "Do you have any of those little cheesy bacon things I like? No? Well, why the hell not?"

The two Withering Wyldes each place a hand at the top of William's back and guide him across the floor. The slight pressure makes him feel like he is wearing shoulder pads made of toilet paper. He listens closely to their speech and leaves the translation machine behind. He does not need it. It is an operational façade for the dangerously gifted. William understands every subtle nuance, every potential deceit in their altered tongues. The Withering Wyldes seem temporarily lost in their own sorrow, then regain their composure and take turns speaking to him, one voice sometimes switching over to the other mid-sentence.

TRANSLATION DATA: *Correction—we no longer serve anyone. Rest in peace, Dr. Dorian Wylde, our dear late king. Let your deceptively wispy ways inspire in the afterlife, oh father of our cause. Your wise man's beard grows to great lengths in the tomb. Your struggle for the attainment of a supreme modern nirvana will not be in vain.*

William understands what it is like to lose a father—his own committed suicide two years ago, not long after his mother spiraled into schizophrenic lunacy. He has lived with his aunt ever since.

The Withering Wyldes navigate him through their communal space. The high ceiling is decorated with helium-inflated balloons and party streamers, though William can see no sign of a ladder. They reach the back of the main room, which leads to a pathway protected by crushed-taffeta curtains. The Withering Wyldes pull the curtains back and allow him to enter a hollowed tunnel that does not look like it has any right to belong to the same building. The tunnel curves so he cannot see the other end, but he thinks—hopes—he sees tiny trickles of light in the distance. The texture of the walls within is similar to diagrams William has seen of the inside of a vaginal membrane.

TRANSLATION DATA: *We apologize for the doctor's untimely death. It is our fault. No. It is not our fault. Our attorneys remind us that we had no hand in his passing. We plead the Fifth. Regardless, we feel responsible. Dear Doctor, you merely wished to cure society of its obesity plague. We promise to carry on your vision to the end of time, like a brilliant blue torch on the blackest of nights.*

William wonders why they have suddenly ventured off on this tangent, referencing their founder in the midst of filming, then realizes—remembers from his research—that today is Dr. Wylde's birthday. He would have been forty-five.

The tight, esophageal shape of the tunnel brings William to a near claustrophobic state, but is thankfully not as long as it first appeared. It soon opens into a dimly lit cave, and William steps into a private world the camera's eye is contractually bound to not see.

Dozens of other members of the hive—those not fit for television's consumption—are curled and woven into one another along the walls, legs to arms and arms to legs like discount tapestry. The insect harmony is more pervasive here. At first glance there appears to be some sort of orgy occurring, but William quickly discards that idea. There are no thrusts, no insertions, no pleasurable moans. The members of the hive concentrate on one another, speaking rapidly and in fresh tongues that even William has yet to master. He realizes the Withering Wyldes have likely escorted him back here in an attempt to convert him. They use kindness as their Kool-Aid. William feels it is a noble attempt, but he is only interested in them for linguistic purposes. He observes the activity in the cave for a few moments longer and changes his opinion again—this *is* an orgy. An orgy of minds.

The two Withering Wyldes accompanying him offer a rickety chair. He sits and it bows dangerously downward even under his waifish weight. Both of the tall, thin, sentient trees whisper into his ears. His body temporarily locks up. His throat tickles as if he is contracting laryngitis. The Withering Wyldes shove a framed photograph into his lap, the first real aggression they have shown. An image of the late doctor, relative youth forever trapped within the stained wood and smeared glass. His face chiseled like the monoliths at Easter Island, subtle wire-rimmed spectacles, a perfected five o'clock shadow, a creamy white lab coat and pinstripe bow tie.

TRANSLATION DATA: *Look. Can you see? Dr. Wylde was fashion forward. Always remember. Never forget. Of course we will never forget. We are he and he is we. The Withering Wyldes. A media-bestowed moniker. A badge we wear with pride.*

William nods and sets the frame down on a folding table. He murmurs some guttural grunts that almost reach the grace of a primal song. *Thank you for sharing this with me.* He stands and begins to make his way back to the main warehouse. Before he reaches the tunnel he passes an open pantry stockpiled with pill bottles and a padlocked mini-fridge. He knows leaving so quickly will not offend the Withering Wyldes. They are not much for small talk. They have already joined the others along the wall. Living, breathing hieroglyphs.

Once William arrives back on the set, he finds that the filming has continued without him.

"Where have you been, kid?" Garth asks. "I can't tell what the hell these freaks are saying." A sudden hiss tears through the warehouse, a sound like an angry quiver of king cobras.

"Just because you don't understand them doesn't mean they don't understand you," William says.

"The boy is right," Harris says. "You might want to be more cautious with your words in the future."

Garth darts his eyes and adjusts his testicles. "Okay, let's keep this circus rolling!"

William returns to his machine, to his miming, mimicking act. The remaining Withering Wyldes simmer down and face the camera once more.

TRANSLATION DATA: *We feel fat. The world is a greasy tub of lard. America is porcine. Obese. Gargantuan. Butterball. Humanity is Epicurean. We do not wish to follow the gluttonous path, for we are right. Righteous. We seek the higher taste. We prowl the streets. Never sleep. No time for winks, for REM, for crusted, sandy eyes when we have a laudable gospel to spread.*

We distribute hand-assembled pamphlets stating our hopes for the universe. Perhaps you have been given a copy by one of our representatives or viewed one pasted to a telephone pole. Thirty percent recycled paper. Biodegradable inks. Environmentally friendly adhesives. The Withering Wyldes are green. Our flesh is a desirable green-grey-blue. We create petitions. We seek to add Witherix to required Daily Food pyramids. No flesh. No filth. No toxins. We start small. We start local. Today, Sweetville. Tomorrow, the People's Republic of China. No borders. No limits. No excuses.

"Hey, Harris," Garth whispers, "Between you and me, I've never been too fond of these creeps. Self-righteous diet crap. I mean, I'm a man who likes a good burger, you know?"

"I don't doubt that you're in the majority, Mr. Childs. Sweetville may wear a veil of tolerance, but I've had enough direct experience with this city and its denizens to see things with a bit more clarity. It's unfortunate, but it's also reality. Why bother choosing to work with them, if you don't mind my asking?"

"Well, the pay is pretty damned nice."

"Yes. Yes, it is."

TRANSLATION DATA: *We will settle for nothing less. The future of man relies on our plan. Open your mind, you might successfully view the blinding light.*

"You know," Garth says, "this sure is going to be a hell of a lot of text to have crawling across the screen."

"Don't worry about it," Harris says. "The Institute employs an excellent voiceover expert. He'll take care of it."

"He's the one who sounds like Bela Lugosi, right?"

"If you say so."

TRANSLATION DATA: *Do not fear us. Do not believe the news fed to you by the television cube. We are not media monsters. We are calm. We are gentle. We are koi fish. We are tall. We are alpine. We are eucalyptus trees. We are thin. We are lithe. We are high-fashion models. We are not weak. We are beautiful.*

William nods. He agrees, he believes.

TRANSLATION DATA: *Do not accept the accusatory hype. We are not a cult. Cults offer false solace. We are the future. We are evolution. Be like us. Be us.*

A balloon pops somewhere in the warehouse, followed by an animalistic shriek. Both sounds morph into a single echo.

"We can cut that in post-production," Garth says. "No problemo."

TRANSLATION DATA: *We offer a stable dietary plan free of charge for any new members of the fold. Our plan is suitable for any man, woman, boy, girl, infant, elder—insert preferred identifier here. Abstain from most examples of traditional sustenance. Read our pamphlet for more specific information on what is acceptable and what is not. Subsist almost solely on Dr. Wylde's miracle drug*

Witherix. Resist temptation to binge and purge. It will only come back to haunt you later. Follow strict regimens of caloric restriction. Reference our impeccable, infallible charts for proper intake. Weekly fasting offers promise of euphoric mental states. Attend any of our Wednesday meditation meetings if you seek group support. Fly higher than a Rüppell's griffon vulture and never feel required to stay glued to the ground. It may initially be rough to harness your willpower, but soon you will be sublime. You will be blessed.

The Withering Wyldes shift positions again. The one who is now in front wiggles and points a caricature of a finger directly at the camera. Something that resembles a shell of a devious smile molds onto its lips.

TRANSLATION DATA: *A message to the devoted pill-poppers: we know you are plentiful. We appreciate you more than we can ever express, for you are our flaxseed bread and non-hydrogenated coconut oil. We recommend avoidance of all forms of Sweet Candy. This drug is equal to heresy. Witherix is to be deified and revered. The only exception to this rule is Witherix Lite. Featuring a hint of aspartame, this version is designed for those with severe allergies to natural sweeteners.*

William stops pretending to use the machine to translate. He scratches at his upper lip, brushing at the beginnings of a half-hearted mustache. He feels a slight tugging sensation near his temporal lobe.

TRANSLATION DATA: *Do not be frightened by our appearance. Witness the feathered wings of an angel estranged from Heaven for the first time, it might be startling as well. But you would eventually grow accustomed to even that. The fantastic becomes mundane. Commonplace. We are peaceful, pacifistic. We teach by example. We are the next natural progression of human existence. Darwin would be in awe. He would take extensive notes. Vast volumes would be written about our perfection and how to mimic it. Someone will write our tale. Perhaps it can be you.*

William whispers to himself, "Yes, of course, why couldn't it be me? I'm more than capable. It *should* be m—" Another jarring jab inside the left of his skull.

> TRANSLATION DATA: *Do not despair. The Reverse Cocooning Process—hereby referred to as RCP—is harmless. Less restricting than has been reported in the past. No casualties. Not anymore. The process has been perfected. Practice for the eventual act with this popular simulation: bathe your body in warm white glue; make certain you have a long straw to breathe through while your face is submerged; allow glue to dry completely, then peel the tight layers back to reveal fresh, smooth epidermis. It is imperative that this be done slowly. RCP is akin to this experience, only more wonderful and with proven results.*
>
> *Surface regression becomes human progression. You must abandon the need for traditional fashion, for any learned sense of archaic language. Allow your natural scents and pheromones to lead you to your multitude of mates. It is not noisome, but natural. Aluminum in antiperspirants causes Alzheimer's. Parabens in toothpaste lead to breast cancer. Our approach is holistic. The body, the mind, the spirit of we. The few function as a collective one. The hive is sacred.*

William stands up, his fingers massaging his temple. He looks lost, dazed.

Harris offers a token look of concern, but does not lift himself from his chair. He whispers, "Damn." He has witnessed similar effects on lesser minds and knows his helping hand will be for naught.

> TRANSLATION DATA: *This does not vary from individual to individual. Idiosyncratic concepts do not exist in our belief structure. We as a whole are one. We are connected. You will never feel alone. Through withering we will persevere. Join us. We promise*

you will never regret the most important decision of your existence. Welcome to the new world. Welcome to your—

William topples to the floor, foam rising from his mouth like volcanic matter.

A sound like a tongue endlessly flapping dominates the room.

"God damn it!" Garth says. "Who the hell forgot to bring the extra film stock?"

April 17, 1989

"Maybe...you weren't really supposed to be my little boy after all. At least I can...die knowing I had a good, special daughter... for what that's worth. Stay happy. Be careful."

That's what Mom whispered in her final hours. Something to that effect. Maybe a little less eloquent and coherent due to the heavy morphine dosage, perhaps a little less Afterschool Special than the way I've worded it, but that's how I prefer to remember her last words. She hated the way my life was heading, never showed even a little support, then had a sudden slight change of heart right before she died. Could have been a worse eulogy.

She was diagnosed with pancreatic cancer. Metastasized to the liver. Unresectable.

I'm using a lot of fifty-cent words now, Miss Diary. Got myself a thesaurus. Deal with it.

Vibrant pink cheeks became skeletal voids
Once thick ropes of maize hair shed and

Collected in greyed mats
in the corners of sterile hospital pillows
Soon to be property of the Reaper

Just some sucky poetry I've been working on, Miss Diary. God, I feel like I'm trying too hard to be Poe or something. Death is morbid, breathing life even more so.

Mom was buried one week before my "sweet sixteen." Yeah, I'm being sarcastic, Diary. Haven't you figured that out yet? It was a lovely funeral, as they cliché say. Black clouds and white stargazer lilies. A stainless steel coffin that I know Hank/Dad/Asshole can't afford, offering decent rest and comfort, as well as rust resistance. An easel displaying an enlarged black-and-white photo of Mom in her prime, circa 1965, when she was just a high school cheerleader named Judith, a mile-wide smile gleaming on her face, bouncing on a tattered trampoline. Hank forced me to show up in boy mode "out of respect for the rest of the family." I've pretty much convinced myself this was the final official public appearance of ~~Thomas~~, whereabouts now unknown.

It's been almost a couple of months now since Mom was lost to the sick, and Hank's writing entire dictionaries that give new definition to abuse. I don't even know how I can manage to scrawl these words down right now—or ever—but I guess I can try. I have no one else I can tell. No one besides you will believe me, Miss Diary. Mom had enough clout within the confines of the house to keep him in league with the human race on rare occasions, but that power died with her.

Hank has never been a Norman Rockwell father by anyone's stretch of the imagination—bottles of the cheapest malt liquor forever at his bedside like guardian angels, a ribbed muscle shirt stained with Rorschach blots of chorizo grease, the education level of a trained chimp, a blue-collar job at the Sweet and Sourdough Factory, which he claims is the direct source of his disdain for immigrants. Or, as Hank so eloquently refers to them, "wetbacks and sand niggers." Really? Who the fuck talks like that? Oh, yeah. My dear old dad. Real classy. Now, as my sole guardian, he's got nothing holding him back from doing his damnedest to try and force me back into ~~Thomas~~ mode.

On any given night, if I'm returning from a few hours of perfect escapism, he'll usually snarl some obscenities in an alcoholic haze. He never was much good with people. Here's a few choice examples:

"Well, lookie here. The fruit fairy has arrived and delivered me a dainty little homo son underneath my pillow."

or

"Goddamn queer disappointment. Get out of my house before I kick your dick to kingdom come. You'd like that, wouldn't you?"

or

"Quit your baby-ass cryin! Wash that clown paint off of your face, you fucking fudge-packing freak before I introduce you to my five closest friends."

Ladies, gentlemen and those somewhere in between: my father, Hardass Hank the Wordsmith Wizard. Who am I kidding, Miss Diary? You're the only one who's ever going to see these words.

Tonight there's a plum shiner painting my eye for the offense of being caught in the wrong clothes again. All lines of deviancy crossed, the laws of parenting lost. Various atrocities performed, accompanied by the unspoken caveat that no one will believe the words of a "faggot in a dress" anyway.

And when this happens, I lose all ability to defend myself. All righteous power flushes right down the toilet. I shut down.

"You want to be a girl so bad?" he asks. "Well, c'mere. Let me show you how to behave like one, you little slut."

The sound of a belt buckle clicking, a zipper's teeth unlinking, a monster moaning.

I don't think I should write about this anymore, Diary. I don't think I—

Fuck.

No.

The specifics are best left forgotten. Let the darkest reaches of the mind fill in the blanks. Then multiply that exponentially.

Life is hell, amphetamines are swell.

June 30, 1989

Crushed some Zolpidem and mixed it into Hank's glass of Brass Monkey last night. Couldn't take his shit anymore, Diary. Don't know how I even managed as long as I did. Sometimes it takes unfathomable circumstances for bravery to finally poke its way through the body. I pilfered his sock-drawer savings during co-matose snores. Surprised, and thankful for, how much he had stashed away—a few hundred and some change—considering he hasn't really been working a hell of a lot lately. Layoffs loom-ing or just plain laziness? I couldn't care less. The cash should, I hope, last me for at least a few weeks before I have to start fending for myself. Something tells me there's not going to be much more where this came from anytime soon, but I'll figure something out. I found a box cutter in his toolbox and—get this, Diary—I actually held it up to his neck while he was dozing. Like I'd actually do anything, right? Well, whatever. I kept the damned thing. Might come in handy later.

I took an overstuffed duffel bag packed with too much fluff, too few essentials. I really *am* a girl, aren't I? Don't worry,

I'm not going to forget to pack you, too, Miss Diary. Obviously I didn't 'cause I'm writing in you right now. No note left for Hank. No major worry about him even trying to look for me. Sweetville's not exactly the biggest bustling metropolis in America, so I guess he could find me if he really wanted to. I know he won't bother, though. He'll be glad to see his little disappointment has bailed on him for good.

Tough to believe that there was a time that Hank might have actually given a shit about me. I don't think I've ever told you this story, Diary. I'll never forget the day when I was six and he took me ice skating. I didn't even have to beg for it. We got up before the sun did and made a big trek out to some enormous, gorgeous forest. Must have taken us a few hours to drive out there. I don't even know where the hell it actually was, to be honest. Never bothered to ask. Hank made sure I was bundled up so warmly that I don't think the cold had a chance. Tons of kids there. So much fun. Easily one of the best days I ever had, so long before I consciously realized there was something different about me.

Hank turned around for just a second to chat with one of the other parents and my leg broke right through the ice and took a dip. I was wrong. The cold **definitely** had a fighting chance and I was losing badly. I screamed for him and he didn't hesitate to hustle out there to save me, even as the ice was beginning to crack beneath his weight. He could have hesitated, somehow found an excuse to let me drown or freeze and save his own ass. He could have avoided the future, his huge mistake of a son.

But he didn't.

When I think about that day now, it feels like I'm watching a scene from a movie. Some feel-good shit that would still manage to jerk a tear or two out of me. It's like it wasn't me that day and it wasn't him either. Because who you are really only counts in the present, doesn't it?

And the present's all I have to focus on right now. Hard to worry about the future when it's so uncertain. I've gotta stay positive, though. Downtown Sweetville better watch out 'cause here I come. I'm going to find my place, wherever the hell that might be, and it's going to welcome me with open arms.

CHAPTER SEVEN

DR. JULIUS KAST TRIED TO IMAGINE what the man now inside the Reverse Cocoon once looked like. The man—if he could still be referred to as such—was currently in transition, neither here nor there. The Reverse Cocoon itself was still vaguely shaped like a man, something that was once a man but would soon become something new. Something better. That was the idea, at least. Kast certainly couldn't fault the Withering Wyldes for trying. He *was* in the business of cosmetic surgery after all.

He couldn't help but wonder, though, in this man's former life had he been a ginger or a silver fox? A slightly or perhaps morbidly obese child? Had he loved his mother dearly? Had he been a record store clerk or a stockbroker? Had he impregnated his high school sweetheart or had he been sterile? None of this mattered anymore, which fascinated Kast to no end. He was enamored with the fact that a man could decide to take on a new life, a new version of himself, and never look back. The old self erased, possibly forgotten, eradicated from the yearbooks and census polls and Employee of the Month photos and frequent eater clubs. If that much had changed about a body, was it even the same creature anymore? And did the soul follow suit?

Kast lightly brushed his fingers across the shell of the Reverse Cocoon, careful not to scratch it with his multitude of rings or his overgrown nails. It looked thin and membranous but felt hard and sticky, like a lollipop that had been given a few lazy licks and was then left out in the sun. Its color was a mix of creamy white and mucous green. There were nickel-sized air holes poked straight down its middle, and the sound of breathing sucked in and out, soft like a baby snoring.

"It really is beautiful in its own way, wouldn't you agree?" Kast asked, turning to the matchstick of a man he knew only as The Angelghoul.

"I'm not sure we have the same tastes in art." The Angelghoul did not turn when he answered. He was focused on puffing a clove cigarette that made the immediate space smell like Christmas.

Kast scanned the wall the Reverse Cocoon was attached to and observed dozens more scattered from one end of the stark grey warehouse to the other, going on for about a hundred feet. If there was a pattern to their placement, he couldn't figure out what it was.

"Shall we?" He politely stepped out of the way and allowed The Angelghoul to walk ahead of him.

"I suppose. Let's get this over with. I have places to be. Pieces to eat."

"Don't be in such a rush all the time, my boy. There are many pleasures to be had in patience."

They turned a corner and passed through a small doorway, The Angelghoul leading the way. They entered what appeared to be a small factory. About twenty or so Withering Wyldes were working as part of an assembly line. Or, more accurately, an inspection line. Wispy drones in the concrete hive. Tiny, white Witherix pills, no bigger than a child's pinky nail, bounced down a conveyor belt. Some of the Withering Wyldes picked the pills up to check for defects, others counted out a quantity of ten and dropped them inside small Ziploc baggies and others supervised. Kast was in awe of their consistency, their dedication to their craft.

Kast stepped up on his tippy toes, tried to peek over the back of The Angelghoul's leather jacket. Even with The Angelghoul clomping around in that hunched-over manner of his, there were still too many inches between the two of them. He grunted, gave up and asked, "How are your implants faring?"

"Itching's finally stopped. They've almost healed. I think they'll do the trick."

Though The Angelghoul had natural bumps on his shoulder blades, they were little more than nubs. Allegedly grown as a result of his spiritual devotion, or so The Angelghoul claimed, but Kast believed they were actually just a genetic deformity. However, he would never speak that thought out loud. The paying patient was always in the right.

The Angelghoul had come to Kast in desperation, claiming his group of Eaters had dubbed him a false messiah because those nubs of his had never sprouted their promised feathers. His acolytes and sycophants had left him high and dry, causing him to swallow his pride and ask Kast for assistance.

Kast knew how much The Angelghoul hated working with him, even though he had done nothing but good deeds for the selfish, skinny man over the years. Granted, he had made The Angelghoul pay handsomely for each slice of kindness, but that did not demean them in the slightest.

As an act of good faith, Kast had granted The Angelghoul one favor gratis: surgical implants to enhance his fleshy cysts. It had been a simple enough surgery. He had used a combination of steel for strength and periosteal bone samples for realism. The scarring was minimal—unnoticeable without prior knowledge and a quality magnifying glass. As impressive as the craftsmanship was, apparently even this development had not been enough for The Angelghoul's original group of Eaters to continue believing in him. They had already lost their faith and nothing, no matter how convincing, would bring them back into the fold.

One of the Withering Wyldes glided up to The Angelghoul and chirped incoherently, waving its spidery fingers at a NO SMOKING sign on the otherwise barren wall. The Angelghoul calmly lifted his foot to the opposite knee and put out the cigarette on the sole of his boot, then showed the butt to the Withering Wylde, perhaps in case it wanted proof. It seemed pleased, but the too-large smile took on a simian playfulness, revealing teeth that looked as though they were laced with chewing tobacco.

"Yes, I'm sure your new devotees will be considerably impressed," Kast said. "We'll begin designing the wings whenever you're ready."

"Designing? There'll be no need for that, gnome. I'm confident they'll come in on their own."

"You'd be wise to watch that tongue of yours. Never forget that a surgeon knows all the right places to cut when necessary." Kast fumed inside, tried his best to not let the name-calling distract him.

He consulted a clipboard hanging near the conveyor belt. A paper attached to it appeared to contain a partial ingredient list. Ephedra, bitter orange, grapefruit extract, guar gum, hydroxy tea, chilled tapeworm eggs. Kast turned the clipboard face down before The Angelghoul had a chance to look at it. He flashed a devious smile at his tall and lanky business partner and they moved on, heading toward the other side of the factory.

"Besides," Kast continued, "I thought we were friends."

"Don't get yourself confused, Kast. I don't exactly call you up to talk about the weather."

Kast pulled a bag of Swedish Fish from one of the pockets of his pea coat. He held the bag out to The Angelghoul, deciding to make amends despite the insults. His Catholic father would have been proud. "Would you like?"

"No thanks. Trying to quit."

"Hmph. You know, what I'd really like is a bar of white chocolate with almonds. Why is something so fabulous almost impossible to find in the Sweetville city limits? I don't think I'm asking for too much, do you?"

The Angelghoul just stared at him, his eyes small, dark and dead. "So, have you figured out how to communicate with them yet?"

Kast decided to curb the small talk. It obviously wasn't building any sort of rapport, no matter how cordial he was being. Why waste unnecessary breath? "Until recently, my understanding of their language has been rudimentary. I knew enough to survive, so to speak, but naturally that wasn't enough. However, they've introduced me to someone very special. Young fellow by the name of Ekkert."

"What do you mean by 'special'? Like Corky Thatcher?"

"I can't say. I've never met this Mr. Thatcher you speak of. But my new friend, he's been invaluable in helping me further decipher their language. Trying to figure out why it devolved along with their bodies. That poor, brilliant lad, I tell you. Suffered so much. He's just—"

Kast craned his neck around The Angelghoul's rawboned frame and watched in surprise as one of the Withering Wyldes snatched up a

Witherix pill from the conveyor belt and flicked it into its skeletal maw, swallowing it dry, likely thinking no one had noticed. But it was wrong. Another member of the hive, this one only distinguishable from the rest because of a pencil wedged in the top of its paper-thin, pointed ear, snuck up behind the thief, smacked it on the side of its head and hissed. The Withering Wyldes at each end of the assembly line pulled levers and pressed buttons and the conveyor belt slowed. The other workers turned around almost in unison. As the machinery came to a halt, the warehouse was nearly silenced, the only sound coming from the buzzing of the hive.

The thief backed away. Its expression was stern, its body language betraying its fear. The group of Withering Wyldes crept toward the thief in dancelike steps that almost looked choreographed, but the movements were from no dance routine Kast had ever witnessed. A few members of the hive encircled the thief and pounced. A brief moment passed, then a horrible shrieking made Kast jump back a half step. He covered his ears and looked away, but he noticed The Angelghoul watching with calculated interest.

The shrieking continued for what felt like agonizing minutes before tapering off. Then a dull shredding sound, like a saw blade ripping its way through dead bamboo. When quiet resumed, the Withering Wyldes left their comrade in the corner and returned to work. Whether it was comatose or a corpse, Kast could not say.

"Hmm," he said, trying to regain his composure and not appear skittish. "A pity, yes?"

The Angelghoul chuckled without emotion, if such an act was even possible. "Well, all I know is I wasn't expecting to see that today."

"The Withering Wyldes do not tolerate deviations from the hive. They are trustworthy business partners. But, then again, some of the individuals who worked with Al Capone might have once thought the same thing."

"I can respect that."

Kast changed the subject ever so slightly. "They've been experimenting with synthetic pheromones, you know. Both sweet and savory scents. Injecting it beneath the loose skin around their torsos, leaving some sort of small air pockets in order to release the pheromones later. I've seen it in action and it seems to work. Quite an intricate process, really, and it likely wouldn't even be physiologically possible if they were still—"

"Can we please get to the point of this meeting?"

Kast motioned for The Angelghoul to follow him. They continued walking through the seemingly endless warehouse, eventually passing through a doorway trimmed with tiny motion-activated lights and entering a room that had been hollowed out into something more closely resembling a cave. There was a pantry, a padlocked mini-fridge and not much else save for a few fluorescent lights hanging from the carved ceiling. This was where the Withering Wyldes slept. The walls were covered with a material similar to Velcro where they attached themselves, huddled together and entered one another's dreams. However, it was not yet time for bed. Still so much work to do in the day for the Withering Wyldes. Their work ethic reminded Kast of a song his mother had sang to him when he was still in diapers.

The busy little beavers chop wood, wood, wood.
They'd stop and take a break if they could, could, could.

Kast fished around inside one of his pockets, then another. He grew frustrated and patted around his pea coat until finding a small bronze key. "You deal directly with Junkie Creeps, do you not?"

"What, you mean like the Big H?"

"That *is* their preferred heaven, yes?" He unlocked the padlock, opened the refrigerator and wedged half his body inside as if searching for last night's half-eaten sandwich.

"Yeah, of course I deal with them. That's where most of the money is. Aside from some bored trust fund babies in the Sweethills, the Creeps are my bread and butter."

Kast retrieved a small plastic tub of little baggies filled with grey powder. He passed them to The Angelghoul.

"What's this?"

"This is one of your new products. Not terribly different from what you're used to peddling. However, it *is* laced with just a hint of Witherix. I'd advise against imparting that information to your buyers, though."

"Huh. So the Withering Wyldes are using covert recruiting methods now?"

"You could argue that."

"Not like I care one way or the other. As long as they pay and I get my share on time, all is right in the world." The Angelghoul shoved the baggies into his jacket.

"I have something else for you here as well." In Kast's other hand was a Ziploc bag containing a smattering of Sweet Candy.

"Why is that here? I thought these freaks were total Candy naysayers."

"Shh." Kast giggled, pressing his finger to his chapped lips. "Public relations, my friend. Our little secret, okay?" The Angelghoul shrugged. "This is their own formula. A sample for you to try before you sell."

"Business is business." He held out his hand, awaiting the offering. Kast tossed it to him.

"I think you'll be pleased with this new development. The psychedelic qualities far surpass the previous versions."

"I thought you didn't do this stuff, though."

"No, no, of course not. An old heart like mine wouldn't do well with something so…fervent. This is just what I've been told."

"Let's just hope your little translator knows what the hell he's talking about."

Kast closed the door to the refrigerator. "Are you ever going to tell me your real name?"

"Are you ever going to stop pestering me?" The Angelghoul lit another clove.

"Touché." Kast beckoned for The Angelghoul to follow him. "And, of course, there's more where that came from. From what I under—"

A ritualistic chanting echoed from the other end of the warehouse.

"Oh, what the hell now?" The Angelghoul asked. "That's fucking it. I've got what I came for. I'm dust."

Kast's purple eyes filled with childish glee. "Oh, my. I think one must be hatching. What an honor to be here right now. Do you want to—" He turned around and realized he was speaking to himself. The Angelghoul had crept away in a matter of seconds, skittered off into the shadows. He would enjoy this birthing spectacle alone.

When he arrived back at the long room filled with Reverse Cocoons, there were nearly a hundred Withering Wyldes gathered around, more than Kast had ever seen in the beryl flesh in one place. It appeared as though the chamber was now overgrown with weeds. A few members of the hive were using hacksaws and pry bars to remove a Reverse Cocoon from the wall while another barked orders. After a minute or so of what may have been swearing in their language, they pulled it loose and their chanting grew louder. It did not even sound like words to Kast, more like a discordant hum.

One of the Withering Wyldes was in a corner away from the rest, fiddling with something behind what looked like a sound booth. Sparks flew and the Withering Wylde shrieked in response. The fluorescent lights in the chamber blinked out for a moment, and when they returned there was music seeping out of the speakers. Highly synthesized and pro-grammed, upbeat and quirky, almost in perfect time with the bizarre chanting.

Kast watched as the last bits of the Reverse Cocoon were peeled from the wall. A white, viscous fluid seeped from its edges. With its shell now fully removed, a newly born Withering Wylde was attached to the wall in a broken Christ pose. It looked tired and drugged, but it was real. It was what it was always supposed to be, what it had yearned to be for all its former life.

Other members of the hive poured mineral spirits on its newly stretched body, then caught it as it dropped face forward. They wiped off what bits of the wet goo they could and backed away, giving it room to breathe. Its new flesh was so fresh and clear blue that Kast could almost see right through it. It opened its eyes and shrank from the lights. It was beautiful, fully realized.

The chrysalis was complete.

Kast couldn't help but smile.

and now a word from
OUR SPONSOR

V/O: "Having misgivings about your questionable weight and size? Feeling disappointed with your shape? Wishing you had a hard body that all your peers would envy? Our researchers have the perfect solution."

JINGLE: ♫♪♬ *Witherix* ♫♪♬

V/O: "A revolutionary new diet pill, developed by world-famous surgeon and dietitian, Dr. Dorian Wylde. Two pills daily, taken with one gram filtered water and a quarter ounce of flaxseed bread. You'll never have to exercise again."

JINGLE: ♫♪♬ *Witherix* ♫♪♬

V/O: "Enlightenment has been achieved. Clear your mind of life's troubles when your body is slender and perfect. No more counting calories. Just counting the jaws that drop and the heads that turn to look at you."

JINGLE: ♫♪♬ *Witherix* ♫♪♬
♪♭ *The path to a godly body* ♪♭

V/O: *Witherix can be found in any drugstore near you. May cause a variety of side effects, including bulimia, diarrhea, constipation, dark urine or stool, clinical dementia, hallucinations, dysphoria, hypnotic regression, unnatural hair growth, decreased libido, painful erections, increased menstruation, obsessive anorexia, irregular heartbeat, hives, abnormal dreams, dry lingual paste, severe rectal rash, cinnamon/vanilla scent emission, unusual bruising, infertility, yellowing of the eyes or skin, morphemic vertigo.*

July 5, 1989

So I made a friend out here already, Miss Diary. I know. I'm just the kind of person everyone wants to be around, right? Yeah. On Mars...

   Anyway, her name's Gwen. I'm lucky I found her so quick-ly. I haven't been able to find any work, even part-time. No one feels sorry enough for me, I guess. I don't think I would've lasted another week alone on the street, and the last thing I'd ever want to do is go crawling back home. I felt an immedi-ate magnetism toward my new companion, though. There was some sort of charismatic aura seeping from Gwen's pores when I first ran into her, some impossible-to-fake coolness when I first met her and she tried to bum a smoke off me that I didn't have. From far away, Gwen's an averagely pretty girl about two years or so older than me. Amazonian height, nondescript facial features. Hispanic mix, I guess. A failed cheerleader's body. Slight stubble on her jawline. Lets me know I'm not alone in Transition Hell. I guess Gwen more or less saw the same in me and was cool enough to take me under her wing.

Our relationship hasn't really developed into what one would typically call friends, yet we still make it work. She can barely tolerate my relatively virgin naïveté. There's that whole cooler-than-you thing popping up again. Well, so what? To be honest, I think she's a bit impersonal. Of course, like I said, this is still a colossal step up from my home life. I'll take it. Aside from a few slight clashes, we basically force ourselves to accept the other pea in the pod and act as each other's protector. Strength in numbers.

Mom would've said Gwen's a bad influence since she's been encouraging me to go out palming with her. But it's kind of a necessity. And it's not like I've never done it before. My old dis-count wig was, as they say, "free 99." Acrylic of questionable quality, not exactly capable of recreating a perfectly fashionable 'do. But it was the best that next-to-no-money could buy. It was also kinda itchy. Thankfully I don't really need that any-more since my hair's finally getting close to shoulder length. Don't even know why I bothered packing it. We've been heisting from Modyrn Gyrlz. Gwen taught me a great scam. I'll arrive to the store in arguably androgynous apparel, sneak into the dressing room with two fierce little numbers, then put my fa-vorite of the two on underneath my street clothes, return the other to the racks and hope that no one notices the extra bulk as I'm leaving the store. Thank God they don't use those alarm tag thingies.

We've been wandering the streets together past dusk and beyond, congregating at the mildly popular trick spot of Fifth and Quail. Gwen's an old pro at this point, which I suppose makes me a contradictorily eager and unwilling pupil.

I don't think I'm ready to learn these particular ropes just yet, Miss Diary. Can you blame me?

Hooking up with Gwen also comes with the bonus of a rented studio-sized room at the Friendship Motel, all utilities paid and a barely operational kitchenette, with just enough room on the floor for me to squeeze into a sleeping bag. It can be kind of terrifying sharing space with the creepy crawlies that I never see, yet sometimes feel tickling and brushing across my cheek in the few moments between sleeping and waking.

I'll eventually earn enough to rent my own room, probably in the same motel. I just wish I could find some sort of regular job soon. Baby steps. At least Gwen has a crappy boom box and some cool tapes she lifted from Tower. Stuff I've never heard of before, but I think I like it. Yeah, I really do like it. For some odd reason, all of her favorite bands seem to be from England or somewhere. The Smiths, Joy Division, Siouxsie & the Banshees, The Cure. It's different, but different is kinda what I need right now. Dark music for dark times.

Gwen's been explaining how things work on the street, so it'll be easier to adjust when I'm ready—*if* I'm ever ready. Where to stash my cash and condom variety packs in case the cops show up. Which public restrooms are good for cleaning up quickly between tricks. How to receive return business by appearing grateful to the hungry older men after being barely compensated for my grand performance.

How to find solace in stoic nights. How to erase the events that have just transpired. How to forget.

August 1, 1989

Last night ended up being my first night of "work," which amounted to watching from the shadows. It's taken me a while to even build up to that. We showed up to Fifth and Quail at about midnight. Gwen says there's no point in showing up much earlier. She's the expert. Bertoberto's Tacos was just shutting down for the night, the last lights of safety in the general vicinity. A grey Bronco picked Gwen up about ten minutes after we arrived, but she was brought back pretty quickly after a spin around the block. Just a window shopper or a nervous first timer, I guess. Gwen says that happens a lot. Just part of the game. A red Mazda came next, and she was gone longer this time, long enough to earn at least part of her night's pay.

Gwen was cool enough to share a turkey sandwich after we got back home, but my gurgling stomach ended up being my strongest motivator to pull my own weight. If I'm not careful, the money I stole from Hank is going to be nothing but pennies pretty soon.

I can't go home, Miss Diary. Ever.

So tonight had to be the night.

Hair teased, sprayed and crimped just a bit. A look I don't think I'll ever completely commit to or care for, but one that ultimately seems to do the trick. Four-inch heels—note to self: only a good idea if I'm not planning on doing much walking. I'm really more of a flats sort of girl if I can get away with it. Navy blue capri tights with runs behind the knees and fraying near the bottom. A black miniskirt and matching spandex top, and a purple pleather jacket. I looked like an extra from the dance party scene in a straight-to-video teen sex romp.

But it worked.

My first customer was drawn to me like I was a Siren.

He was old enough to be my father. Meaty head with an obvious combover hanging around on the top. He was wearing a faded red T-shirt that read: WORLD'S COOLEST DAD—a sentiment I really hope was just ironic. Remnants of junk food snack packs and cigarette butts were strewn around the floor of his car.

I introduced myself by my street name—"Ariel." What, do you think I'm going to give any of these guys my real name? You're crazy, Miss Diary.

My host was named Ken, or at least he was at that moment. I learned pretty quickly that street identity changes as frequently and nonchalantly as underwear. Ken drove me into a carport a few blocks away. I was a little worried that whoever normally parked in that spot would come home. But let's be honest, that wasn't the main thing I was worried about.

Ken was nice enough for my first trick, I guess. He didn't over-degrade me or whatever, if there's such a thing as degrees of degradation. He also apparently didn't bathe or trim his pubes regularly. Is this what I have to look forward to every night? Fuck.

I felt ill afterward. Still kinda do. After I finished, I slipped my earnings into my bra, threw Ken's car door open, winked and mumbled a goodbye. Then I hurried to the alley to vomit. Luckily no one was around to witness that humiliation.

The shame will eventually subside.

It has to.

October 22, 1989

So this is destiny, huh? I can't shake the feeling that someone's been playing a cruel joke on me. Was I really supposed to end up here, Miss Diary? This is the plan laid out for me by God or Zeus or Shiva or whoever? If this is supposed to be some sort of test, then I'd rather just flunk out of school. It's only been a couple of months since the streets became my new home, but this "temporary solution" continues to be my only option.

It's ideal when the johns are forgettable, when they just get what they came for and drop me back off. Sad when that's the best treatment I can look forward to from a guy. I gave up on expecting politeness after this one john gripped my neck and held my head down the whole time I was working. Not fucking fun at all. Gwen checked me out afterward and I already had a couple of bruises forming at the top of my neck. Bruises shaped like fingertips.

A few weeks ago, I started offering full service. I was really dreading that eventuality, but I needed the money. A girl's gotta eat. I brought him up to Gwen's place. Does it count as my place too, Miss Diary? I **am** paying rent now, doing my best to pull my weight. Anyway, I left the guy out in the hallway at first because I knew Gwen was still inside, cleaning up from her last trick. I asked her if she could just hang in the bathroom for a couple of minutes while I took care of this guy.

So I told him to lay his cash on the end table, and I started working on him down below because I wanted him to be good and ready when we went all the way. I wanted the second part to be over as quickly as possible. I got lubed up, pulled up my skirt and lay on my stomach, facing the wall at the head of the bed. I tried to paint pretty pictures on the wall with my mind. Rainbows, unicorns, mermaids, anything to take a vacation from reality.

As soon as he entered me, he told me to call him Daddy.

I choked. I couldn't even begin to handle that, so I pulled away from him and pulled my skirt back down. I said I was sorry and tried to give his money back. He was kneeling at the edge of the bed, his fleshy flag already flying half-mast. He said no, he didn't want the money. He wanted what he paid for. I begged him to leave, told him I was feeling sick, but he wouldn't budge. His face turned pink and he told me not to be a fucking bitch, to just lie back down and let him finish.

I was holding back the tears, ready to swallow my pride in case he was going to try and hurt me. I didn't know what the hell to do. Suddenly, from behind us, Gwen told the asshole to get the fuck out before she cut his goddamned balls off. She was just inches away from him, holding a toothbrush with a razor blade duct-taped to the end of it. The guy threw his hands up, said it was some kind of misunderstanding. She shoved the razor closer to his package and his pathetic little prick shrank down to the size of a peach pit. Ha! She was not fucking around.

He pulled his pants back on and ran out with his fly still down like he was trying to escape a fire. He even left the money. So win/win, I guess? At least we know he's never going to come back trying to press charges or something.

Gwen later told me that she always keeps a small arsenal on hand. Pepper spray, homemade shanks and shivs, whatever might stop some loser from taking advantage of her. I didn't have to ask if she'd ever used any of the weapons before. Her eyes told me she had. She's even savvier than I already thought. I owe her big time. Try to think of a present I can lift for her, Miss Diary. I'll scribble down some ideas later.

I wish so badly I had better options. I don't think the shame of what I'm forced to do will ever go away, but I guess survival's drive can push it back into the furthest corridors of my mind. It's easier to pretend I enjoy the work. It's easier to ignore the fine lines of exploitation. It's easier to become the lie.

CHAPTER EIGHT

TRIXIE FIDDLED WITH THE CRUMPLED NAPKIN. She had been carrying it for what seemed like months, protecting the marker-scrawled phone number like sacred numerical scripture. In reality, less than two weeks had passed since Christopher strolled into Audrey's Diner and into her lonely life. Was it even reasonable to say he was *in* her life at this point? Seemed a bit obsessive to even consider that before getting to know more about a guy beyond a pleasant face and a name. And even before actually calling him. For now, he was just on the outskirts of her life. Why dwell on the possibilities unless there was a valid reason? Their moment might have been fleeting, a connection that was never meant to be. It was up to her to take the leap of faith. Maybe, just maybe, this could be a real shot at happiness.

She decided this mysterious thing called "happiness" was only possible for people who were not her, but she also figured following such a foolish dream had the potential to be fun.

Once Trixie discovered the ink was smearing from spending too much time in her pocket, she folded the napkin up and left it at her apartment, nestled within a cherry oak jewelry box. Now she freed the napkin from its wooden prison and stared at it, trying to figure out if there was some hidden code between the numbers that would offer guidance on how to approach this situation and avoid all dangerous missteps. A potential attraction also had the potential for sheer destruction.

She decided to send caution packing and risk it.

Baby steps toward her telephone. A glance at her black Kit-Cat clock. Almost noon. Surely it wouldn't be too early to call. It was a safe time. She picked the receiver up, checked the numbers on the napkin, checked them again, started to dial the first few digits, then hung up. It felt like Suzanne Somers was squeezing the Thighmaster deep within her bowels, though that would have been less nauseating.

Trixie decided to change her course, opting for a trip to the kitchen to treat herself to a piña colada wine cooler. She found the least spotty glass in the cabinet and poured the drink slowly, buying precious time. She burrowed into her couch and sipped the cool mixture, letting it flow between her teeth. It was so well chilled that it triggered the sensitivity of her incisors. She shook off the shivers and tried to fool her brain into thinking the drink was relaxing her. She picked up the phone again and pretend-dialed, then adjusted the receiver along her cheekbone as if finding the most comfortable spot would somehow summon charisma.

Federico crept out of nowhere and silently floated up into her lap. He purred inquisitively and his piston paws worked on her thighs until he found a comfortable spot to curl up into. His tail writhed and danced in the general vicinity of her crotch like a long, furry phallus under the control of a snake charmer.

"Okay, Rico. Now I think you're just trying to mock me. Not cool."

The cat meowed playfully, as if confirming her accusations. Trixie brushed his tail away and scratched behind his ears. He seemed to get the point and went along with the new plan. His head dug into the palm of her hand, begging for eternal affection.

"So what do you think, baby cat? Should I call this guy? He's sort of cute, he seems nice enough, he gave me the time of day, he's a single male and he has a pulse."

Federico scuffed her fingers with the papillae of his tongue. Trixie took any sort of a gesture from him as a yes simply so she could pretend she was momentarily brave. The slight buzz from the wine cooler didn't hurt either.

Trixie always knew she was a lightweight when it came to adult beverages. She wished she had some Sweet Candy on hand to balance out her buzz, but that could lead to the possibility of dealing with The Angelghoul—never a pleasant experience and one she had managed to avoid for quite some time. She had met with other dealers instead, but the availability of these new jacks had been dwindling in recent months. Freddie, the guy she usually hit up for her Candy fix, had mentioned The Angelghoul was starting to corner the market on the drug again. A solid reason to think, at the very least, about quitting the habit. That guy gave her the creeps. She had never seen what he really looked like. He was always hiding somewhere in the darkness while one of his lackeys traded the pills for the cash. Gwen had apparently dealt with him directly. Just once. And she had not mentioned very much about the experience. Trixie remembered it was the first and last time she had seen true fear in her former friend's eyes.

She grabbed her phone with gusto and dialed the full number without pause, then wrapped the cord around her arm like a heroin tie-off. She realized she had not bothered to plan her first words just as the other end was picked up.

"Sweet-E Donuts." The voice sounded like it was being transmitted via a paper cup and a string.

"Oh. Hello. Um…I'm not sure I have the right number. Is Christopher there?"

"Say huh?"

Trixie shoved the napkin closer to her face, hoping she had translated the scribble correctly. She could smell traces of Sharpie still emanating from the paper.

"I'm trying to reach Christopher. Does he work there? Christopher Faith?"

"Oh yeah. We got the cinnamon glaze."

"No, I don't want any donuts. I mean his last name is Faith."

"Oh yeah. We got, like, many kinds. Chocolate glaze, sugar glaze, honey glaze."

"I think I dialed wrong. Sorry to bother you."

She hung up the phone and couldn't help but giggle afterward. With this small amount of tension now released, she found her focus and dialed each number from the napkin carefully this time, like it was a passcode to defusing a bomb.

One ring. Two rings. The third seemed even louder than the first two combined. A fourth would give her the excuse to hang up.

"Hello?" A voice like Kermit the Frog on methaqualone answered. Trixie winced. She should have known Christopher would be the type to stay up late and sleep in. That was probably the norm for a guy in a band. Staying up until the crack of dawn practicing or going to see other bands or something like that. She was tempted to hang up and came close to making that move, but then began to stress about the possibility he might Star 69 her.

She paused, tried to think of the perfect thing to say and then said, "Hi, is this—can I speak with Christopher, please?"

Not even drinking a gallon of oil could have smoothed the squeaks in her voice. She felt like her months of rigorous vocal therapy had been worthless, that her voice was now devoid of any proper gender.

"Uh...yeah. I'm the droid you're looking for." Christopher's voice suddenly sounded invigorated. Trixie could practically hear him shoveling Mr. Sandman's crust out of the corners of his eyes.

Trixie attempted to compose herself and turn her flirty femininity up to eleven. She glided to the window, carrying the phone with her as far as the cord would allow. She peered out at the fire escape. Still nonoperational, but she couldn't help but feel paranoid about the possibility of someone waiting out there for her these days. "Oh. Hi. This is Trixie. We met last week when you came into the diner that I—"

"Oh. Hey! What's up? Sorry, I didn't mean to—"

"No, that's totally fine. You go first."

"Well, it's just... I was hoping I'd eventually hear from you. Cool. How are you?"

"Good." Her response came out sounding like a question. Anything she had initially planned to say next had taken a taxi straight out of her mind and into Nowheresville. This was too early in the conversation for such an awkward pause, but lo and behold, there it was. Like passing gas in church.

She smeared the dust on the windowsill with her finger. It felt like frosting that had been left out for days without a top. Outside, two cars honked at each other as if engaging in their own little chat. "I'm sorry if I woke you up or something."

"No, don't even worry about it. I needed to get up pretty soon for work anyway."

A few hushed seconds. Trixie couldn't figure out what to say. She was starting to feel foolish and regretted making this call.

Christopher filled the silent gap and continued. "Hey. So, I hope this doesn't come off as *too* aggressive, but I wanted to see if maybe you'd like to hang out…uh…go out sometime?"

Trixie felt like she was going to throw up. A reasonably swell guy was asking her out. Could this really be happening? She warily welcomed the possibilities, though, and did her best to put on her cool face. Thankfully the phone's presence nullified the need for this and made her job a hell of a lot easier.

"Oh, sure. I'm down." She was in the groove now. Pretending to be cool and calm could sometimes be just as effective as the real thing.

"Well, what are you doing tomorrow night? Do you have to go to work or anything? I hope I'm not being too pushy."

"No, that's fine. I'm about as free as can be." She mentally cursed at herself multiple times. Coming off so desperate was a terrible move. She should have casually told him she needed to check her calendar first and call him right back. Of course, she soon remembered she did not even own a calendar.

"Okay. Awesome. Would you be into going to see a movie with me? *Fire Walk with Me* is playing over at the Livingston."

"What's that?" Enormous stomping and shouting came from the apartment above hers. A slight drizzle of plaster dust drifted down to the carpet.

"The *Twin Peaks* movie. I've been really excited to check that out. Sound good to you, or is there something else you want to see?"

"Oh. Okay. No…well, yeah. That's fine. I'm totally game for that. Let's do it."

"Nice. Shoot me your address. I'll come pick you up around, say, seven?"

"Make it eight. Just to be safe. I *am* a girl, after all."

Trixie gave him her address and said she'd wait out in front of her building. She could not summon up the bravery to tell him The Truth. Not yet. Why ruin a nice night by outing herself before she had a chance to sabotage it by other, less dramatic means? She felt twenty degrees of awful. The last thing she wanted to do was trick him. But it's not like anything was going to happen. Just go to a movie, hang out, and start getting to know each other as friends. The revelation of hidden appendages could wait.

For now.

Forever, she wished.

Christopher laughed. It sounded like he was blowing air between his teeth.

"Yeah, I know the drill."

* * *

Jujubes. Licorice whips. Popcorn, lightly salted and heavily buttered. Large Cherry 7UP with two straws. More than a few reasons to share some skin space.

Trixie was somewhat confused by the film, having never watched the *Twin Peaks* television series, but she was fond of the way Christopher was engrossed in it. Out of the corner of her eye, she observed his filmic obsession with a mixture of awe and apprehension. It was like his soul had left his body and was surfing the 35 mm film as it moved through the projector. She definitely considered herself a movie fan, but wondered if her tastes strayed too far into Lowbrow City, if movies like *The Goonies* and *Beetlejuice* would be capable of stimulating impressive conversation with Christopher.

The film ended and they took a walk along the streets of downtown Sweetville, where even the accumulated filth in the gutters seemed romantic. Trixie felt Christopher's hand guide her by the small of her back as they crossed the street on a yellow light. She had thankfully never been terribly large—even now she was only five foot eight, 130 pounds. Her size was the only bone God had tossed in her direction. Though Christopher likely did not outweigh her by too much, Trixie was relieved that he was the clear winner in the Height Olympics.

A light mist fell from the sky and peppered their faces. Nothing severe enough to wish there were an umbrella handy.

"So," Trixie said, "you're really into movies, huh?"

"Yeah. That's an understatement."

"What's your favorite?"

"Hmm. Well that can change depending on my mood. Lately it's been *Friday the 13th Part 4: The Final Chapter*."

"I didn't even know there was a part three."

"They're actually up to like eight or so now. Pretty hit and miss as a series. Part four is a total gem, though. Crispin Glover's dance scene is one of the finest moments in the history of American cinema."

Trixie felt at ease when she realized that Christopher's interests were not as obscure and artsy as she had initially feared. He told her he could find some worth in almost any film. It was there, somewhere, but you just had to be patient enough to look for it. The hammy expression of an extra hovering behind the two leads during a botched romantic interlude. Terrifyingly real gore effects amidst a sea of subpar acting, bad editing and plot holes. A quirky score that had no right to be accompanying the flickering images, yet somehow worked regardless.

Trixie wasn't used to strolling the streets proudly. Though it had been well over a year since Fifth and Quail could have been considered her "place of employment," she still felt like the shape of her Mary Janes fit too perfectly in the confines of the concrete. Her perspective had changed as well. Now she was able to absorb her surroundings as a spectator, and here was a guy who actually went out of his way to at least try and look presentable for her. Trixie was awed by the fact that Christopher was here to spend the evening with *her* specifically. He wasn't just some random guy paying for an orifice that could have belonged to anyone or anything.

They stopped to sit on a bench near a small plaza, a general hotspot for people-watching on any given weekend. A homeless man used a stoplight pole as lumbar support. Sketchy, searching eyes peered through greasy strands of hair. Clothing that looked more planned than naturally disheveled. His curiously well-constructed sign claimed, with near perfect penmanship: "Y LIE? PIZZA SOUNDS GREAT, BUT SOME CANDY WOULD REALLY B SWEET. GOD BLESS. ✪." Skate rats thrashed their boards on a nearby curb, turning destruction of public property into an art form. Trixie noticed Christopher doing his best to not be distracted by the tricks they were attempting to pull off. A young couple had a brief tiff next to a malfunctioning streetlight. Police and ambulance sirens roared through nearby streets, most likely much too late to their destination. Groups of fashionable young men and women spilled from the clubs only to filter into whatever other club happened to be closest. Trixie thought she saw someone in the crowd she recognized but ignored the possibility. Across the street, a Jesoid wearing a papier-mâché crown of thorns and a shirt proclaiming LISTEN TO ETHEREAL JAZZ barked confidently through a megaphone.

"If you are a heathen, a homosexual, a drug user, a criminal, a liberal—repent now and save your soul. Feel the glory of God or feel his fearsome wrath. It is not too late to face the light. Our God is an awesome God. You, too, can be awesome. Join the Prophets and absolve yourself of sin." The Jesoid wielded a professionally printed sign with his other hand, advertising for PAUS: PROPHETS AGAINST THE USE OF SWEET CANDY.

Trixie and Christopher continued learning about each other, elements that seemed to be only important on the surface but actually led a direct path to their souls. They gushed about some of their favorite music, and even though Trixie was unfamiliar with the names Christopher spoke so highly of, she felt it was refreshing to be able to talk so openly about passions for sound. Music had been there for her during her darkest moments, had been more of a savior than any bible could have ever been. They promised to make each other mix tapes reflecting their respective tastes.

Trixie caught sight of something on the corner catawampus to their spot—a young, well-dressed couple squealing with drunken delight as they waited for the light to change. Despite the fact that the woman's face was mostly obscured by the man's hulk of a body, Trixie was certain there was something familiar about her. Her voice. Her movements. Something.

"Want to go over to Lucky Larry's and grab a drink?" she asked, nodding her head toward a dive bar in the opposite direction of the couple.

"Oh…well…I don't drink, actually. But we could still go. If you want. I don't mind."

"Oh, that's right!" She mentally slapped herself. "I remember now the rest of your band was borderline wasted that night I met you, but you were totally sober."

"Ha! Yeah, those guys love their brewskies."

Trixie kept sneaking subtle glances at the mystery woman who finally shifted enough for her to catch a good glimpse, and her identity became clear. A ghost from the past shivered across the nape of her neck. A name—almost forgotten to her, but still capable of crawling out of the corridors of her mind.

Britt.

Difficult to recognize without what had once been her trademark street outfit, and it looked like she had gone under the knife a few more times. Somehow she had found new crevices in her body where she could craft more womanly features. Her breasts were big enough to smuggle infants inside, and her face was simultaneously ravishing and cartoonish.

Trixie turned her whole body toward Christopher, hoping it had been so long that Britt wouldn't recognize her, wouldn't *want* to recognize her.

"So what's the deal with that choice?" Trixie's voice dropped to a whisper, her eyes wide. "Did you…have a problem before?"

Christopher laughed politely. "No. Nothing like that. I get that a lot, though. Never been drunk or high in my life, actually. Holds zero interest for me."

"Wow. Gotta say, I'm impressed. Sorry to say I haven't been quite the saint you have."

"No biggie, really. Just a personal commitment I made and stuck with."

"So are you like…straight-edge or something, then?"

Trixie heard the crosswalk beep meant for the blind and noticed that Britt and the side of prime meat she was attached to were now crossing the first street. She hoped they would either keep walking straight or hang a right once they reached the other side. Anything to keep her from being noticed and inadvertently outed. This near-perfect night could go so wrong so quickly.

"Yeah, you caught me." Christopher offered an earnest grin that almost made her forget about the possible confrontation. "I don't usually go out of my way to mention it since a lot of people either don't know what the hell I'm talking about, or they hold some kind of grudge against it or whatever. I'm not militant or anything like that. No preaching. I do this for me and me only."

Fierce laughter bounced off the dilapidated buildings, almost cracking their windows further before reaching Trixie's ears. She could practically feel the heat of Britt's breath caressing her shoulders.

"Sorry," Christopher continued, noticing her distracted expression. "That didn't come off as self-righteous or anything, did it?"

"No. It's just that I've never met anyone like you before. I mean, I remember a couple of straight-edge guys in high school, but they were sort of jerks I guess."

Trixie heard Britt's laughter fading away. She stole one final glance in that direction and could see Britt's backside being swallowed by the darkness. She was safe. Temporarily. She allowed herself to relax and focus on the date. Her life, now more than ever, amounted to always keeping her eyes pushing as close to the back of her head as she could manage.

"Yeah. It only takes one bad egg, right?"

"Unfortunately."

"I don't eat meat either. Is that weird?"

"Well, no. I guess not. Not really. Caring about animals is a bonus." Trixie made a conscious note never to eat a burger in front of him. That was not going to be easy.

"I can try and cook you one of my mean veggie stir-fry dishes sometime. You might like it."

"I think I already do." She tossed him a flirty smile. Their eyes met, and Christopher tore his away first. Someone had to.

"Speaking of high school, you didn't go to Sweetville West did you?"

"No. I was an Eastern girl."

"Yeah, of course. What am I thinking? I would have definitely remembered you if you were a former Westie. Bummer you had to put up with Sweetville East. I went there once for summer school and it was a total dump. No offense."

She worried for a few moments that Christopher might have known Aron, or at least crossed paths with him, but dismissed it as less than likely since they came from different crowds. Completely different worlds, really.

"Don't sweat it," she said. "I totally agree. Your family live in town?"

"Yeah, my folks live on the outskirts of the Sweethills. You know, nice enough to be a respectable neighborhood but also right before it stops being affordable?" Trixie nodded and they both released some light laughter. "Not in the same house, though. They split up when I was in junior high."

"Oh, that sucks. Sorry to hear about that."

"I've never really been super close with them, but I was going to my mom's house a lot because my cousin lives…uh…lived there until kinda recently. But yeah, he and I are buds. And my older brother Adam and I are pretty tight, too. He owns this really cool video store a few blocks away from here, actually."

"The love for movies runs in the family, huh?"

"Ha! Yeah, I suppose so. I'd take you there now, but he's closed on Mondays."

Trixie swelled with temporary pride. She had never met a guy who wanted to introduce her to anyone in his family before. Never even believed that was possible. "That's cool. Maybe some other time?"

"Absolutely," Christopher said with a sincere smile, and Trixie flushed at the idea of future plans with him. "So what about your parents?"

She paused for a moment, choosing her words carefully. "My mother's been dead a long time. My father…well, he might as well be."

Christopher froze. "Shit," he said, his hand landing atop hers. He gently caressed her knuckles. "Sorry to hear that. Didn't mean to stir up any rough memories."

Trixie flipped her palm up so her fingers linked with his. "Been so long since I thought about any of that. It might as well be someone else's life."

"Hey, I know we don't know each other that well yet, but if you ever want to talk about that stuff in the future, well, I'm a damned good listener at the very least."

Trixie nodded vacantly. No matter how much she tried to avoid it, all fresh starts still had trails of breadcrumbs leading back to the past. "It's cool. I don't want to be a burden or anything."

"I don't see how anyone could ever think of you as a burden."

A few seconds of silence in their little bubble as the cacophony of downtown surrounded them, creating a white-noise soundtrack to their budding enchantment. Their fingers remained loosely locked. Trixie was relieved she had remembered to use a double-dose of lotion before the date. Her hands had been so uncharacteristically dry lately. Perhaps she should have been concerned about the fact that her hands were, unfortunately, not much smaller than his, but she was too entranced by the moment. They gazed at each other and the quiet between them continued, waiting to be filled by words, actions, natural disasters. Yet this time it was not awkward. It was a clue. A sign for Trixie to partake in the first truly brave moment of her life.

"So," she whispered, "you look like you want to kiss me."

The blood drained from Christopher's face.

"Uh, well, yeah. I think…I didn't know you wanted me t—"

"What are you waiting for?"

Christopher stopped waiting.

The homeless man by the stoplight applauded and whistled.

* * *

Though it had been difficult to pick the lock between their lips, it wasn't long before they arrived at Christopher's apartment. The first thing Trixie noticed as she entered the living room was his turntable—the dust cover wallpapered with stickers—a Vans shoebox packed with 7-inch records and a milk crate full of LPs. Taped to the wall above this were battered posters and flyers of punk bands she had never heard of. Near his television was a framed lobby card of an exotically gorgeous woman. The text below her face read: *I PUGNI IN TASCA*. He noticed her interest in the picture.

"That flick's a good one. From '65. Real quirky. Her name's Paola Pitagora. She's not really well known in America, much less Sweetville. She's kind of a celebrity crush of mine."

"I can see why."

"She was untouchable back then. Pretty much perfect." Christopher's eyes glossed over into an embarrassingly dreamy haze. "You know, you kind of remind me of her from this era. Your eyes, your facial structure, even your hair a little bit."

Trixie almost spit out a too-loud laugh.

"Yeah, right," she said. "I wish. Even on my best day I couldn't look half that good."

"Hey, the eye sees what the eye wants, and it's typically the uncanny truth." He grabbed her lightly by the shoulders and this time he took charge of the staring contest.

Trixie was terrified but even more terrified of breaking the gaze. Christopher brushed her cheek with the back of his fingers, gently grasped a swirl of her hair and pressed his lips to hers. Trixie's toes curled. It was even better than the first kiss. Raw, hard passion. Lips linked, set to never let go. Tongues exploring uncharted territories, shifting and sliding like tectonic plates. She wrapped her arms around him, pulling just tight enough to feel his body heat. Her movements were gangly, but her arms eventually hit their target. Their embrace was more comforting than mother's milk.

The phone rang.

Christopher tore away from the kiss and craned his neck in the direction of the interruption.

"Just let the machine pick it up," Trixie whispered, giving him her best pouty look.

"Well, you don't have to tell me twice." He eased right back into the kiss.

After a few rings, the machine's message started rolling. When the message ended, a voice on the other end began to respond.

"Hey, Chris. What a goofy machine. I'd keep it simpler, if you know what I mean. Pick up, man. It's William, not Terry Gilliam." The voice continued to ramble on and Christopher's eyes went wide.

"Crap. I'm sorry. Hold on just a sec. That's my cousin. Let me get rid of him real quick."

"Sure. No prob."

Christopher sprinted to the phone like it was an emergency, grabbed the receiver and shoved it to his ear.

"Hey, bud. Are they letting you call this late now?"

Trixie could tell Christopher was trying to keep his voice down. She did her best not to listen, to not invade his business, but it was almost impossible. She tried to zone out from the one-sided conversation and distract herself by flipping through his records. More stuff she didn't know, for the most part, but then she stopped at a copy of *The Queen Is Dead* and smiled. They had something musically in common after all.

"No, no. Tell them to wait until Adam or I can come sign the papers, okay? They can't legally do that."

Trixie wondered what they could have been talking about. It sounded important.

"William, I'm sorry. I've gotta go. I've got company." After a few seconds he hung up the phone, then paused, removed the receiver and set it down on the table. The dial tone hummed. "No more distractions tonight. Sound good?"

Trixie gave him a thumbs-up and he returned to her, seemingly trying to figure out where they left off. Christopher's fingers began exploring her back, dancing firmly along the edges of her spine.

"Mmmm," she said, pulling away from the kiss just enough to release a mumble. "That feels kind of amazing."

"Yeah? Lie down. I'll do a real good number on you right now, and I'll even waive the masseuse fees."

Trixie giggled. "Hold on a sec." She turned around and removed her top, feeling like she was going to faint as she bared her back but still holding on to her brave face for dear life. She was no stranger to seduction, but this was the first time in years—or maybe ever?—that she was using those powers for something real.

From behind her, Christopher released a quiet "Whoa."

As Trixie lay face down on the bed, Christopher mentioned that he liked her tattoo—a simple, silver dollar-sized yin yang on the small of her back. He began the journey of his fingers there and moved along the thin curvature of her torso up to the contours of her shoulders. She moaned. It felt like her body was experiencing multiple external orgasms.

Unfortunately, she was also feeling arousal in the worst place imaginable. Her hormones usually nullified what remained of her male libido. She hadn't experienced an inappropriate erection in forever, probably not since her encounters with the Zane brothers. She had invested in a collection of tight gaffs that successfully smoothed the surface of her crotch, and were much more effective than the homemade ones Gwen had taught her to construct. In its tucked position, her penis should not have been allowed enough blood flow for a fully functional erection. But still it stirred, doing its best to burst through the gaff like a girl from a giant birthday cake.

She focused on keeping control, thinking of anything else but the pleasure. *General Hospital. Hammerhead sharks. Federico's litter box. Russian dancers.*

Christopher paused for a moment, as if he could feel her body tensing up and wasn't sure how to continue the massage. Trixie took the opportunity to spin around and face him. She beckoned to him with her long finger.

They tumbled around in the bed, pawing at each other with wild rapture. The sheets became twisted, intoxicated ghosts. Christopher's hands tickled at her tummy, hovering just below her small breasts, which were still secured in a black bra. Trixie nudged his hands closer to them, giving him the okay to take a handful or two. Better that way than the other direction. He touched her and kissed her at the lowest point of her cleavage, and she sighed with pleasure.

More distractions passed through her head. *Hemorrhoid commercials. Clowns with deodorant caked in their armpits. Shoplifting mascara. Bill Cosby in a tutu.*

"I don't want to make you do anything you don't want to do," Christopher whispered.

"I want this. Trust me. Just…nothing below the belt. Not yet. I'm… I'm still a virgin."

He looked temporarily dumbfounded but quickly shifted his expression to one of understanding. She wanted to slap her own face. How much deeper of a hole could she dig for herself? Probably pretty damned deep if her past was any indication.

"I hope that's okay," Trixie said, disgusted with herself that she now had to follow through on this tall tale. At least for a little while, until she could summon her guts and tell him The Truth. And Christopher seemed like such an honest guy, so much that it made her gut drown in a thick, guilty syrup.

"No problem," he replied. "I'm having plenty of fun as it is. I'm down for doing whatever makes you happy."

"Oh, trust me, I've still got a few tricks up my sleeve. I'll make sure you won't even notice what you're missing."

"I like a good challenge."

Trixie never lost eye contact as her hands guided Christopher to his back and unzipped his jeans in one swift motion. Sliding into third base, heading toward a home run that could easily spell D-I-S-A-S-T-E-R.

Old habits die hard.

February 13, 1990

Wow, Diary. Life has been a total trip lately. Gwen, both directly and not so much, has been introducing me to an unfamiliar world that's slowly bringing some much needed changes to my body and soothing thoughts to my mental state:

1. Black market hormones, androgen blockers, oral estrogen—purchased from the most undesirable scum. Gwen "knows a guy who knows a guy." Sometimes paid for in hard cash, others traded for sexual favors. Don't really have much moolah in the ole Reassignment Funds Savings Account, so guess which form of payment I end up having readily available most of the time? The golden road to achieving my womanly desires. Yay. Seriously though, Miss Diary, do you ever detect my sarcasm? I always worry about how that comes across on the page.

The changes from the hormones are heaven, though, and they feel almost instantaneous. It's only been a couple of months, but I'm already developing some breast tissue.

Just give me some time and I'll blossom into a respect-able B-cup. So much better than those mail order silicone domes I was using for so long. God, I can't believe I used to have to pilfer Hank's wallet and call some toll-free number in the wee hours just to order some low-budget breasts that I could wishfully mold into legitimate flesh. I don't even want to get into how stressful it was racing home from school every day to make sure I beat the 'rents to the mailbox. I used to think the weight of those things felt almost natural. I guess. But what the hell did I know? It's not like I ever compared the genuine article with a kitchen scale.

2. Sweet Candy, the latest designer drug introduced into Sweetville courtesy of this mysterious guy called The Angelghoul. Whoever *he* is. I thankfully haven't had to do anything with that weirdo yet and hopefully never will, but Gwen said she gave him head once for a few doses. Said it tasted like he ate way too much protein. So gross.

But these pills. Oh. My. God. *So* good. Tart like a ripe cherry with a hint of key lime. Shaped like the cutest little lips and hearts. If they had special little sayings written on them, I'd feel like it was Valentine's Day whenever I swallowed some. Oh. Wait. It's V-Day tomorrow, isn't it? Weird. Maybe I'll get some flowers from my imaginary boyfriend.

Anyway, back to Sweet Candy. Saliva dissolves the out-er shell and the tongue sizzles from the tang of the gum-my center. Pure pill-popping bliss that allows me to make it through each week of street horrors. Alters my person-ality and tweaks my libido just enough to pretend that my new "place of employment" is appealing. The estrogen

I'm taking isn't addictive in and of itself, but this stuff, well, let's just say I need to keep an eye on myself. It isn't just an issue of addiction, though, but one of necessary sustenance. I'll never use anything else again.

3. The Sweetville Free Clinic. I'm as safe as safe can be with the guys who pick me up, but you can never be too safe, you know? I get tested once a week, just to be sure. Hey, the price is right and it's discreet, so it'd be stupid not to take advantage.

4. Brief visits to the LGBT center. Uneventful at best. Not even remotely helpful most of the time, to be perfectly honest. The leader of the support group is this guy named, well, his name is literally Guy. He's got endless energy farting out of his ass like it's going out of style. He makes Richard Simmons seem like a real mellow cat. Unfortunately, Guy's not terribly sensitive toward trans issues, and as far as I can tell, no one else like me ever shows up. The T support is sorely absent from these meetings. I'm not finding any consolation in the one place where I should be swimming in it. Gwen tried to warn me, but I guess I had to experience the disappointment for myself. As far as the LGBT center is concerned, I wasn't just born on the wrong side of the tracks but on the wrong side of the sex.

5. Tips about working both the familiar south side of Sweetville at Fifth and Quail, where our anomalies are sought and bought, and the more dangerous northern side, where my birth gender has to remain shrouded in secrecy. Gwen told me they pay higher rates up there. Twice what I get down here. But I should only offer head, though. Full service would be bad news up in that part of

town. They def aren't looking for what's really between our legs. They wouldn't be too pleased about it, either. She said to catch them when they're coming out of the bars so they don't know what they're getting into. She only gives it a shot when it looks like she's coming up short on rent. Way too sketchy of a sitch. She thinks I'm totally passable, though, so I shouldn't worry as much as she does. Said she'd give anything to have my figure. She got a little bitchy about the whole thing, but whatever.

There's occasionally a few other girls who work Fifth and Quail on any given night, sometimes stretching their legs a bit by taking a stroll around the block.

Britt is a true original. She's kind of gorgeous. Enormous breast implants that I would probably murder puppies for if my hormones weren't already starting to treat me right. Long legs that would send a giraffe into fits of envy. Looks like she's probably had some work done on her face, too. You can only tell if you squint, though. Maybe some brow bone shaving. Rhinoplasty. Gore-Tex lip implants. A bit of a facelift or something? She must have some sugar daddy taking care of her on the side because she definitely couldn't afford that on our salary. Though, now that I think of it, I've heard Gwen mention some local underground "surgeons" that will perform some of these procedures on the cheap. Sketchy stuff. No thanks.

Britt also has this really peculiar shtick that apparently drives the men wild: she only works in roller skates, hot pants and knee-high socks. Well, she wears a top, too, but that varies from night to night. Just wheels herself up and down the streets. Oddly brilliant in a way. I'm kinda pissed I wasn't savvy enough to come up with that.

Then there's Angel. She's about six foot two and 230 pounds, makeup applied just a tad over-tarty—even for *our* profession. She speaks almost no English, and I used to take naps in Spanish class, so I try to deal with her as little as possible to avoid awkward linguistic dilemmas. She always seems to eat a carne asada burrito and chat with the guy working the counter at Bertoberto's before she starts her "shift."

And Joi, a twig in size to Angel's tree, who's somehow managed to survive the streets despite the fact she only ever works in a rarely washed baggy shirt and stained sweats, wears almost no makeup and is not even remotely pretty. I swear this is *not* jealousy invading my thoughts. A proboscis monkey in a pink tutu might be as appealing as Joi. I mean, I feel bad about saying stuff like this since Joi is a nice enough girl, but—

Really, girl, try a little harder maybe.

June 5, 1990

Fuck. Last night was horrible, Miss Diary. I don't know who else I really feel comfortable talking to about this.

Took me forever to work up the nerve to try working the north side, and this is what I get for my bravery? And my fishnets are all torn now. Dammit! I hope Gwen has some clear polish to fix that.

Doesn't look too different up there from what I'm used to. North Ozymandias Boulevard is a pretty long strip where the working girls gather. The buildings have fewer piss stains on them, and some of the cars that screech by are closer to Porsche than Pinto. It's near the community college, too, so there were a lot of future frat-guy types wandering the streets on drunken adventures, ignoring me like I was triple invisible.

The competition up there seemed pretty fierce. Lots of beat-looking bitches, but they own those streets so I kept my opinion to myself. Don't I always? Still, they all got picked up pretty quickly and I didn't have to strut along Ozymandias too long. Some guy pulled up to me less than twenty minutes after I showed up! Should have known it was too good to be true. Always is.

He didn't seem any more or less socially inept than any other johns I've "dated." Didn't say much aside from asking how much he was going to have to "donate." Didn't even offer his name. It's not like I'm dying to socialize with these guys, but it at least makes me feel like half a human being when they try and ask my age or where I'm from or tell me I'm pretty. Something, anything, to at least pretend to be natural.

We went up to his hotel room, which I don't usually like to do. Safer to be on my own turf. Granted, the north side was already far from anything remotely my turf. But he insisted, said he'd make it worth my while. Made me an offer I couldn't refuse, which included a dose of Sweet Candy. Why am I such a sucker? We got up there and he dropped his pants and smirked like he was expecting me to get all giddy or whatever. Sorry, curlicue pubes and an uncircumcised prick don't impress me much. He got closer to me and started panting. His breath smelled like pepperoni and garlic. I told him I was only available for head, no full service, and his expression changed. He started saying he knew how to fucking please a woman properly, and he'd fucking make sure to pay me well. Then things got really bad. That bastard grabbed my crotch! Zero warning, with fingers like little jackrabbits. No time to react.

Doesn't matter that I was tucking like always. Dammit Gwen, your homemade gaffs suck so badly! This guy just knew something wasn't right, and he knew what that something was. He sort of stood there, frozen like some hideous statue, his face twisted like he'd just consumed a pound of lemons.

I should have run when I had the chance.

Whatthefuckwhatthefuckwhatthefuck is pretty much all I remember hearing for the next few seconds before I got cracked on the side of my head with his fist. Would have been nicer if I had actually seen stars or little tweeting birds like on *Looney Tunes* cartoons. Instead, it was more like quick flashes of darkness as he smacked me and I tried my best to defend myself. I started getting scared that it was going to stay dark permanently. It's terrifying enough when an enraged 250-pound gorilla starts attacking you. It's even worse when that gorilla is supposed to be a part of the human race.

In a perfect world, this guy would have been more understanding, just backed off, and we could have gone our separate ways. No harm, no foul. At worst he'd tell me sorry, baby, not my kinda thing. Is that so hard? I have thick enough skin at this point in my life to deal with that. The irony is that this scumbag wanted to take me in spite of not being "his thing." But it wasn't lustful. God, I wish it could have just been simple lust. *That* I could have dealt with. This was evil, dominance and rage all wrapped up in a big, greasy, stinky tortilla. I wasn't asking for that. No woman wants that.

He was too huge for me to be able to fight back and have any shot at winning. He gripped my arms, threw me to the bed, flipped me on my stomach, pulled up my skirt and pressed all his weight on top of me before I had a chance to try and scratch his eyes out. It felt like I was trapped under a dozen sandbags. I started screaming and I felt another smack on the back of my head, this time with something that was definitely not his fist. He told me to fucking shut up, that it would be over quick. I could feel something with the weight and shape of a corn cob pressed up against the crack of my ass.

Lucky that I noticed my purse was within reach. Lucky that asshole was too busy trying to get inside me. Lucky I had the pepper spray I "borrowed" from Gwen, or I might have become just another statistic. I sure as hell believe in luck now. Luck was my lady tonight.

Didn't tell Gwen about this, or anyone else. I don't feel like even thinking about this anymore, much less talking or writing about it.

Did this really happen, or am I just trying to impress my diary with my creative juices? Maybe better if I pretend it's fiction. Doesn't matter I guess. You decide, dear Diary.

CHAPTER NINE

GREYSON ZANE WAS BORN on February 28, 1960 at 11:50 p.m. His brother Orin first witnessed the light of this vexatious world fifteen minutes later.

It was a leap year.

If one wants to get technical about these sorts of details, this makes Orin now eight years old in real time, while Greyson has just begun enjoying his thirties. While this has clearly not affected Orin's physical growth or his actual age accepted by the general public, his confidence as an eventual grown man has still been harshly stunted. Though this confusing concept occasionally enters conversations, Greyson had never gone out of his way to make it a bone of contention during their youth. This infrequency does not offer Orin much relief, if any at all.

Needless to say, as absurd as his situation may be, Orin feels more than a little bitter resentment toward this calendarized technicality, a sentiment that is oftentimes passive-aggressively redirected toward his more fortunately birthed "older" brother. When they were younger, their parents—God rest their souls—always offered their best efforts to make the brothers feel equal on their special day. Always a cake with both names in sugary cursive, the same numbered candle representing both boys. Almost without fail, some cruel child—usually some neighborhood brat

Orin didn't even know, but was invited to the party regardless—had to bring the topic up in a taunting tone and spoil everything. Birthdays tend to be so very important in one's formative years.

Today just happens to be their birthday, or at least the day both of their birthdays are officially celebrated. The heavy clouds in the sky form their cake, the sinking sun their burning candle. And today there is a gift strolling along Swallow Street, heading in their direction. A gift from the past that is now a present in the present.

"Grey," Orin says, nudging his brother in the rib cage, "look who I see." He points down the street with one hand and absently straightens out his slacks with the other.

"I don't know what—"

Orin grabs Greyson's face, smashing it with the palms of his hands and turns it in his desired direction. He points again to a girl on the sidewalk, blending in with the other pedestrians. "Look familiar? Hmm?"

"Oh. *Oh.*" Greyson swats Orin's hands away and dusts off his blue bamboo-leaf polo shirt even though it has not been touched. "Been a while since we've seen this one, hasn't it?"

She has headphones on. She is bobbing her head. She does not notice them. She is no longer part of the walking crowd. She is five feet away when the twins step in front of her. She looks up and almost runs right into both of their iron chests.

"Shit!" she says.

"Hello, *Ariel*," Orin says. "Oh, I'm sorry. My mistake. I mean hello, *Trixie.*"

Trixie's face scrunches up, her eyes squint in disgust. She removes her headphones. The muffled music escapes and she turns off her Walkman. "Oh, God. Are you serious?"

"Whatever do you mean?" Greyson asks. "Are you trying to say you're not happy to see your favorite old flames?"

"Ugh. Don't flatter yourself. No. You know what? Actually, I *am* glad I ran into you jerks. God, the fucking nerve of you two. I can't believe—"

Orin holds up the palm of his hand as if he is Diana Ross asking her to stop in the name of love. "I'm sorry. What exactly are you babbling about?"

"Why would you tell that little troll about me?" Her voice drops to a whisper. "About my past?" She is almost in Orin's face now, but since she is a few inches shorter she has to stand on her tippy toes to come off as intimidating. Orin can smell her breath. It stings like fresh wintergreen.

Orin looks over to his brother. Greyson just shrugs. He is no help.

"Honestly," Orin says. "We have zero idea what you're talking about."

"Kast? Ring any bells?"

"The cast of what? Are we talking a play here or something you put on a broken leg?"

"Stop fucking with me, Greyson."

"Orin. I'm Orin."

"Yes, dear," Greyson says, finally ready to join the party. "*I'm* Greyson."

"Whatever," Trixie says. She looks right at Greyson now, giving Orin a chance to breathe. "Do you really think I'm that stupid? Did you even have to say that?"

"I'd still like to know what you're accusing us of," Orin says.

With each word, Trixie shoves Orin. "You. Told. Him. About. Me." Orin stumbles back a step with each battering. "About The Truth."

"Told whom?"

"Kast!"

"Oh there she goes about this 'cast' thing again," Greyson says. "I'm at a loss here, brother."

"This is a person you're talking about?" Orin asks.

"I guess you could call him that."

"Well, we'd never betray your trust. I can promise you that much. Too many good times to taint all that."

"And we hold no grudges," Greyson adds. "Honestly. And we do miss you dearly. Why don't you come with us after our last stop of the evening?"

"Oh, what a good idea for once, Grey. Yes, Trixie, how would you feel about coming back to our place with us? For old time's sake. What a sweet reunion!"

Trixie fakes a gagging sound. "No fucking way. Are you kidding me?"

"When have we ever been known to joke?" Greyson asks.

"Doesn't matter. I'm seeing someone else now. And it's serious, so don't even bother."

"Well now," Orin says. "So sorry to hear that. I'm sure he's a lucky fellow. Would love to meet him sometime."

"Don't hold your breath," she says.

"At least come with us over to Video Drones and help us pick out something we've not seen," Greyson says.

Trixie's face goes pale. "What?"

"Yes," Orin says. "Please do. It's just back the way you came. You must have passed right by it."

"Wh-why are you going there?" Trixie has stopped making eye contact with the twins. Orin sees she has lost her composure, but cannot determine why. He attempts to get her attention again but fails.

"Well, you know what today is, don't you?" he asks.

"No. Don't care either." Some of her bite has returned, but she is still clearly shaken.

"Well," Greyson says, "we've just installed a theater in the east wing of the estate as a celebration for a certain *day* that happens to be today. We want to celebrate with the cinema and you are cordially invited. We'll put you on the list in case Fredo doesn't recognize you after all this time."

"I do think he's going blind in one eye," Orin says.

"Can I go now?"

Orin and Greyson step aside, parting ways like a steel gate. Trixie does not immediately pass through the space they have provided her.

"Please do come visit sometime," Orin says. "Our theater will be so lonely without your lovely face to view it."

"Yes," Greyson says. "Our doors are always open for an old friend."

"Okay. See you on the fifth of Never." Trixie places her headphones back on her ears and shuffles off. Orin still cannot determine what has her so bothered, exactly who this person wearing a cast is and what part of their body may have been broken.

"Well, that's too bad now, isn't it?" Greyson says.

"Yes. Well, we have ways of figuring out who this new beau of hers is."

"In due time."

Orin grabs his brother's hand and links their fingers together. A woman with a small child passes by them and looks at them as if they should be burned at the stake. They both smile at her.

"Grey, do you remember the first night we met her?"

"I've never seen that woman before in my life."

"No, you recalcitrant lout. Our girl Trixie."

"Oh. Of course. It was quite wonderful."

"Yes. Yes, it most certainly was."

"Methinks our friend Trixie doth not agreeth."

* * *

Three or so years earlier.

A spoiled boy can never have enough toys and attention.

And a man can never have enough holes to thrust himself into.

The damp alleyways of downtown Sweetville offered many pleasures. An abundance of secret underground clubs, both under the noses of the authorities *and* physically below the surface of Sweetville proper. Soliciting sex was a nightly adventure due to the individual workers and their respective genders rotating almost as frequently as the Zanes' soiled silk boxer briefs. Seemingly endless supplies of Sweet Candy available at a moment's notice. Masochistic and, perhaps to a lesser extent, sadistic desires a mere phone call away. The Zane brothers considered themselves connoisseurs of deviance. Most of their pursuits had become passé, yet still they dragged themselves out of bed each day to search for and concoct carnal fantasies, hoping to unearth these hidden treasures or something similar amongst the pupu platter of secret sex offered downtown on any given night.

"Lyle, please take us to Fifth and Quail," Greyson requested of their chauffeur. "Or somewhere in that vicinity. And don't dilly-dally. We've had a bad streak the last few nights, so we prefer to stay focused. Tonight's the night, old chum!"

Lyle was paid very generously for his driving services. He was contractually bound to be discreet. He was also what one might, if they were kind, refer to as homely, truthfully only a step or two above Attila the Hun on his best days. Eyes spaced too far apart to ever be worth gazing into lovingly, reverse-puckered lips like a contracting anus, patchy facial hair that he usually neglected to groom with any effort. Despite this, he was no virgin, and his employers knew he was appreciative of the special times they treated him to a gorgeous, high-class call girl for his loyalty. These women were grand actresses that never revealed their disgust for his appearance. Nothing but the best for those devoted to the Zane brothers.

The Zanes' pristine black 1940 Packard Super Eight glided through the streets of Sweetville, a hunter on the scent of its prey.

"Orin, my boy, we're trying something new tonight. I think you'll be impressed." Greyson placed his hand on Orin's leg, walked his fingers like the itsy bitsy spider, leaned over and nibbled at his brother's ear. Orin remained stoic.

"Don't call me boy. I'm not your *boy*." Orin politely removed Greyson's hand like it was a turntable's tonearm leaving the precious grooves of a re-cord. "And I can't recall the last time you successfully slayed me with any of your findings. You *do* understand the definition of 'new,' don't you?"

"Why, of course I—"

"I believe you're slipping. Boring, boring, boring. I can't take much more of just the two of us. Do you really feel like being the bottom again?"

"Ye have little faith, Oreo. Don't be such a Negative Nancy." Greyson stared narcissistically at his twin, in lust with his mirror image. It was impossible to tell the two men apart, either via a quick glance or an ob-servant stare. They were identical archetypes. Hair fascistly greased and coiffed into impenetrable black helmets. Diamond blue eyes. Perfectly manicured hands with not a stray cuticle in sight. Bodies toned and craft-ed from obsessively rigorous exercise routines, stuffed into custom-tai-lored grey seersucker suits. Matching genuine Nile crocodile wing-tips. Beneath the wardrobe were corresponding birthmarks on their left breasts that, if one were to squint, slightly resembled a wolf's head.

The Zanes could easily seduce men or women of their choice, yet the normal and the bourgeoisie types they associated with in the day-light hours had become just plain humdrum over the years, their ulterior motives predictable. Never-ending yattering about Swiss bank accounts, summer homes in the Hamptons, private jets, aged caviar. It made both of the Zane brothers ill with ennui. The more interesting encounters came from the people who did not brag about how much they paid for their new Rolls Royces or their Versace gowns, but rather those who had price tags dangling from their own sleeves. The hardest working people within Sweetville's city limits. Those with tales of blood, sweat and seminal leakage.

"And, of course I'll bottom up if I have to," Greyson continued. "Better bottomed than blue-balled, naturally. Isn't that right, Lyle?" He leaned up toward Lyle's seat and patted him on the shoulder.

"If you say so, sir," Lyle replied. "I'll respect your choices, but you know where my tastes lie."

"Fair enough," Greyson said. "It's your prerogative. But I still think—"

"Since when do you get to make the decisions, Grey?" Orin asked.

"My special little brother, how soon you forget that I am your eldest surviving relative, the closest thing you have ever had to a guardian. Don't make me put a hold on your trust fund."

"Yawn. Same old empty threat. Please try again."

"Well, regardless, I deserve respect every now and again."

"You deserve a good kick in the privates," Orin muttered, which Greyson was too self-absorbed to notice.

The Packard slithered through the filthy south-side streets of Sweetville. This section of the neighborhood was a dank swamp robbed of nearly all its fluids. Street lamps with broken bulbs that would never be replaced. Roaches and rodents splashing through the shallow gutter puddles. Homeless campers huddled in their cardboard like eggs in a carton. The meat market at Fifth and Quail appeared to be all but shut down, not that there was usually a large crowd. Only one girl tonight.

"Oh, yes. I want her!" Greyson cried out, briefly clapped and pointed like a child picking out a brand new puppy that he'll never remember to feed.

Orin rolled his eyes. "Lyle, please stop here."

The girl noticed the car nearing her and gave a subtle, flirty, practiced wave. She wore Mary Jane flats, a jean skirt that came to just above the knee and a plain grey tee that comfortably hugged her undernourished torso. The shadows made her shoulder-length hair resemble the color of a Bing cherry.

The well-tuned Packard came to a silent stop beneath the oscillating beam of a broken streetlight. Lyle pulled it close to the curb, careful not to scratch the hubcaps. Greyson cracked his window six inches, his dark eyes leering over the edge. The girl cautiously looked from side to side, as if preparing to cross the street.

"Darling, would you like a ride somewhere?" Orin once again rolled his eyes at his brother's cloying behavior. No matter how frequently Greyson demanded center stage, Orin was never content to accept it.

"Are you a cop?" the girl asked.

The twins knew this was only a formality. Cops almost never bothered with the sweetmeat offered on this corner. There were far more pressing issues developing in Sweetville. A few prostitutes just trying to pay last month's rent and fill their shrunken stomachs were very low on the Sweetville Police Department's priority list. Not that arrests didn't occasionally occur in order to appease the taxpaying public, but the instances were few and far between. Greyson shook his head to the girl's query, opened his door, allowed her to step in. Her straight auburn hair tickled the side of his face as she sat. He cooed softly.

"Lyle, carry on," Greyson said. "Let's head back to the estate." Then, to their guest, "What's your name?"

"Ariel."

"Pleasure to make your acquaintance, Ariel. My name is Greyson and this is my dearest brother Orin." He nodded in Orin's direction and leaned back a few inches, which revealed the sudden simulacrum. "Try not to get us confused."

"Um, I'll do my best."

* * *

The Packard purred as it switched from neutral into drive. Trixie's fingers danced across the grey leather upholstery.

As "Ariel," Trixie did her best to internalize her fear and disgust. Her profession was more profitable if she allowed herself to become the role she was supposed to be playing. She had never been with twins before. Never been with brothers. Never been with two men together. Period.

Where exactly did this fall on her "wrong" scale? Was she even able to gauge that anymore?

"Don't worry, Grey," said the brother called Orin. "She'll be able to tell us apart when it comes time to pay the bill. She'll figure out you failed remedial math."

Greyson shot his brother a glaring look, then turned back to Trixie. "How old are you?"

"Eighteen." She was still inching toward that number, but she remembered what Gwen had recommended when she was first starting out.

When they ask your age, always say eighteen. Even if you're still doing this when you're well into your twenties, cling on to that number as long as you can. The darkness is a great cover for wrinkles. Barely legal's a cash cow. They don't even care if you're telling the truth most of the time. It's all for fantasy's sake, right? Just go with it.

Trixie hesitated, cringing at the next requirement of working this part of town, then turned her switch to put on her best pouty performance. Even though the majority of potential customers who drove to this destination knew what they were getting into, there was always the off chance an unwary straggler could make his way here. This could result in either a simple awkward exchange or perhaps something more terrifyingly savage.

Fear of sexuality—both of one's own and that of others—could be a powerful rage inducer. She had encountered other transgender girls who seemed to revel in seducing and hooking up with as many intoxicated straight guys as they could. Blurting out The Truth in front of the guys' friends after the fact, just for embarrassment's sake. It was like an outtake from a bad talk show.

Trixie knew from her recent experience on the north side of town how quickly a meet-up with a trick could shift into a violent encounter. She had managed to avoid anything sketchy since that night and didn't plan on it happening again. However, she knew danger was always a distinct possibility. She had seen the fading welts and bruises on Gwen's body and the very slight curved scar on her left cheek—unwanted gifts given to her because of who she was. It needed to be stated outright, though. Lying could result in even worse than a harsh beating.

"You guys are looking for a transsexual, right?"

She loathed the word. Being reduced to someone's fetish. Feeling like a reject from the blackest corner of the sticky porn shop. "Shemale" wasn't any better. Even the less harsh term transgender made her feel ill inside. She wished she could be privileged enough to just refer to herself as a girl and call it a day. Self-hatred, unfortunately, allowed her to eat and pay the bills.

"Sure, that's perfectly fine, dear." Greyson stated this with such nonchalance that Trixie felt she could have just as easily asked if they were seeking an octopus in a nightie or a mannequin with its fiberglass chipping and it would have been "perfectly fine." She wasn't so sure their indiscriminate nature was such a great quality. Greyson allowed a smile to escape his Ken-doll face and placed his hand on Trixie's exposed thigh. "And don't be concerned about payment. My brother was just making a little funny. You'll be generously compensated. I never cheat a new friend. Or an old one, for that matter."

Orin extended his hand, which was filled with a colorful spectrum of hard-shelled, chewy-centered pills. He shook them like lucky dice.

"Would you care for some Candy?"

If nothing else, Trixie knew she would at least have that to hold her together for the night.

* * *

The Zane residence was a lush, restored Victorian mansion in the Sweetville Hills, an area aptly dubbed The Sweethills by the locals. No neighbors within an approximate acre of land and no numerical address. The property was a street unto itself named Steamer Duck Lane, thus the postal street address for the mansion was simply Steamer Duck Estate.

The driver dropped them off at the front gate and remained in the Packard. A sneering gargoyle statue greeted the trio, its left palm held up as if awaiting a high five. Fittingly, Orin placed his right palm against the gargoyle's stone. A soft gong echoed from a source unknown to Trixie, and the gate began to creak open. The brothers locked arms with hers on each side. Not like prison guards, but like gentlemen. They trekked along a fifty-foot flagstone pathway that led from the gate to the front door. It was lined with bushes trimmed like animals, but not like any Trixie had ever seen before. One had the head of a wolf and the body of an eagle. Another appeared almost human, but with a serpentine tail trailing off behind. Yet another had no discernible physical qualities of any animal she had ever seen in the zoo. The Hedges of Dr. Moreau.

Scaled shingles decorated the outer walls. The four domed dormer windows that protruded from the second story resembled a spider's eyes. There was a turret to the right, like a life-sized rocket prepared for lift-off. Though green was the mansion's dominant outer color, splashes of purple throughout kept begging for Trixie's attention. Purple made her tingle inside. The Sweet Candy was already getting down to business.

Once they reached the front door, Trixie arched her head back to see if she could view the top of the house from this position. She failed. The door itself was made of solid burgundy oak. *VANITAS VANITATUM, OMNIA VANITAS* was carved into the door's center. An oval piece of stained glass featuring two aqua Abyssinian lovebirds crowned its top third.

The door creaked open without anyone from the outside touching the handle. A portly, middle-aged butler with a pencil mustache greeted them.

"Hello, Fredo," Orin said. "We'll be in for the remainder of the evening. You may retire to your quarters." Fredo nodded and allowed them to enter. He was apparently either a man of few words or one who favored another tongue.

The foyer was empty, save for a waist-high wooden table with cast-iron legs. On the table lay a stack of pamphlets advertising Citizen Zane Property Investments, with a picture on the front of the twins in full Sears-portrait mode. Argyle sweater vests. Glistening dental hygiene. One tilting his head up as if contemplating the meaning of life, the other staring almost directly into the camera with debonair eyes that seemed to be begging, "Trust me with all of your goals and dreams. And feel free to fuck me. You will not be sorry."

Greyson noticed Trixie's curious gaze at the pamphlets.

"Oh, don't trouble yourself with that," he said. "We're just proud of the sound financial decisions we've made over the years. I'm sure you can see why." He gestured to the general vast space of the house. The echoes of his voice scurried off to uncharted hallways and hidden rooms.

"I feel like I should be charging you guys extra." Trixie felt that a flirty joke here and there often endeared a client to her. "You know, just because you wouldn't notice."

Greyson bellowed out a hearty laugh that, leaving anyone else's mouth, would have sounded forced. He brushed Trixie's cheek lightly with the back of his knuckles. "You don't 'charge' in the House of Zane. We *invest* in you. No lowball offers here. We are businessmen, and we believe in our stock."

"You make it sound as if she's cattle, Grey."

"It's okay," Trixie said, "I guess that's probably a better deal for me in the long run, right? Return business and all that."

"Well, we certainly hope so. We prefer to build long-lasting relationships, with emphasis on 'relationship.' If you work hard, if you perform as well as your face is pretty, then you'll be welcome any time and *all* of the time. We—"

"Brother," Orin interjected. "May we stop flapping our tongues and escort our guest to the master suite now? Please?"

Trixie noticed that Greyson and Orin's slight British accents came and went, as if their proper manner was affected, a mere ruse to make the brothers appear more sophisticated than they actually were. She figured as long as she wasn't being paid in pounds instead of dollars, it was none of her business.

"Yes, let's," Greyson said. "But first…Ariel, is it? Would you be so kind as to prepare us some tea? Orin and I are going to head upstairs to get the room tidied up. We'd be ever so grateful. Chamomile, please. I tend to break out in hives from chai. The kitchen is at the far end of the west wing. Tea is in the pantry. The French press and china in the third cabinet on the left, second shelf. Then just come up these stairs here. The entire second floor is our private penthouse. You're an angel. Thank you *so* much."

Greyson shuffled away. Orin remained behind for a moment. He leaned toward Trixie's face for a whisper. His eyes were like those of a mischievous cat.

"Never mind what my brother just said. Bring the chai."

* * *

The first kiss was Orin's, a flavor like mint leaves, a texture like used sandpaper, a gentle eagerness. Then Greyson, a scent like freshly smashed pumpkin, a nibble like a vestal vampire, a clammy wetness swimming between gooseflesh. The sounds of Def Leppard's "Love Bites" seeped through unseen surround speakers. A few moments of writhing, tangled bodies sans plastic Twister mat, and Trixie tried to imagine the twins were only one man. She used both of her talented hands to simultaneously stroke and paw at each of their waistlines, which proved they were well beyond aroused as well as pelvicly gifted.

She found herself plunging into The Necessary Zone: the discovery of indulgent pleasure and feigned intimacy in an effort to avoid a complete mental breakdown. This was almost exclusively a mind trick that made the work tolerable and convincingly enjoyable. Some girls claimed they had the ability to black themselves out of the situation, like specters watching down disdainfully on their empty performing bodies, thrusting and lusting, trysting and fisting and orificial resisting. However, in this rare case, The Necessary Zone was an unnecessary act. Her Sweet Candy dose lubricated all inhibitions, loosened her like a rusty bolt saturated with WD-40.

The Zane brothers roused some dormant shrieking beast within her, and she abandoned her concerns and let the primal urge take the reins. Their sex was an exquisite sundae, the payment would be a bonus cherry on top. A few moments of heavy petting and the twins tugged playfully at the worn denim of Trixie's skirt. She unconsciously disputed despite being contractually obligated. A "may I," and a "please." A lip sync of "Pour Some Sugar on Me" with a response of, "sure, just nothing painful," and it soon became clear that all intentions were quite the opposite and that pleasure was currency within the walls of Steamer Duck Estate.

Months and years of consuming androgen blockers assured avoidance of almost any and all accidental erections, but Trixie was strangely enkindled, so she stopped battling the throbbing hardness that was stirring down below and let the brothers have their manly moments. Greyson was pure animalistic lust, jagged edges of teeth and all, enjoyed his quick fill of flesh Popsicle. Orin was comparatively tender, like a well-practiced virgin doing his best to make a good first impression. And then it was time to switch out so Orin stood up, removed his belt, dropped his pants. Trixie twisted her body around so that she was now on all fours, doing all she could to own the role—save howling at the moon—and took his semi-erect shaft into her mouth like a pacifier. It quickly transformed from silkworm to stone and Orin groaned and moaned like a chanting ghost. Greyson planted himself behind Trixie, lubed himself generously and grinned and leered only somewhat perversely. He caressed the barely-existent curves of her ass, squeezed her hips and the side of her stomach and accessed her secret entrance, which resulted in a light, surprised squeal that teetered between delight and discomfort and was also muffled by her mouthful. A sickening sandwich made of twin brother bread and Trixie turkey.

Greyson's arm extended inches longer than it should have ever been allowed to and clawed at his brother. Orin did not pull away but instead smirked deviously, so Greyson pulled out of Trixie before climaxing and shoved his brother roughly to the bed and began passionately kissing him like he was his wife on the first night of their honeymoon. Greyson flipped Orin over with beastly aggression, or maybe it was Orin now doing this to Greyson, but there was soon certain penetration. The brothers clutched hands, and someone's knuckles cracked. They pumped faster, harder, a flesh locomotive. And Trixie just leaned back, found a comfy pillow to hug.

It was like she wasn't even there anymore.

and now a word from
OUR SPONSOR

FADE IN:

INT. SOUND STUDIO — DAY

A miniature scale model of Sweetville sits atop a
walnut dining table. It sparkles beneath professional
lighting. The background is draped in silver velvet.

GREYSON ZANE, a debonair chap in his early 30s,
stares deep into the camera. His eyes are sly and
seductive. The gel in his hair glistens like moonlit
mud. His bespoke navy blue suit perfectly hugs every
bend of his body.

The beginning notes of an instantly recognizable
Jacuzzi jazz song meander in the background.
Saxophone to soothe the soul.

                    GREYSON
          Hello, I'm Greyson Zane.

ORIN ZANE appears immediately behind Greyson. He is
an exact replica. Not a trick of the camera's eye.

                    ORIN
          And I'm Orin Zane.

                GREYSON AND ORIN
          We are the CEOs of Citizen Zane
          Property Investments, here to make all of
          your financial dreams come true.

The view alternates between each man so they
eventually become almost indistinguishable.

                    GREYSON
Have you ever wondered what to do with
the extra money wasting away in your second and third bank accounts?

                    ORIN
Just purchased a treasury bill with an
unfortunately large IOU from Uncle Sam?

                    GREYSON
Stocks paying out high dividends?

                    ORIN
Or are you a recent beneficiary to a trust
fund that is now burning a nasty hole in
the pockets of your Gucci slacks?

The brothers double clap in unison.

                GREYSON AND ORIN
We can help!

                    GREYSON
We have the inside track on how to properly invest your money with little to no
headache.

Orin casually thumbs a stack of hundred-dollar bills,
folds it into a silver money clip, places it into the
inner pocket of his suit jacket, then straightens his
tie.

                    ORIN
Yes, my brother is correct, if not
somewhat modest. With Citizen Zane
Property Investments, you can rest
assured every dime you entrust us with

will be put toward real estate that will
profit you greatly. No lemons, no money
pits, no ghetto shacks here. Only the
finest homes in the Sweethills and awe-
inspiring brand new, high-rise
condominiums downtown, all just waiting
to be remodeled and/or rented for maximum
profit margins.

                    GREYSON AND ORIN
          Gentrification is purification.

INTERCUT MAP OF SWEETVILLE

A community map of Sweetville fills the screen.
Pushpins highlight the most desirable areas within
the city limits.

SUPER (flashing): "ACTUAL PROPERTIES MAY VARY"

INTERCUT GREYSON AND ORIN

                         GREYSON
          The key is location, location, location.

                          ORIN
          We'll never pressure you to purchase. We
          want you to have peace of mind that your
          investment is secure. We'll treat you
          like the best of friends.

                         GREYSON
          Or the closest of brothers.

                          ORIN
          At Citizen Zane Property Investments...

                    GREYSON
        ...we keep it in the family.

The brothers stand side by side and reveal wide
Cheshire Cat smiles. Their teeth gleam and sparkle
like precious ivory.

They clasp each other's hands and take a deep bow.

SUPER (scrolling): 555-ZANE

SUPER (flashing): CALL NOW FOR YOUR NO-OBLIGATION
CONSULTATION

November 28, 1990

Been hanging out a lot with Greyson and Orin, the most generous and peculiar of all customers. Sorta kinda my friends now, I guess. Sugar daddies? They sure do throw money, gifts and companionship around like those things are breadcrumbs and I'm the duck. So I'll just keep on quacking for now. Maybe these were the guys paying for Britt's goods? Hmm, the plot thickens.

Oh hell, I don't know. Britt's been gone from the streets for a while now. Hopefully that means she got her shit together and moved on to greener pastures. It's what we all want, what we deserve. Right, Miss Diary? Or does this new situation just make me a slightly higher-class call girl? It's an upgrade I guess.

Seems like Gwen knows the Zane brothers pretty well. Or knew. By the time I met them, she had already serviced them into boredom and had little left to offer. When I told her about hooking up with them, she became really cold and wouldn't open up much about her experiences. It only went downhill from there.

Gwen and me. Hell, we've already become sorta distant ever since I moved out. It's not like I moved that far. I'm just down the hall, girl! Why's she acting like I went away to college and fucked her boyfriend? Okay, so maybe you could argue the second one happened. I wouldn't. Whatever. It doesn't matter anyway. I think the Zanes must have noticed the same creepy behavior in Gwen that I've just begun to see. Girl's got issues, to say the least. Makes me feel like I'm a well-adjusted success story. I'm pretty much over watching her walk the tightrope to self-destruction.

I have to admit, though, Diary, being spoiled rotten by the twins has been a wonderful change of pace. I never have to worry about keeping up on my hormones or Sweet Candy. I'm about as hot as can be right now. Pretty much a full-blown girl these days. Except for, well, you know.

Being with the Zanes is the closest thing I've felt to love since Aron. It's nice to pretend at least. It's not like that word really means anything. Kinda sad, right?

Fucking pathetic is more like it.

January 21, 1991

I feel so disgusted with myself every time I look down between my legs and see what was never meant to be there. After all this time, you'd think I'd just get used to it or at least tolerate tucking it away with itchy, scratchy duct tape.

No way. Not even close.

I want it off of me so fucking badly it makes my whole body hurt. Sometimes I even feel like I'm going to puke when I see it. I have these insane fantasies where I just tie a tourniquet around those boy parts, set them on a cutting board and let a nice sharp cleaver do what it was born to do. I'm not stupid. I know that would probably kill me or leave me deformed. Sexless at the very least. Not the results I'm looking for. A more appropriate fantasy might be wishing my penis were made of Play-Doh so I could mold it into its proper form. I'd probably even manage to screw that up, though. I've never been good with my hands. I could barely put together a mud pie when I was a little kid.

You know what's really been ticking me off, Miss Diary? Those people, those *things* that have been all over the news for a while now. I can't even change the channel today without seeing them because some creepy scientist guy died. Everyone's calling them the Withered Willies or something stupid like that. I dunno. Well, what upsets me so much about them is the fact they were able to take control of their bodies. Why do they deserve that privilege and not me? A few simple pills and they've been able to transform into what they apparently felt they were always supposed to be. If you ask me, I think what they've become is totally unnatural, but I guess I'm the last one who should be talking. A lot of people probably think the same thing about me. Jealousy's a real bitch. But we all evolve in some way, right? Isn't that how life is supposed to work? When's my fairy godmother coming to give me my glass slippers?

It's just so unfair.

I feel like I'm so close to being who I should be, but the penis always gets in my way. How's that for double meaning? Yeah, there's the obvious choice of professional surgery, not the underground kind where you end up in the hospital and die later from complications. How the hell would I ever be able to afford something legit? Makes the illegal approach much more attractive. No matter how much I save up, my transformation just seems so far out of reach.

I don't know what to do. I wish someone would help me through this, but I wouldn't even know where to start looking.

A Discarded Letter Found in an Alley
near First and Ozymandias

Dearest Trixie,

   If you are reading this letter now, I am either still standing directly in front of you—which might be a tad awkward, so I hope you have opted for waiting until I have vacated the premises—or my associates have already safely escorted me through the darkness back to Lower Sweetville. Again, I apologize for intruding upon your personal space. It is not my preferred method for approaching potential patients, but sometimes my prospects can be a bit elusive. That is why I have typed up this letter, so that I might be out of your way as soon as possible and allow you time to dwell on the information you are about to read.
   Obviously, by this point, you must have deduced that I know both *who* you are and *what* you are. Do not be alarmed. I am not here to judge you or to "out" you, whatever my demeanor may indicate. Quite the contrary. I know you are willing to protect your privacy at any cost. I understand and respect that choice. I am on your side. I am sure you are curious about my sources, and you have every right to be. However, how I have happened upon this personal information of yours is classified. For now. Do not be concerned. Where I come from, we of the surgical persuasion have a variety of ways to obtain critical details about those we seek out. What you should

be concerned about is that I am more than capable of helping you achieve true womanhood. You have the potential to carry yourself above and beyond this special sort of chrysalis you've encased yourself in for years. Absolute completion of self. No more secrets, and no more need to lie to the world.

Is that not what you have always dreamed of, sweetness? To finally blend in? The dream you have strived for your whole life is attainable.

I assume you were already familiar with my associates, the Withering Wyldes, before we so rudely intruded upon your abode. So I will do my best not to bore you with too many of their details. I'd be utterly shocked if you hadn't heard of them by this point, considering how prevalent their little pamphlets are around town. Between you and me, I don't understand how they can refer to themselves as "environmentally friendly" when the litter from said pamphlets covers the streets of Sweetville. But I digress.

The Withering Wyldes are useful for a wide assortment of other purposes. Many of them come from scientific and medical backgrounds, much like their former mentor and my close personal friend Dr. Dorian Wylde—may he rest in peace—and they have seemingly omnipotent brains. Recently, they have been not only experimenting with new uses for their flagship drug Witherix™, but have also been researching new avenues for surgeries that are often unaffordable to those who may need them most. Body modification as a way of correcting nature's mistakes. They have such a terrible media reputation, but ultimately I am confident that they work for the greater good. This move will boost their public image at the very least.

This is where I come in. They have personally selected me to implement their plan and have given me *carte blanche* to help those who I have chosen. I am a practicing, self-made surgeon. My credentials are not from any accredited university, and you would not be familiar with any of my most reputable references. But rest assured I received nothing short of the utmost professional training during my ten-year stay in Thailand.

I can provide to you the equivalent of gender reassignment surgery via an advanced technology, and at a rate that is guaranteed to please. I determine many of my payments based on a sliding scale. You will spend considerably less than you might even in Bangkok, and I also offer a convenient payment plan if necessary, free of interest. No requirements for a psychological evaluation or pesky letters of recommendation. I have also undergone extensive psych training that allows me to carefully choose my patients, only pursuing those who are clearly in dire need of my assistance. I have treated a number of young individuals in a similar plight to yours, and all have been successful. I pride myself on pleasing my clients. Here are a few testimonials. I have omitted the full last names for privacy purposes. Hopefully they will make your decision much easier.

> *"Dr. Kast has made me the happiest woman in the world. Whenever I used to look in the mirror before, I never saw the real 'me,' but now that's what I look at every day. Now I'm both content* and *confident."* — Grace H. (Madison, WI)

> *"Seamless, professional work. No one will ever know you weren't born this way."* — Carrie K. (Eugene, OR)

> *"I never thought I'd be able to afford SRS, that it was just a pitiful dream never to be fulfilled. That all changed when I was referred to the*

Monarch Metamorphosis Syndicate. The prices were so reasonable, and Dr. Kast even threw in a complimentary forehead re-contour! I've never felt so feminine in my life!" — Rebecca M. (Toronto, ON)

"Dr. Kast has become more than just a surgeon, he has become a friend. I owe him my life." — Alejandra G. (San Ysidro, CA)

As you can see, many of these clients have traveled from other regions. Medical tourism has become a lucrative business in recent years. However, it is always a treat to be able to perform this procedure on a lovely local such as yourself, something I've had the pleasure of taking part in only a handful of times. I enjoy giving back to the community and all of that.

If, for whatever reason, you still cannot afford my generous offer, do not consider all hope lost. I am confident we can find a solution that will be beneficial to both parties.

I truly hope you will consider my offer, not simply because I desire payment, but because I find honest joy in the ability to assist in a much deserved transformation. Please contact me if and when you are ready.

Yours,

Dr. Julius Kast

Dr. Julius Kast, M.D.
Monarch Metamorphosis Syndicate
99 Sweet Pepper Lane, Suite D7
555-5278

"God's hands alone are not worthy of change. We must take the malleability of the flesh back into the power of our own grasp. Only then will we begin to understand the true intentions of the heavens." —Dr. Dorian Wylde

CHAPTER TEN

Samuel finished the final bites of his most recent Taste Subject. It was exquisite, a rare delicacy.

The final piece was always heartbreaking to him. He knew he would have to fast between Subjects for a few weeks if he wanted to reach pure Consumption Enlightenment, but his willpower was weak. So he had started the tradition of saving and freezing a sliver acquired during Layer One. Always a slice from where the buttock meets the thigh, so ripe with fat and flavor. Fried before it could thaw, just enough so the frost evaporated, then seasoned with turmeric and sea salt. A pity there was no more left in his freezer. He wished he had not only saved this small piece for tonight's meeting, but also another morsel he could have enjoyed in private. Tasting and Eating had never been much of a social activity for him, not like it was to some Eaters. It was in solitude he found his true religion.

As he swallowed the last bite, he could see the torment in the eyes of each of the four pledges that sat before him. He could not have—would not have—shared a single taste with any of them. Not yet. They were not worthy. He took a toothpick to the stalagmites and stalactites in his mouth and picked out some short strands of black, wiry hair that had not cooked out of the meat.

"Tell us more about the Layers, Master Angelghoul sir. Please," one of the pledges begged. Rudy. A grotesquely obese middle-aged man with a nose like a beefsteak tomato ravaged by rot and a bald spot on his head that looked like it was creating its own natural tonsure. He had all the makings of a fine lackey. Unfortunately, Rudy was wearing the same tattered clothes he wore to every meeting. Samuel could smell him from across the room.

Samuel took a sip from his bottle of seltzer water. He normally loathed talking so much, but had to make an exception so he could increase his ranks once again. He was dressed down for the meeting. His mohawk was washed, dried and pulled back into an awkward ponytail. The group met in the neutral space of his living room, still somewhat filthy, but far away from the areas of his home that were littered with punk rock garb. He needed to act professional. It was going to be a long night.

"Well," Samuel began, "the consistency of Layers varies somewhat between Taste Subjects, but over the years I've come up with an overview of how they usually play out."

Samuel Haines had earned the honorable nickname of The Angelghoul just five short years ago at age twenty-five. His meals of fresh flesh were divine-derived, part of a quest that was not merely a matter of dabbling in taboos, but a yearning to reach a spiritual zenith. The meat of the willing elevated him to a meditative state in which he gained a greater understanding of both himself and the world around him. To an outsider, the processes of Tasting and Eating might appear violent, but to Samuel it was perfect peace.

"Layer One is like licking a salty Fudgsicle bubbled in the sun." He saw Judith taking notes already, the same as she had done during the other meetings she had attended over the past few weeks. Judith's appearance was jarring amongst the other pledges. All business, her hair in a bun so tight it gave her a facelift that made her ageless. She seemed to write faster than he could speak.

"Layer Two is copper-ridden, like a mouth full of wet pennies." He looked directly at the youngest and newest member of their group, a Hawaiian boy. His name was Kai, and he had a shocked expression glued to his face that seemed to intensify every few minutes. Samuel already knew Kai wouldn't last through a respectable poker game, much less the journey they were on this evening. He had seen his type before. Doing this on a dare to impress his friends, acting as if the whole thing was just some big silly joke, not realizing he was getting himself into something much more raw than he could have imagined. This boy did not realize the sacrifice that Tasting and Eating entailed, what it took to reach Consumption Enlightenment. Samuel's soul had lost its way, so the solution was to absorb the souls of others to feel whole again.

At least temporarily.

"Layer Three can be gristly and chewy at times, but is good with curry and lentils."

"So this is like the Eucharist, then," said Charlie, a thirty-something, bearded redhead who looked like a pirate that had yet to earn his patch and peg leg. His interruption was no question. He seemed certain he was correct.

"No," Samuel replied, trying to maintain his composure despite Charlie's condescending tone. "Catholic transubstantiation is nothing more than a fraud. Why settle for tasteless, stale bread when legitimate sacramental flesh can be had for a price?" He paused for a moment to let it soak in. "Did you get that, Judith?"

"Yes, sir," she replied without so much as removing her eyes from her notepad.

When Samuel had first connected with his original group of Eaters, they were unorganized, sloppy. His intelligence and his dedication to the cause had quickly made him a figurehead, they his loyal followers, and soon they became little more than peons. His pious approach to mastication methods, combined with his atrophied appearance, had made it simple for him to advance in rank all those years ago, and for the other lowly Eaters of Sweetville to bestow his special name upon him. Samuel accepted the term of endearment with stoic glee. Once he officially became The Angelghoul, he would watch from the sidelines as they did his dealings for him, and he reaped the majority of the benefits.

Samuel had not always found himself in such a respected position in life. It had taken great work to achieve this status, a status that had waned once his wings had failed to grow and his group had lost faith in his leadership, but one he knew would once again flourish. He was well aware the new group he'd assembled was a pack of misfits, but that was also what made them so appealing. They craved his guidance and carried none of the old baggage. They believed in him, or were at least on the faithful path.

His original Eaters had once thought him to be a Christ-like figure— an ironic assumption. Little had they known the lovely, long brown locks and bushy beard he wore at the time were actually inspired by Jim Morrison. A far cry from his current appearance, it was a look that had worked well during his days as Sweetville East High School's junior custodian, where no one cared to see his face or know his name.

The students at Sweetville East had been near negligible to Samuel, nothing more than snacks in training—he had already been researching his spiritual quest at the time. After a year of uneventful employment, he fell under the scrutiny of the school's administration. Students of both genders had reported that Samuel often spent too much time lingering in the restrooms when they were clearly occupied and his cleaning was already complete. The police became marginally interested in the case, but there were no concrete crimes to pin on him. Samuel pleaded that he was only trying to perform the duties of his job, that he was wearing headphones and was unaware there were children relieving themselves in the stalls. Ultimately, he was forced to resign.

"And what about Layer Four?" Rudy asked. The fat little frog looked so eager, so hungry that Samuel wanted to shove his fist down his gullet, see how he liked the taste.

"Ah, the final Layer. Well, the feral dogs in the alley usually seem to enjoy it."

"How do we know this isn't a ruse?" Charlie asked. "That what you ate tonight wasn't just something you picked up at the butcher shop?"

"You're free to leave," Samuel said, taking another sip of his seltzer. There was a skeptic in every crowd, and they always came around to become the most loyal slaves. "Or you can learn more about Tasting and Eating. Learn from someone who has failed, succeeded and become equally powerful from facing both ends. Do you want the opportunity to reach Consumption Enlightenment?"

Charlie stared at him, twitching with what was likely a mix of fear and anger. Samuel took that as an answer of yes.

He told them about his various unsuccessful Tasting and Eating attempts, those that occurred long before he had finally achieved the beginning stages of Consumption Enlightenment. As other Eaters had informed him when he was a budding beginner, such edification became obvious the moment it was reached. Samuel had been told it would move slowly through his mind with a direct line to his soul, and he was not lied to. Each failed attempt had been a grand learning experience, a baby step toward some semblance of nirvana. He had been a fast learner and was soon well educated in the art of Tasting.

The first of his failures seemed like it was meant to be a gleaming success. It involved one of the Junkie Creeps, a teenage girl named Sara. His Eaters had all been occupied with other business that night, and so he had met Sara by himself in an alley off of Third and Raven. She was looking to purchase some Sweet Candy instead of the standard H. The drug was still fairly fresh on the scene at the time and all of its flaws had not been rectified yet, but it was already exploding in popularity. Sara paid and popped a couple of pills on the spot. The effects at the time were dangerously immediate, and so she had invited him back to her squat a few blocks away for some fun.

Thankfully, the other Creeps in her clan were out somewhere being creepy, so Samuel and Sara had the whole top floor of the abandoned apartment building all to themselves. The dust on the walls might as well have been part of the décor. It was so thick he had wondered if it would have been possible to scoop out a spoonful and make some tea. Sara's bed was a ratty mattress that was more spring than cushion—covers and pillows not included. He had slept on worse, so he barely blinked at the temporary discomfort. He had avoided Sara's sloppy kissing and crotch pawing advances with professional stealth and casually proposed the idea of partaking in some bite play. She thought it kinky, so Samuel decided to take advantage of the situation before she sobered up, if that would have even been possible for her at that point. A quick nibble at her nipple, just enough to draw a trickle of blood, and Samuel had been able to enter her psyche from that tiny taste. It was a revelation of hidden truths.

He discovered that, despite her street urchin façade, Sara secretly came from a life of privilege, a bratty rich girl cliché. She had rejected her brand new convertible Bimmer given to her by her parents for her sweet sixteen, her trust fund in progress, an enormous bedroom in her parents' house in the Sweethills and her crispy clean laundry that magically appeared in her closet every third day, courtesy of Marta, the live-in housekeeper. She once had a face that could have been prominently featured in *Vogue Italia*, but she also had a brain that told her hanging out with the worst of the burnouts in Sweetville just to piss off Daddy was a grand idea. Win some, lose some.

Sara had donned the traditional blue Junkie Creep jumpsuit and never looked back at her pampered life, at least not in public. Clean, rosy, youthful cheeks soon resembled those of an aged chimney sweep, then began their descent into near-leprous pockmarks. Track marks had developed in the soft crevices of her elbow crooks, puckering, pustule-covered tattoos that she'd never rid herself of. Her flesh emitted a stench resembling carp left to rot on asphalt. Not particularly pleasurable in Samuel's discerning opinion. A chemical imbalance, boredom and good ole honest American teen rebellion. Sara's family likely never knew for certain why she felt the need to turn her back on such a cozy birthright. The destitute companions she ran with on the streets likely never knew her upbringing. They would have maimed, ravaged or killed for just a day's worth of the comfort she had been born into.

He had moved further down Sara's body and attempted one minuscule bite the size of a water chestnut on the back of her thigh, which made her squeal. He had been unsure why she reacted this way. His numbing agent, a gel with a sweet scent resembling a fruity car air freshener and a cool sensation like a slightly thawed ice pack, had been applied generously. His taste test had lasted a few seconds before he spat the chunk back out onto the floor. Palatal poison left as a snack for the rats and roaches. In her Candy-fueled haze, Sara had probably never noticed this new little defect on her body before it had the chance to heal, so it really didn't matter much.

Samuel took another sip of seltzer. The bottle was almost empty. In his trip down memory lane, he had not noticed that Kai had fled from the meeting. Samuel was certain that would be the last time he'd see him. Judith was still scribbling away like a good student. Rudy's mouth sat askew in dumb, perverse glee, and Charlie was enraptured, a soon-to-be true believer.

He went on to tell the brief tale of the second failed attempt, which had been with a flirty mannequin posed in the window of Modyrn Gyrlz. A plastic, flawless goddess. Samuel had been high on a three-day binge of Sweet Candy at the time and barely knew his own name, much less the difference between a human being and a fiberglass facsimile. He had taken a ravenous bite of the mannequin's shoulder, chipped one of his incisors, torn open his lip and swallowed his treasure. He had bled all over the clearance rack and was promptly booted from the store by management. The fiberglass had seemingly gone down smoothly, but Samuel had shat blood for two days after. He had refused to go to the hospital and instead meditated, perhaps fallaciously attributing his quick healing to a growing ascendancy within his epidermal shell.

Then, the *piéce de résistance*.

Wangombe, a Kenyan man who had been out of work for three months and in desperate need of finding a way to support his wife and two daughters. Dr. Kast, who Samuel had only recently met at the time, had introduced the two of them, and to this very day, that ugly dwarf would not let him hear the end of it. Though Samuel still owed Kast for leading him to the wonders of the liquor of human ichor, he still loathed the little turd. How convenient for Kast to earn himself a 15 percent finder's fee, too. Where had that sideshow reject gathered such nerve? Because of this, he had to pay Kast *and* the Taste Subject for their services. No real matter, though. It was only business, and he had to respect that to a degree. Samuel always had a surplus of cash to blow from peddling the potpourri of designer drugs that constantly crept into the city limits of Sweetville, so the extra payment was ultimately a non-issue.

He did, however, leave that part out of the story for fear the fledgling Eaters would lose any respect he had gained from them.

When Samuel had first met Wangombe, he was apprehensive about tasting a man rather than a woman. The sensation did not attract him as much, but he had not been very successful with female Tasting and

Eating at that point, and he knew he needed to separate his sexuality from his blissful ascension into The Angelghoul. The desires of an almost-god knew no sexual preference. Divinity and carnality were mutually exclusive concepts.

Initially, Wangombe had allowed himself to offer only small pockets of Layer One, in less painful areas that could be bandaged easily without his wife discovering. Wangombe had worked in an injection molding factory and often sliced up his fingers on the harsh gears of the machinery, so Samuel stripped those to the bone over the course of a week. Wangombe had concocted a lie about picking up an odd job during that time, feeling confident that his family would never raise their eyebrows at his recent wounds. Or, at least by the time they began to notice something was wrong, it would have been too late.

Layer Two had been far more difficult—without plasma a man tends to grow weak. Samuel had made sure he had an economy size box of sugar cookies on hand to feed to his Subject after each serving, which, over time, resulted in a crisply saccharine taste to the blood. A pleasant bonus.

At Layer Three, Wangombe had received greater compensation up front, with the caveat that his family would be hunted down and harmed if he intended to keep the money and run or attempted to leave any sort of information that could trace the authorities back to Samuel or Kast. It was not uncommon for Taste Subjects to get the last-minute jitters, especially when approaching Layer Three, so there needed to be some sort of insurance policy.

Days later, it was time for Layer Four and there was nothing left of Wangombe after that, save a slew of HAVE YOU SEEN ME? flyers sloppily wheat-pasted to random telephone poles and mailboxes along Quail Street.

It had been an acquired taste for Samuel, but a necessary one. It soon became an experience to relish. He had known then, deep down as he knew now, that angelic blood surged through his veins and he was beyond sick of his useless humanity. The more willing flesh he consumed, the closer he would come to true Consumption Enlightenment. He would earn his wretched wings, growing them from the cartilage absorbed into his bloodstream.

He grinned wide, making eye contact with each of his new Eaters, except for Judith, her pointed nose buried in her notepad. "I have compiled a distinct list of personal directives. I suggest you take them into consideration and highly recommend you *all* take notes, not just Miss Judith over there."

Judith finally looked at him. He thought she might have been mildly offended, but her tight face was devoid of expression. He almost feared what she would look like with her hair let down, that her face would crumble like a mummy released from its tomb.

"The first directive," Samuel continued, "is fairly simple: you must consume sacred flesh. You all know this already. The second: you must excrete the remnants of souls. Screaming spirit shits."

Rudy chortled at this, but Samuel ignored it. That last thing he wanted to do was acknowledge and potentially encourage disruptive behavior.

"And the third," he said. "You must be selective with Taste Subjects, based on levels of need, desperation and will." Samuel believed he was relatively good at heart despite the foul reputation other Eaters often carried with them. It did not pay to be cruel. Fairness was a virtue. Like a true addict, he shed a tear each time he stole a taste, then wiped his eyes with hopeless pride and moved on to the next high.

None ever truly satisfied.

When no volunteers were readily available, the freshly dead had sufficed in a pinch. The scent of formaldehyde, the chill of autopsy tables and the visions of supine cadavers in the Swell Rest Mortuary had become a tad too familiar for Samuel's liking. It was like dining at a restaurant in a foreign country: he might not have understood much of what was on the menu, but he ordered something regardless. Kincaid, the mortuary's night watchman, was prone to looking the other way if his palms were greased well enough. He had even allowed Samuel to taste of him just once, on a trial basis. A nibble from the webbing between his thumb and forefinger. It had not proven beneficial to either party. However, occasional use of the crematorium was helpful in disguising some of the bland tastes. Between the flambéed flesh and the added dashes of cumin, cayenne pepper and poultry seasoning, the cadavers were often delectable. He had begun to understand the appeal of Sweeny Todd's infamous meat pies, and wondered if he couldn't open up his own lucrative business one day. However, the dead were empty Twinkie calories while the living were filet mignon. Both deserved their place in The Angelghoul's balanced food pyramid, but it was clear which of the two choices would help those two small, malformed bumps between his shoulder blades grow more quickly and properly.

"Any questions?"

Samuel was not just working hard to earn his blessed wings, he was entitled to them.

"Good. I think you'll all work out just fine."

CHAPTER ELEVEN

TRIXIE FLOATED AT THE THRESHOLD between her bathroom and bedroom, brushing her freshly washed hair, still damp like a dishtowel. Her face was made up just enough to accent her feminine features. Christopher sat at the edge of her bed, digging his teeth into his cuticles.

She studied the white wall across from her bed, barren aside from a tacked-up, shoplifted poster of The Smiths—a shot of the boys in their prime, lounging in front of the Salford Lads Club—and a naked Wishnik troll strung up by its purple hair, showing off all of its anatomically aberrant glory.

"So Trix…who's Thomas?"

Trixie dropped her brush. It made a soft thud on the bedroom floor.

Did Christopher really just ask what she thought he had? Was that a knowing wink in his voice? Maybe all of the subtle clues were finally starting to form into a Sherlock moment for him, a seed in his brain blossoming into a possible flower. Trixie knew it was only a matter of time until The Truth became a billboard plastered across her forehead. She just wished she possessed the power to postpone the inevitable ruin of her relationship, or the strength to be honest with him and hope for the least amount of agony. Even though their relationship—if it could be called that—was still in its infancy, after just a few short weeks she felt she owed Christopher at least that much. There had been a few close calls at being brave enough to spill the beans, but her chicken feathers always started flapping whenever an opportune moment presented itself.

She sat next to Christopher, leaned down and played with her toes as a way of avoiding direct eye contact. She looked up toward the wall and saw that Federico had somehow managed to curl himself up on a lone shelf that had no convenient cat access.

"What are you talking about, Chris? Thomas who?" Her voice cracked uncontrollably. She coughed and cleared her throat, buying her at least a few more seconds to think.

Things needed to stay the same. They just *couldn't* change. It would murder all of the positive points she had built up since the night of their first kiss. She couldn't lose Christopher now. He had become her oxygen, her reason to get up in the morning and feel worthy. How could something so wonderful shift into something so stressful in a matter of seconds?

"I was, uh, looking in your dresser when you were showering."

"What? Why would you do that?" she asked, upset. Snooping was way off limits in this apartment. Who knows what he could have seen? What the hell was he thinking?

"Sorry. Just wanted to see if you had any gum or whatever. But I saw a picture of some kid in there. It was sitting on top of a notebook. 'Thomas' was written on the back, so by some difficult deduction I figured that had to be his name. Weird that it was crossed out, though."

Her stare burned through him.

"Geez, Trix, I really am sorry."

Trixie turned away. She didn't want to cause a big stink. It was far too early in the game for them to be fighting about something so stupid. But was it really stupid, or was she going to let him off the hook because she felt even the smallest confrontation could chink away at the shale of their relationship? Trixie wondered what kind of person goes fingering through someone's drawers for gum, but she needed to remain calm.

Deep, meditative breaths.

It was nothing. Only a stupid mistake. Christopher was a guy, and guys never understood the magnitude of their actions, especially when it came to girls and their private matters. Yelling at him about it wasn't going to help the situation.

Trixie allowed herself a sideways glance. Christopher's apologetic guilt stretched his face into a crescent moon. She felt slight, temporary relief. Maybe he knew nothing at all. Maybe his intentions were pure and real. This was just an innocent question, and he didn't seem like the type to be a good liar.

But then one word from his apology suddenly appeared in front of her in block letters.

Notebook.

Notebook meant diary, and diary meant the spilling of all of her scrawled secrets onto the floor in front of her. She could have sworn she had locked the diary away in her safety box. The situation had now escalated to Code Purple: Worse Than She Ever Could Have Possibly Imagined.

Trixie knew exactly what picture he was talking about, of course. Taken when she was still that lost and confused little boy who begrudgingly went by the name of Thomas. Nine years old. A perfectly posed soccer picture during a stint with the YMCA. The Sweetville Red Deer. A shiny burgundy jersey and black shorts. Shin guards with Velcro that barely stayed stuck together. Scuffed and muddy cleats that had left uncountable puncture holes in the field. A rice-bowl haircut and an adorably goofy smile. The seeds of a young man who would never exist.

She cursed herself for keeping that ridiculous picture, the only physical remnant of her former life. She should have burned it long ago, completely rid herself of all ties to the past. She made a mental note to install a lock on her dresser in case Christopher might have another hankering for gum in the future. She hoped that she would still have the option.

"You didn't open the notebook, did you?" Trixie asked, still trying to structure a passable poker face before turning around. She got up from the bed and approached her Smiths poster, praying to the visage of Morrissey for poetic advice. His handsome face could only offer her a lyric about all men having secrets. Trixie supposed that sentiment applied to all women as well. It sure as hell did to her. Here was her secret, and she should let it be known.

"No. *No.* Of course not. I know better than to stick my nose into a lady's business. I'd never invade your privacy. Well, not any more than I already did." Christopher laughed.

She felt the comfort of a crisis averted. Her chest relaxed and she turned around to face him. His eyes were freshly polished marbles.

"I didn't know you were into writing, though," he said. "You ever work on anything else besides the diary?"

"No, not really. I tried a little more when I was younger, but to be honest I haven't had a lot of time to write much recently. Even in the diary."

Not true. She had been writing about *him*, more than could be considered healthy. It would have been terrible enough if he happened to read any of the recent mortifying moments where she had been gushing about how amazing she thought he was. It would have at least been a blessing if he hadn't managed to venture beyond that. If he had seen any info about the big *T*, this would not be such a tranquil conversation.

Another scare surged through her body. She worried that Christopher might have continued his search for gum in her jewelry box. Kast's letter was still folded up inside. She had read the letter only once, the same night he had mysteriously appeared in her house with the Withering Wyldes, and filed it away. The temptation of his offer, however, had never left her mind. She couldn't remember if she had locked the jewelry box either. It was frustrating beyond belief that she required so many keys and combinations in her life.

"You know how it is," she said. "Gotta pay the bills. It was mostly some pretty bad poems and attempts at stupid little stories that never really seemed to work out."

Christopher hopped off the bed and closed the distance between the two of them, sliding his arms around her waist.

"Aw, I bet they weren't as bad as you think. We're always our own worst critics, right? I've been dying to make a short film or something, but I have no idea where to even start on a script. Doesn't help that I'm terrible at writing. Or that I can't afford the camera equipment. You ever try writing a screenplay or anything like that?"

She shook her head. "I guess I'm just better at writing out my inner demons privately and truthfully. Maybe I've had enough crazy things happen in my life that I don't need to fictionalize them."

"Fair enough." He nodded, and a brief moment of awkward silence passed. His lips were in the perfect position to press against her forehead, so he let the magnetism take control. "Anyway, sorry again about getting into your stuff. I can't apologize enough. I owe you some flowers or something."

"Add some chocolates to that and consider yourself forgiven." Trixie pouted, then smiled.

"Done. But yeah, I was just curious who that kid was. He kinda looks like you. You got a little brother you haven't told me about?"

"Um…no." She paused, begging her mind for a brilliant excuse. This was something she had become an expert at. When a woman could fill volumes with her secrets, fabrications were a genuine requirement. "Thomas was my, uh, cousin. He passed away a few years ago. I don't really like to talk about that. It's just too—"

"Shit. I'm so sorry, babe. I had no idea." Christopher placed his hands on her shoulders, massaging them with a marching cadence. "Look, if you don't want to talk about it, that's cool. Just know I'm always here if you ever want to talk. About anything."

His mini-speech was so simple and comforting that any outside listener would argue it had to have been scripted. But no, Trixie had learned over the last few weeks that this was just Christopher's way of showing he was a genuine, caring person. Simple and effective, whether intended or not. A questionable superhero, this one. Flowing capes, heroic tendencies, muscles bursting from gaudy spandex, these did not apply to Mr. Christopher Faith. However, he most certainly *did* rescue her from the villainous clutches of the single life. His romantic appeal was gut-tingling enough to allow him to cross over into Ultimate Boyfriend territory. She hoped it was not just because the relationship was new. She also thought Christopher should be careful for what he wished for. Trixie felt she had more baggage than the average girl, more than Christopher deserved to deal with.

She felt horrible about withholding The Truth from him. Again. And this time she had outright lied. How many lies were enough to keep her skeletons safe? How many versions of her past had to die before they came back as ghouls prepared to rip off her flesh and expose her raw innards?

Christopher kissed the side of her neck, just below her jaw. Guilt-ridden goose pimples made the translucent hairs on her arm stand at attention. Strands of her damp hair clung to her cheek. More than ever, she was relieved she had not been born with a prominent Adam's apple. A tracheal shave would never have been an affordable option. Unless, maybe, that was something included in Kast's surgical plans?

Trixie released herself from his embrace, flattened her body onto her bed and sprawled her limbs out. She stared at the ceiling, trying to summon some deeply repressed psychic power that would cause a spiraling helicopter to crash though it. Something, anything to get her out of this mess.

"Chris?"

"Mm-hmm?"

"You really mean what you said?"

"I don't just throw promises around. At least not on purpose." He cracked a smile and joined her on the bed, straddling his yardstick body around her waist, hovering over her like a protective shield.

"Okay." She fiddled with his belt loops, fitting her thumbs through them and tugging them tightly.

"Why?"

A few moments of silence. Christopher was a patient boy.

"There's something I've been meaning to tell you."

* * *

Of course, as usual, Trixie's attempt at honesty failed miserably. After more prolonged reticence that was wearing out its welcome, she opted for a distraction instead, caressing Christopher's crotch without much warning, pawing at it like a professional until he grew to full size. This was a quick process. One booming success of a blowjob later, she was sure he would have forgotten all about her need to blurt out The Truth. A narrow escape.

She snuggled up to him, slid her fingers up his shirt, scratched at him like a playful kitten, and twirled his light, almost invisible chest hairs.

"So, yeah, that was pretty awesome," he said after recovering from his stellar orgasm, a smirk stretching across his face. His half-flaccid penis was now tucked back into his underwear. "No complaints here, as usual. Far be it from me to refuse such a generous gift. Now that we've gotten that out of the way, though, what exactly was it you were about to tell me beforehand?"

Trixie's brain melted into nacho cheese.

"Oh, nothing."

"Seriously, I wasn't kidding around earlier. I want you to feel comfortable telling me whatever. In fact, I've gotta be honest. I wish you'd open up a little more. Not that being a mystery's a bad thing, but, well, you know. Gotta dish out a few clues every now and then."

Trixie turned her gaze back up to her popcorn ceiling, white and empty save for an adventurous daddy longlegs. Federico perked up at the edge of the bed and froze into a comical statue. The cat watched the arachnid creep and crawl, likely trying to work out a way to chase and catch it.

"It takes a while to get to know me."

"Oh, I'm aware," he said. "And it's been worth every excruciating moment." Trixie socked him in the shoulder. He winced in pretend pain.

"It's just…" Again, she had to think on her tippy-toes, search into the safety deposit box of her mind where she had stored away more than a few fibs over the years. "Well, you know how I haven't been comfortable enough to let you see me fully naked yet?"

"Mm-hmm."

"I wasn't totally straight with you when I said I was still a virgin."

"Oh. That's all? I kind of figured you weren't."

"What the hell do you mean by that?" She geared up to give him another light beating. Christopher held up his palms in surrender.

"I didn't mean it like *that*. Hey, I'm no angel either. It's just that a special, beautiful girl like you has probably had to beat the guys off with a big stick. I'd be really surprised if you hadn't reciprocated with at least a select few."

"Hmm." Trixie tried to hide her grimace. She surrendered her silly fists and ran her fingers through his hair, pulled it closer to her face, relishing in its mandarin scent. "Nice save."

"I'm not going to lie. I really, *really* want to take things further with you. I think about it all the time. Just want to be clear about that. But I'm cool with waiting until the time's right for you. I totally respect your comfort zone. And I'm not going anywhere."

Trixie was in awe of these words. She wondered if he was wearing a wire, if someone was feeding him these flawless lines. She couldn't believe she was graced with such a sweetheart, a guy who didn't fall prey to male cliché. Hell, she was just pleased to have someone who put up with her.

"It's more than just that, though," she said. "I was…I was kind of abused when I was younger. I'm not ready to get into the details yet. Maybe someday. But that's why I'm so freaked about totally sharing my body. It…it wasn't a willing virginity loss."

Trixie believed this to be the worst lie she had concocted thus far. Though it was technically not a lie, just slightly tampered truth. At the very least, it bought her more time until she could come clean for real.

Christopher's face turned white. His eyes reddened and dampened. He remained mute, took her in his arms, clutched her hand. "Trix… I'm…I'm really…I didn't…" There were no words that could have prepared him for this revelation, nothing that could come even close to comforting her, and it was obvious that he quit trying to search for a solution. He cradled her, a force field made of flesh, the two of them against the world.

"It's okay. You couldn't have known. I can't expect you to read my mind. Just keep holding me for a while. Don't let go. Please."

Trixie adhered herself tightly to his torso. He squeezed back, and she wished she could tell him The Truth. But her mouth couldn't form the words.

She studied his breaths. After a few moments his pattern became calm and steady. The CD changer made shifting and clicking sounds before "It Makes No Difference" by The Darling Buds began to shimmer in the background. Trixie changed the subject and asked, "What are you doing tomorrow?" The mundane, the banal was all that could save the day now.

"Gotta pick up a couple of extra shifts at Mad Mario's. One of the drivers quit yesterday."

"Bummer."

"Yeah. Way too many flakes at that place. I'm free Wednesday, though. Maybe I can stop by Video Drones and bring over some questionable cinema."

Trixie allowed a tiny burst of fierce laughter to escape. "No good. I'm working graveyard at Audrey's again. What about Friday? Can we go out and see a movie or something?"

"Shit. I need to go visit my cousin on Friday."

"That weird cousin who seems to call every time I come over to your place?"

"The one and only."

Trixie's eyes were morphing into those of a jilted puppy dog.

"But," Christopher continued, "that's during the day. Do you want to come meet him? I think you'd like him, actually. We can go catch something after. I think *The Crying Game* is on second run at the Livingston. Nominated for a shit-ton of awards I guess, but I don't really care about that stuff. My brother said there's some crazy twist in it, but he didn't want to spoil it for me."

Trixie felt like a swarm of centipedes was scurrying down her spine. "Nah. Stacey at work said that one was no good. Let's skip it. I think there's a Twilight Zone marathon on that night, though."

"Hey, works for me. Hopefully they'll show 'The Lonely.' That one's my favorite."

Relief. Sweet, soothing relief after far too many hours of a tiring juggler's performance. Trixie knew her circus act was only becoming more difficult with every new flying knife she dodged. But Christopher was worth every tiny ulcer she earned from her deception.

July 17, 1991

I need to get the hell out of this life, Miss Diary. You know all the dirty details, so I'm sure you agree. As much as I want to avoid the sentiment, I fucking hate myself and I'm starting to regret ever leaving home. Can you believe that? Is that really what it's come down to?

Remember that girl Joi I told you about? The homely one who wore sweats? Gwen told me the cops found her face down in the gutter before the sun came up this morning. Throat slit. It had been raining. Some of her blood flowed away to the storm drains and is now living another life down in the wet darkness. I could end up like her. Maybe I want to.

Cutting myself doesn't help. Believe me, I've tried. It just fucking hurts. Gwen said that sometimes the slice of a razor in just the right spot makes her stop feeling whatever she's got going on inside because she can focus more on the temporary physical pain. Dulls the emotional turmoil. Doesn't work for me one bit. Especially when I'm well aware that I'm deliberately slashing my wrists in the wrong direction and not quite deep enough to leave any permanent scars. I keep thinking maybe I need to save up my Sweet Candy for a couple of weeks, use it for just the right night and have one last hurrah. Better to go out partying, right, Miss Diary? Would you even miss me?

All I want is love, and all I get is fucked. Would the real world be any different, or would the only difference be that I wouldn't be getting paid anymore? I'd have nothing to show for my pain aside from the pain itself. Maybe that's how it's supposed to be. Some people aren't destined for decent lives.

I was staring through the window of MOXY tonight. Saw some girls kinda like me, but not really. I mean, they're only girls for a few hours. Painted pretend pretty. They're gorgeous, though. Seems like they have a lot of fun in there. There's my old pal envy again. How much is that doggie in the window, right? It must be easier to live as a man in the normal world and be paid to entertain as a woman. Leave the wigs and girdles behind after the audience bails. They can go home, remove their makeup and their drag and just be themselves. But then, which self is the real self? I only have one real self, and I can't escape biology no matter how hard I try.

God fucked me just as hard as any of the nameless johns I have to deal with night after night.

If God can't save me, who will?

CHAPTER TWELVE

Chelsea, Manhattan

Honey.
Girlfriend.
Bitch.

Don't ever let anyone tell you tuckin' ain't no art form. I got a mother-fuckin' terminal PhD in that shit.

Dios mio. Alls I can think about after I'm clockin' out is I'm dyin' to unleash the girdled beast so I can go gets me a cheeseburger and onion rings. Some *carne asada* fries or somethin'. You ever have a taped up *pito* ticklin' your *culo* and some *huevos peludos* chafin' your tuppy?

No? Well, *cállate* your face, *güero*. It ain't fun, know what I'm sayin'?

You know, I may be Ms. Major League New York City Jessica now, but I was *papas chiquitas* before I decided to move out here to the Big Adam's Apple. I know it seems like I been the Big Time Bitch here *siempre*, but it wasn't even all that long ago when I started takin' over this town. Just a few months, really, but it feels like *una otra vida*. Used to live in this *caca* little city called Sweetville. Never heard of it? Shit, girl, neither had I, and I was born there.

You wanna, like, build some character, you get your start in that dead-ass town. Wasn't all that bad, though. Not totally. Enough tasty man meat to go around, but you know I ain't picky. Pretty much ran the show at this low budget joint for a couple years, too. MOXY was the name. Such a hole in the wall, and I'm not talkin' 'bout the glorious kind, you know what I mean? I was like King Queen of the castle there, not that I deserve a cookie for that or anything. Unless you got a cookie.

Oye, hold on a second.

Hey! *Pendejo* by the door! Yeah, you lookin' like muthafuckin' Julius Caesar. I see you checkin' out my sexy ass. Come back later when I'm bored. We'll see if you can handle what Ms. Jessica's got for you.

Shit, honey, where was I? *Los borrachos* always want a piece of this pussy pie. I may be servin' fish now, girl, but MOXY was where I caught my first trout. You know what I'm sayin'?

Yo, this MOXY was some *pinche* poky place and all, but it was like my second home, too. The ceiling looked like someone stood upside down on their *cabeza* and peed all over it like they thought it was a respectable work of art. I guess it kinda was. There was only one bathroom. I mean, shit, why bother with two when it's just gonna cause more confusion with all us bitches, right? So *fuchi* in there, though. Too many *pedos* just floatin' around like they tryin' to get back in the ass they came from. Had to kick out way too many twinks trying to score some cream filling. I swear those little *jotos* got no manners. Don't tip worth a shit neither. Some of the new girls live off the tips. Why even show up if you're not gonna help support *las chicas*, right? Coupla oogly-ass bitches that worked in there, too, you know? I mean, it ain't that hard to shave every now and then. Lady Bic. Ever heard of it? Tryin' to be professional around all these amateurs was like tryin' to find a straight guy in a production of *Les Mis*. Bitches tryin' to read me like they got even a sliver of originality. Please. Go back to the library, *pinche mongólicas*. The book you borrowed is overdue.

No, I ain't bein' catty or throwin' shade like some rude bitch. I just take my realness serious. You'd understand if you were man enough to put on a dress some time. Yes, I'm serious. Do I look like I'm jokin' with you, girl?

Oh, so this one night I was finishin' up my show and all of that. Ended with "The Pussycat Song." That one's always a hit with the new jacks. No, honey, I didn't actually *sing* it. You know I gots a voice like a billy goat in heat, and that's on a good night. There was only like a dozen or so freakos in the crowd, but I was like Gloria Estefan *sin* Miami Sound Machine, and they were like my Madison Square Garden. Bitch, I looked fierce that night. Dress so tight I had to use Crisco to get my fat ass into it. *Con muy* slutty lipstick. My drag mama Aphrodite Adonis said to me once, "Girl, you got more spunk than Anthony Quinn, but Zorba the Greek never wore sequins, tacky eyelashes, and size twelve, six-inch glittered fuck me pumps."

Perfecto. High-five me on that one, girl. Not too hard. I don't wanna break a nail.

Anyways, *hubo mucha lluvia* when I left that night. I didn't have no umbrella with me, so I was screamin' through the parking lot like a hurt-ass bitch 'cause I didn't want to ruin my brand new wig and all. So embarrassin'. After I got in my Yugo I saw some poor tiny *chica* hidin' under the awning in the back, and it just broke my heart. See, I'm not the Grinch you think I am. I'm like sentimental and shit, you know? I rolled my window down and saw some bright little doe eyes lookin' back at me. *Preciosa.*

I say, "Honey, you need a ride somewhere?" She barely had time for a nod before she was ridin' shotgun. Girl shoulda been in the Olympics. Her teeth were chatterin' from the cold like a busted vibrator. I asked her name.

She say, "Ariel." Real quiet, like she was afraid she might hurt my ears if she talked like a normal bitch. Then she say, "No. It's Trixie." So I introduce her to myself, the soon-to-be-world-famous Ms. Jessica Chartreuse, *naturalmente.*

We start drivin' and I ask her, "Where you goin', sweetie?" She just look back at me like she don't know the answer to two plus two. No, it ain't five. Take that damn Corona Light outta your ass. You need some coffee, bitch? Pay attention. You might learn somethin'.

I ask this pretty little thing, "You need somewhere to stay tonight?"

She say, "Maybe." I can tell she's hurtin' inside. At this point I feel, like, totally responsible for this poor girl, you know? I also wondered if someone told her she'd grow a cock on her chin if she talked too much.

I pretty much knew what was goin' on already. Seen her type in Sweetville more times than I wish I had, but I asked her anyways.

"You been workin' out there tonight?" She nodded back at me, and I say, "Don't you worry none, *flaca. No hay calles para ti esta noche.* Ms. Jessica's gonna cook you up some of her special *carnitas* tonight." She finally smiled, and she was about the prettiest, soaking wet little *puta* I ever seen.

I never thought I'd ever be a mama or a papa or, well, whatever. But I swear it just clicked with this girl Trixie and me. Like, what do you call that shit? Serpent dippity doo da? Ah, you know what I mean. Don't make me try so hard. Why do I gotta do all the talkin'? Trixie and me, we both needed each other and didn't know it 'til we knew it. So I just gave her leg a little pat and told her everything would be okay. Yeah, maybe I was a little *mentirosa*, but fuck it. At least I was tryin'. I didn't know what else to do.

So we get back to *mi casa* and, of course, it's a fuckin' tornado scene. Wasn't really expectin' company, and I sure don't clean house for shits and giggles. My wig collection was all out of order and shit. You know, I got those things organized by color and style when I gots the time. But, see, I turned on the lights so I could take out my falsies and I really got to see this girl Trixie close up and personal.

Full. On. Fish.

Pescadora.

Like, we talkin' Chicken of the Sea and shit. Girl had legit long hair, but it wasn't no wig, and she had some nice boobies. I mean, they weren't no *grandes melones* or nothing, but hell, it's wasn't no duct tape cleavage neither. The girl had some damn squeezable *chi-chis.* Half a handful at least. She coulda been a model. Well, at least for like a Sears catalog or somethin'.

My mouth went wide open and I say, "*Hijo de puta, Trixie. No eres como yo. Eres el 'real deal.' Soy sólo una ilusión femenina.*"

Her *gringa* ass say, "I'm sorry. I really don't understand very much Spanish." *Ay güey.* She say she dropped out of high school and didn't need to know any for the GED or some shit. So I broke it down for her.

"Honey, we're alike in a lotta ways, but when the lights go out I'm just a big gay boy in a ball gown and fancy war paint. You an almost-girl."

She kinda smiled all weird and sad and say, "I wish it wasn't 'almost' anymore." I just nodded back and grabbed her hand. I mean, I couldn't really relate, but I sure understood. I think I was havin' my man-strual cycle or somethin' cause I gave her a hug and I got all teared up, smeared my makeup in a tissue and shit. Sometimes I think people are slippin' me some estrogen in my *mojitos*. Or, in my case, it's more like a *mojoto*. Yeah, girl. Slap me some skin for that one.

So I obviously had a lot of pull at MOXY. I asked the owner Nico about letting Trixie wait tables part-time there. Nico was a real butch queen. That *culero* got his mustache waxed every week, twice a week if there was a national holiday. He say, "Okay. I'll give her three days a week to start, but she can't fuck it up or it's your ass." My ass? I mean, what was that? One of those In You Intos? It was, wasn't it?

My little Trixie did real fine real quick. Girl, she wanted off the streets. Like bad. Bussin' tables like she could win a prize from it. I made sure she played up her drag look real good and over the top so she didn't look *too* legit, you know? Some of these queens can smell the fish fresh outta the market. People might start thinkin' we hired a bona fide girl. I woulda believed it.

Well, long story short, she eventually got more hours and worked there until the place went out of business a few months later. I was already on my way out 'cause I knew I was movin' out here to make a name for myself.

I even invited her to come with, but she wouldn't budge. Couldn't bring herself to leave that town. No idea why. Scared of change, I guess. I always say she never managed to win any World's Finest Decision Maker awards. Hell, well neither have I, but I own that shit and work it.

Yeah, we still keep in touch a little bit. I give her a call when I'm feelin' sorta homesick. The way things are goin' back in Sweetville these days, I get cured real quick after I talk to her. My girl Trixie, she actually called me up a few weeks ago, soundin' all happy. She datin' some boy now, but he don't know 'bout her, well, you know. Ding dong the wicked witch gives head.

I say, "Girl, *es peligroso*... You need to tell him. Either he love you for you or he don't. Just 'cause you share a common birth, that ain't gonna change nothin'. He right for you or he not. Simple as that."

She say, "I can't, Jesi." She started calling me Jesi after we became tight. Cute, huh? Makes me get all misty and shit. Like I'm her big sister or somethin'. Guess I was the closest thing she had to family. "I can't, Jesi," she say. "I don't want to lose him."

Alls I can do is pray for her at night. Such a sweet little thing, deserves more than she'll ever get. Now I tuck myself into bed some nights and think.

She is beautiful. Love her, straight boy.

Or don't.

CHAPTER THIRTEEN

A long, winding road like an unraveled infinity snake. A domed canopy of thick foliage to protect the path from the harsh burn of the sun, and also from the soothing comforts of the moon. After a drive that felt like a fairy tale journey, Christopher's turquoise VW Beetle puttered into a sparsely filled parking lot and slid into a spot adjacent to a sign claiming:

WELCOME TO THE SWEETVILLE HAPPY HOTEL!
WHERE TROUBLED MINDS REST AT EASE
PLEASE LOCK YOUR VEHICLE
DO NOT LEAVE PURSES, WALLETS, JEWELRY, SPARE
CHANGE, EXPENSIVE SUNGLASSES, TOOLS, COMPACT
DISCS, OR OTHER VALUABLES EXPOSED
WE ARE NOT RESPONSIBLE FOR ANY LOSS OR DAMAGES

"You sure you want to come in, Trix?" Christopher asked. "I'll probably only be a few minutes."

"Well, I already came all this way," Trixie said. She placed her hand atop his and lightly massaged his knuckles. "It's just your cousin. Nothing to be ashamed of."

Through the windshield, Christopher saw a man in an all-white jumpsuit rocking back and forth on a bench in perfect metronomic time. A few trickles of sunlight highlighted a glistening slug of drool escaping from his mouth. A woman dressed in almost identical garb danced barefoot in the courtyard, her arms playing an invisible accordion. An orderly stood nearby, ready to act, but only if absolutely necessary. The grass below their feet was brown and dry, like the top of a Marine private's head.

"I know. It's not that. I invited you obviously. It's just that no one else ever comes to visit him. His mom, well, she got, uh…sick and his dad passed away. My mom couldn't really take care of him well enough after…" Christopher looked distraught. Somewhere in the distance, a shriek almost indiscernible as human.

"After what?"

"Kinda complicated. He's only been in here for a couple of months. He never really had a normal high school life or anything. Even though he's a few years younger than me, we had a lot of classes together since he skipped a few grades. Super gifted kid but pretty much socially inept. He didn't have any other friends, so we used to spend a lot of time together back then, before the…accident. I feel bad if I don't come to see him frequently."

"What happened exactly? If you don't mind me asking."

"No, that's fine. If I can't talk to you about it, then who can I open up to?" Trixie offered a shy smile, proud that she was worthy of sharing secrets. "You ever heard of the Linguistic Fetishists?"

"Is that the band with the video they keep playing on MTV? The one with the really bad claymation?"

Christopher shook his head and clarified that they were a group of brilliant researchers who devoted their lives to the study of all languages.

"Oh, okay," Trixie said. "Yeah I know who you're talking about now." She had seen a brief story on the news about a convention the Linguistic Fetishists had held in town a few months back. Their expertise had seemed so extensive. Primeval unearthed glyphs. Covert slang. Tribal clicks. Uncharted developments of the imminent future.

"Well," Christopher said, "he was interning for them and was apparently doing really well. Deciphering primitive languages and, like, pidgin dialects from places I've never even heard of."

"No way! He could figure out what birds were saying?"

Christopher laughed. "No. P-I-D-G-I-N. Like slang that's specific to a particular region."

"Oh. Whoops!" Trixie wanted to crawl inside the glove compartment and hide. What brilliance would come out of her mouth next?

"But he was working on an infomercial for those Withering Wyldes weirdos when his illness hit him."

"Oh my God. Did they do something to him?"

"I don't really know, to be honest. I mean, I have my suspicions. Sometimes I think he got a little too close to cracking the code to their language, and they decided they didn't like that very much."

"Sounds like he was a mega-genius."

"Yeah, totally. Still is, but he can't figure out how to channel it properly anymore. I guess the major drawback to him being so smart is that it was only a matter of time before something in his brain burst wide open and altered his personality. And now he's stuck in this shithole. Seems fair, right?"

Trixie noticed Christopher was putting up a good fight against the tears.

"Hey," she said, "I've been...I've known people who have been in worse places than this. This is nothing. Really. Hell, I even knew a girl who ended up in here for a while."

"Oh, yeah? Were you close?" Christopher missed Trixie's near flub. He smiled at her with dumb adoration. She pulled down the sun visor and glanced into the tiny mirror. Her hair was pulled back into a tight ponytail, revealing elfin ears. Her bangs were freshly trimmed, but not perfectly crafted.

"I guess. Kind of an old friend, for lack of a better term. Her name was Gwen. She was probably released a while ago. Geez, I sure hope so. But I never came to visit her when she was here. We kind of weren't friends by that point anyway. But still...I pretty much suck." A strand of loose hair intruded on her bangs. Christopher unconsciously brushed it away for her. She leaned over, placed her hand on his thigh, and gave him a soft peck on the cheek.

"No, I definitely get it," he said. "No matter how many times I come here, it still gives me the creeps." He attached his steering wheel lock and exited the vehicle, then hustled around to the other side to open the door for Trixie.

"My, oh my. However did I find such a gentleman?"

"Darling," he said in his best attempt at a Groucho Marx impression, "those are my principles, and if you don't like them, well, I have others."

"Marriage is a wonderful institution," she replied, considerably less successful with the same impression. "But who wants to live in an institution?"

"Could you be any more perfect?"

"I could, but that would take too much effort."

"You're on fire today." He offered his bent elbow and she took it. "Shall we begin down the yellow brick road?"

"I'm ready." They started down the path, which was, more accurately, made of weather-worn asphalt. Fossilized wads of gum formed ground constellations and persistent weeds pushed through cracks, withered fingers escaping from forgotten tombs.

"I probably should give you a heads up, though. I know you've heard a little bit of this from his messages on my machine, but the way my cousin talks now, it's a little odd at first. And that's putting it lightly."

* * *

At the front desk sat a piggish receptionist with a hornet's nest in place of a hairdo. The air in the lobby was humid. Stagnant body odor permeated the space.

"Sign in, please," the woman said, her pitch all nasal, no low end. Her nametag read: RUTH, but the *H* was smeared so it looked more like RUTA. Christopher shook his head and scribbled his name.

"Isn't Linda here?" He tried to peer into the office behind the front desk. "She knows me. I've been coming for a couple of months."

"Nope. Out sick. Who you here to see?"

"William Ekkert."

Ruta the Pig Woman stared at Christopher and then dug through a few papers, pretending to scrutinize them, but not actually paying close attention.

"Which room is he in?" Trixie asked.

"Ah, that's the Dr. Seuss wannabe, right? Room 999. First floor. Okay, go ahead." She waved Christopher in with her ham-hock hand, then glared at Trixie. "Not you, missy. You need to sign in, too." Ruth/Ruta tapped her press-on nail on the desk. Christopher shot her a scathing glare, but she had already returned to skimming her *Reader's Digest*.

Trixie looked down at the sign-in sheet. It read:

SIGNING THIS ABSOLVES US OF ANY AND ALL LIABILTY
ALL GUESTS MUST REGISTER—NO EXCEPTIONS
YES, THAT MEANS YOU

"Don't worry about it, Trix. It's just a formality. You'll be safe. I'm right here with you."

"Says the man who doesn't get paid just above minimum wage to have feces thrown at him on an almost daily basis," Ruth said, her eyes never leaving the page of the magazine.

Christopher and Trixie began their trek down the long, narrow hallway. The fluorescent lights, exuding the full extent of their wattage, highlighted every flaw in the walls. They passed by cobweb chandeliers. Dust bunnies thick as Berber carpet. Peeled paint posing as abstract wall art.

"God, she was a mega-bitch," Trixie said.

"Yeah, well, I almost can't blame her considering where she works. *Almost*. I think it'd get to most people. I know I couldn't do it."

On the right side of the hallway they passed office spaces, a custodial closet and a unisex restroom. The left was strictly for the patients. The first patient room, 111, was open and vacant. An orderly was hosing it down. The space was about fifteen feet square, but there appeared to be another fifteen feet of solid cement wall between it and the next room. Trixie searched for the reason behind that design and came up short. A faint moan crept under the door of Room 222. A face peered out of Room 444, a man with striking amber eyes, grey spittle caking his lips. Soon they passed by Room 777. The door was ajar and Trixie watched as another orderly attempted to coax a catatonic woman the size of a wildebeest into consuming a bowl of mush. The orderly shoved a spoon up against the woman's tight-lipped mouth. The mush splattered to the floor. When they reached Room 999, Trixie could hear a strangely melodious hum coming from behind the door. Christopher knocked and it ceased.

"William, you there? It's me. Chris."

A quick scurry of slipper-clad feet and the door opened a crack. A nervous eye peeked through. When the door swung wide it revealed a young man with a figure so runty and a face so callow that he could have auditioned at a casting call for pre-teens. He wore a long brown pocket tee that fit him like a baggy dress. Thankfully he also wore a humble pair of dark sweatpants to counter this image. A teenage mustache gone wild sprinkled his upper lip.

"Well, hey man, what's the pleasure of this?" he asked.

"William, what happened to your eye?"

William touched the bandage on his forehead as if he had forgotten it was there. "Oh, this is nothing. Just had to question why," he said.

"Why?"

"Yes, why. Why I cry. Pay attention, cuz. I know you don't get high."

Trixie found William's responses disturbing and difficult to follow. She was beginning to understand what Christopher had meant in regard to his cousin's peculiar speech impediment.

"Jesus Christ, why didn't someone call?" Christopher asked.

William held his arm out, inviting his guests into his living quarters. The décor was sparse. A small cot was topped with a bundle of tattered sheets well overdue for a wash. Next to it was a wood nightstand that had been busted and glued back together so many times it appeared to be holding itself together out of spite.

"Dunno. They probably couldn't read the writing on the wall." William attempted a subtle nod toward the partition directly behind his cot.

This piqued Trixie's interest. She glanced at the wall and saw nothing. She wasn't sure if she was disappointed, confused or some combination of the two.

William tapped at his raw, pink knuckles. Though he was barely set to enter his twenties, his hair was thinning from excessive follicle picking.

Christopher whispered to Trixie, "I think I know what happened to his eye. This is what they call SIB. Self-injurious behavior. He's never going to admit that, though." Turning his attention back to his cousin he asked, "William, who did this to you?"

"Doesn't matter," he said. "My words within these walls will never ring true." He lifted what was left of his hair and pointed at a pale scar etched into his scalp. "Not quite a lobotomy. More like transorbital sodomy."

"Fucking hell," Christopher said. "Please tell me you're joking."

"Hard to say exactly where they've been poking." William shrugged, smirked, and returned to his original tangent. "I've always been a healthy boy, only allergic to avocado and soy. I can handle my own affairs, but I think sometimes they're still scared by what they see in my eyes. Realistically, it should come as no surprise."

William was beginning to sound like a bad hip-hop artist. Trixie couldn't take it anymore. A laugh escaped her lips.

"I'm sorry, Chris," she said. "It's just...your cousin's really funny."

William wiped his eye with the back of his arm, scanned Trixie up and down and pushed his tongue deep into his cheek. He nodded approvingly. "So, my man Chris...are you going to introduce me to your honey?" he asked.

"Oh, yeah. I'm sorry. I was just distracted by this whole eye thing, which, by the way, I'm definitely looking into later. Fuck. Hopefully Linda will be here next time I come by. There never seems to be anyone else in charge around this fucking place."

"I know," William said. "It's quite a disgrace."

"This is my girlfriend. Her name's Trixie."

Trixie swooned internally upon hearing those words spoken aloud. The title of girlfriend was so concise. Was that really the first time that official term had been used? Did it actually matter considering it was stated in front of someone classified by the city as mentally unstable?

William did a clownish little bow, grabbed her hand and came within inches of kissing her fingertips. She could feel his hot breath licking her cuticles. The scent of garlic wafted up to her nostrils.

"Nice to meet you, William," she said. He simply nodded and smiled.

"William, if you feel comfortable, would you mind explaining your situation to Trixie, since I already know the drill?"

William began a rapid-fire verbal delivery. "Well, Miss Trixie, if I deviate from the rhyme scheme, my brainwaves kill. I may not always make perfect or even general sense, but that only becomes problematic for the terminally dense. They call it Lotus Aphasia, 'cause my mind's bound like a geisha. Broca's a link in Wernicke's chain, melded into one superior brain. My patterns are mine, my comfort divine. If my brain hurts, the crisis will avert any chance of information transfer, any hope or semblance of satisfactory answers. The doctor's hypothesize that my personality snapped, that the old William is now trapped in this new confused—"

William stopped short, his face wrenched in intense pain. He kept mumbling something, but Trixie could not understand what it was. He shuffled over to a small desk, grabbed a marker and a sticky note and scrawled something onto the paper. He slapped the sticky note on his forehead and returned. The note had one word written on it: S(HELL).

"Chris, what's happening? Is he okay?"

"Don't worry, babe." Christopher lightly massaged the small of her back. "This is normal. He's just having one of his fits because he took too long trying to find a rhyme. Happens pretty frequently, a few times a day depending on how many conversations he's involved in. He'll come out of it in a second. Just got to let it run its course."

William's head convulsed to the right, multiple times, like it was trying to keep time with pinball machine bells. The sticky note came loose and fell to the floor.

"I'd hate to think what happens if someone ever asks him about oranges." Trixie whispered this into Christopher's ear so it wouldn't upset William any further.

As if on cue, William shot his finger in the air. "But, I digress. I've been diagnosed as clinically depressed. Funny thing is, I'm generally content. It's being a prisoner that gets me so bent. It's the doctor's opinion that counts, my words aren't worth an ounce of respect, but what did I expect? No one really understands what triggers my mind to unwind. Once just a normal kid, now I'm the boy with the wayward id. The bottom line is that my mind's mine." He tapped his fingers against his head hard enough to make a thumping sound. "You might argue I'm crazy or perhaps just too lazy to come to grips that what leaves my lips is—"

He looked geared up to launch into another fit when Christopher shouted, "Tourette's poetry!"

William put a finger to his nose and pointed aggressively at Christopher with his other hand. He cracked a smile that could only come from someone labeled mad, then began a series of scattered giggles, and the emotion infected Christopher who laughed as well.

"We've been through this more times than I can count," Christopher said. "If we make it into a game, it's less stressful for him."

"Less stressful, less grim. But that's more than enough of this trivial stuff," William said. He turned to Trixie. "I'm aware why you've come. Do you assume that I'm dumb? No, I know better, because you wanted to see the letter from Dr. Kast regarding The Truth, even if, for him, it was uncharacteristically uncouth."

Did he just say what I think he just said? Trixie thought. She could feel damp pebbles of nervous sweat beading at her temples. *There's no way. I'm just hearing things now.*

William continued. "Of course, I don't even have it anymore. It was confiscated after the cleanup crew found it on my floor. Took the letter straight to the shredder. I believe Dr. Kast stated he was elated. He hoped for quick decisions about desired incisions. Sorry Trixie-doll, but that's all I recall."

Christopher turned to her and whispered, "He talks about this Dr. Kast character all the time. I'm pretty sure there's no doctor here with that name. It's best just to play along."

Trixie feigned ignorance and agreed. She asked William, "Have you had any recent contact from this man? Dr. Kast?"

William shook his head. "However, his flunkies have planted bugs in the glass. Sporadic, metallic. They're listening to my dreams to determine what they mean. The Withering Wyldes are putting me on daily trial. Never finished translating their infomercial, so they keep coming by for further rehearsal. Using too many of my visitor hours, and they don't even think to bring me flowers."

Trixie feared the shroud of her secrets was about to be ripped away. She decided to take a risk and plunge into open conversation with William, playing along with his game, masquerading her reality as part of its rules.

"They've come to visit me, too," she said. "Dr. Kast and the Withering Wyldes. What's the connection?"

"No offense, but I believe they seek imperfection."

"William, come on. That's rude," Christopher said.

"Sorry, dude. Just got into the mood."

Trixie did not find this comment insulting. She simply filed it away.

"And Dr. Kast loves to talk about you," William said. "I've been waiting for his cue. He's difficult to trust, but I comply because I must." This last part was barely audible.

"Wait a goddamn second," Christopher said. "I'm way confused now. What the hell is going on here?"

"Shush, hon. I'll tell you later." Trixie pouted her lips and scrunched her eyes in flirty distraction.

William shook his finger at him. "Listen to your lady, cuz. She's a feisty alligator."

"I mean, I realize I just walked into Cuckoo City," Christopher said, "but this is beyond ridiculous. Should I leave you two alone?"

"No need. The seeds have already been sown." William grabbed Trixie by the shoulder, cupped a hand over her ear and murmured, "I know all there is to know about you. I've always known. Your secret is safe with me. I'm no tattle tale, you'll see." He offered her an exaggerated wink.

Christopher intervened and gently separated them. "William, that's enough."

"Hey now, Chris. No need to get rough." William brushed off the front of his shirt, clearly annoyed.

"You ready to go, Trix?"

Trixie nodded. She was nauseous. She needed air. She needed to be set free.

* * *

As they left the building, Christopher said to Trixie, "That was kind of wild. How did you know how to adapt so well to his game?"

"I guess I'm just a natural?"

"Nah. He seemed to, like, vibe with you in a way I've never seen before. I've seen him behave aggressively a couple of times, but nothing like that."

"I dunno. Maybe he's just girl crazy. I mean, can you blame him?" She playfully framed her face with her hands and stuck her tongue out.

"Maybe. So what did William whisper to you anyway? You seemed kinda spooked."

Trixie was careful choosing her next words. Something cute and humorous that would continue distracting him from the path to The Truth. She needed to state them with such conviction that Christopher *had* to believe.

"I think he was trying to ask me out or something." She giggled. "He said, 'If Christopher is ever stupid enough to dump you, you just give me a call.' Or something like that. I didn't memorize his rhyme. Then he told me when visitor hours were."

"Oh yeah? Geez. My cousin, the failed Casanova. You worked really well with him, though. Brought something out of him I don't think I ever will. You ever consider psychiatry as a career?"

"It'd sure as hell be better than some of the jobs I've had."

As they drove away, Trixie pulled down the sun visor and flipped open the mirror to check her makeup. In the reflection, she could see the decrepit building behind her and hoped the cracks in the stucco were not large enough to allow her secrets to leak out.

They drove back to Sweetville proper, leaving the Happy Hotel behind. The thick foliage did its job, swallowing the path and covering it with a surplus of verdant tongues.

and now a word from
OUR SPONSOR

Family member in severe need of
MENTAL RESPITE?
Has it been difficult, even exhausting, to give them the constant supervision they require?

Perhaps they need professional assistance of the highest order. At the Sweetville Happy Hotel we know relinquishing your loved ones is a difficult decision. Rest assured they will be in competent, caring and happy hands.

Don't hesitate to bring your loved ones to our facility for evaluation. We offer very competitive rates for the housing and care we provide, as well as a variety of fine amenities:

- Central air conditioning
- 24-hour supervision
- Soft beds with clean sheets changed daily
- 3 balanced meals each day
- Communal rooms with network TV and a foosball table
- Daily, supervised exercise time in our lush courtyard
- Flexible visiting hours

You'll never need worry about the safety and comfort of those you care most about within the warm and welcome halls of the Sweetville Happy Hotel!

CALL 555-1134 TO RESERVE SPACE.
We're filling up quickly!

HAPPY HOTEL
— Sweetville —

November 15, 1991

Hi Diary. Miss me much? Believe it or not, life's been treating me a lot better recently. Not a total 180, but I think we're looking at something like a 125-degree turnaround. After everything I've been through the last couple of years, I'll take it. It's just nice to be able to scribble some positive thoughts in here every now and then instead of being such a Debbie Downer.

Jesi's been a total lifesaver. Those who pass through the doors at MOXY may only know her as Ms. Jessica Chartreuse, but "she" is really a he playing a she for paid entertainment. Does that make sense? Her real name's Jesus. Like "Hey, Seuss," not like the hippie who supposedly died for our sins. So Jesi seems like a good enough nickname to me. I've learned that pretty much all the queens refer to each other with female pronouns anyway which, naturally, works in my favor.

Somehow Jesi managed to get me a job waitressing at MOXY. It's only part-time for now. Trial basis I guess, but it's a start. I had to get a fake ID to work since I just barely turned nineteen, but Jesi had a good hook-up for that. Nico, the owner, is kind of a hardass, but I can deal. Gotta prove I'm a reliable, hard worker and carve a more respectable path in this world. I have to pretend to be a drag queen, though, which is kind of weird for me since it's almost like I'm performing a parody of my own femininity. Whatever. I pretended I was a boy for most of my life to appease my family. Camping it up a little bit for the customers so I can keep myself off the streets is nothing. Still, sometimes when I look in the mirror, I *do* kinda feel like I've joined the circus.

Jesi's become like my protective older sister. She's letting me crash on her couch until I can get some more hours and save up for my own place. And she's not even charging me rent! Her apartment's no four-star fancy pad, but it might as well be, compared to Gwen's roach motel. Just having a working heater is reason enough for celebration. It kinda feels like home, and Jesi's attitude is a big part of that. She encourages me to be myself, outside of work at least, and loves me just the way I am. I didn't know it was possible to feel this good. She's got bucket loads of good karma coming her way. I owe her more than I could ever repay.

Even though I've technically been able to stop turning tricks, thank fucking God, I've still been seeing Greyson and Orin every now and then. Does that still count, Miss Diary? The upward transition from random johns to delivering drinks and scribbling down menu orders was a no-brainer, but it's been a little tougher to pull away from the Zanes. Not only do they still fling money at me like I'm a wishing well, which obviously helps me save up quicker, but I also can't help but think I care about them on some level, even though what we share is a dysfunctional relationship. I guess that's better than no relationship at all. Right? They've been getting too clingy and demanding lately, though. So I think it's time to start severing that umbilical cord. We'll see how that goes.

Keep ya posted.

December 20, 1991

Finally rid myself of the needy twins. It took a few tries before they realized I was serious about moving on. They said they understood, but they clearly weren't pleased. They practically begged me to stick around, even offered me a permanent room in the estate. I have to admit, Diary, that was tempting. Sliding around in their silk sheets became sort of a sick comfort, and it would have been nice to have that comfort all to myself. But no. This change needed to happen. I'm on my way to being able to sustain myself with a job that isn't exploiting my body. I'm done with that life for good. I have to be.

Well, I mean, you could argue waitressing is just a few steps away from prostitution, but you'd only say that if you were privileged enough to not have experienced what I have. I'll take a few leering eyes and off-color comments any day. Besides, most of what happens at MOXY is in good fun. Aside from the occasional creep, the vibe is totally different than what I'm used to. It's a wild, colorful party that attracts all of the freaks of Sweetville. Halloween never ends within the walls of MOXY.

This doesn't mean the dating world suddenly became a breeze or anything. Try the opposite. I started seeing this guy Craig, who I met at MOXY a couple weeks ago. He was handsome in a Young Republican sort of way and brazen enough to ask me out, so why not? Don't get all tsk-tsk with me, Miss Diary. I have no room to be picky at this point. He had come in a few times with a group of friends, and obviously everyone who comes to MOXY knows it's just a bunch of queens working under our roof. Well, mostly. I'm in the clear, right? It should have been refreshing to not have to hide certain parts of myself, and at least I knew it wasn't going to turn out like things did with Aron. God, I haven't thought about that asshole in a long time. Little did I know things with Craig were going to go *way* in the opposite direction.

After a couple dates, things started to get more physical with him than just smooches and heavy petting. I spent the night with him so I could give Jesi a break from my mooching. I was a little weirded out about the possibility of getting naked with him, but right away I realized he didn't have any problem with any part of my body. It was refreshing being so sexually open with someone without an exchange of currency. I mean, the Zanes never had a problem with it either, but in retrospect I probably should have realized there was nothing exactly normal about incestuous twin brothers. Amen? Amen.

Basically, Craig started treating my penis like it was his own personal little lollipop. It's a total conflict of interest for me, too. Obviously it feels good. Despite my hormone therapy almost eradicating any erections at this point, sometimes it's still functional if stimulated just right. I wish I could figure out what causes that BS so I could put a stop to it. Blah. But it's just as much a turn off as a turn on because it's supposed to be the little man in the boat that's getting all hot and bothered. I mean, I can only pretend so much, you know? My imagination still has flesh-bound limitations.

I thought at first that Craig was just being selfless, that he didn't expect me to be the only one performing fellatio or something. It's the thought that counts, right, Miss Diary? But no, he became obsessed with it. We couldn't get into bed without him focusing on my penis instead of his. Despite his little guy being about as big as a turtle head peeking out from under its shell, I really wanted things to be the other way around. Eventually I toughened up and said it had to stop, that I totally wasn't cool with it.

So get this. He looked at me like I told him he had to quit eating bacon for the rest of his life. Totally shocked. The room was really quiet for a few minutes and he started sobbing a little bit. Crap. What was I supposed to do then, right? He told me stuff about it feeling so right because he was pretty sure he's gay, and he didn't understand why I was upset about it since I am too. Ugh. Worst. Situation. Ever. I mean, what was I supposed to do, Miss D? I really wanted to tell him that I was sorry to poop on his party, but this isn't going to work out because I'm not gay. I'm a girl. Duh! But I couldn't jeopardize my drag cover at MOXY, so I gave him the ever-useful cliché that it wasn't him, it was me, and broke it off right there. He was pretty upset, but he'll get over it. Haven't seen him around at MOXY lately, so maybe he's out cruising somewhere else. Hopefully he's found his inner comfort. He wasn't a bad guy, just very far from the right guy for me.

This sucks so bad. Maybe I'm just not cut out for relationships. Maybe I'm doomed to be alone forever.

**Civilized Cannibals Set List
@ Club Club 3/20/93**

RESCUED FROM CHOICE

REAGAN'S GEST@PO

IT CAME FROM CHERNOBYL

CHOOSE YOUR FLESH

BLOODFEAST (MISFITS)

SKYNET SYNDROME

FALSE JURISPRUDENCE

SKULLS OF SARAJEVO

~~BEHIND THE DOOR~~
~~(CIRCLE JERKS)~~

CHAPTER FOURTEEN

MACE AKERS PAUSED in front of the stage at Club Club. Steve London hovered close behind him, puffing on a clove cigarette. Made of termite-ravaged plywood layered atop milk crates, the stage was more of a safety hazard than a focal point for impeccable live performance. Their equipment lay dormant on top of it, beckoning them to come ravage it with sonic chaos. After a few flyers were glued to record store windows and passed out at other shows, and some licks to the boots of Club Club's owner and show promoter, Civilized Cannibals were finally graced with the privilege of playing their favorite local venue. In this case, favorite translated to least crappy.

"Has your bassist shown up yet?" The voice of God, or more likely the sound guy, boomed down at them. With the corners of the club enveloped in fists of darkness, neither could figure out where the man with the microphone was hiding. The sound booth could have been practically anywhere—in the air ducts, the basement, the sewer pipes. "We need to do a sound check ASAP."

"No!" Mace hollered back. "He wasn't out back when we were loading our gear in. He's probably around somewhere, though. We'll go check out front." Then, to Steve, he added, "I knew we showed up too early. No way in hell am I loading Chris's stupid gigantic bass cab back in the van after we play."

"Well don't look at me. I could fit inside that thing."

"Yeah, well you could fit inside a thimble and still have room for a big breakfast."

Mace stomped toward the front door while Steve followed behind. His loosely laced combat boots banged against the laminate tile floor like the hooves of a Clydesdale. Thick chains linked around his waist rattled heavily, creating additional percussion against his jeans.

They passed the merch table where the roadie for The Loogs, a semi-popular local gutter punk band, was setting up shop. His long, unwashed hair matted down the back of his neck into a beaver's tail, and his eyebrows had been shaved away and replaced with tribal tattoos. The dirt caked to his arms made it appear as if he was wearing a thermal long sleeve beneath his sleeveless Amebix shirt. He folded t-shirts nice and neat on the table like he was a Mervyn's sales associate. The Loogs had about ten different designs available for purchase but couldn't be bothered to record and release any of their music.

Mace and Steve squeezed through the single-file hallway before reaching the front of the club. Bright neon lights momentarily blinded them. Once their eyes adjusted, Mace spat and cursed under his breath. His head was a teakettle ready to boil over.

"All right. Who's the joker that did the marquee for tonight?" he asked. "I mean, Civilized *Animals*? They couldn't even bother to get the name right? This blows. Fuck!"

"Whatever, Mace," Steve said, his splintered drumsticks peeking out of his back pocket. "Nobody knows who we are anyway."

"It might as well say Puppet Show really huge right above our name, you know?"

"I don't get it."

"You know, sometimes I wonder why the hell I even associate with you. I find your lack of culture disturbing."

"Cool it. We're finally playing Club Club, so just suck it up. We'll probably get paid decently for once. Maybe we'll make enough money to be able to print some t-shirts."

Mace's face lit up, his attitude altered. "And if we sell enough shirts, we might make enough money to record a 7-inch, or even an LP." He was forever a budding entrepreneur.

"Yeah, I suppose. I just want to be able to repay my mom for my new cymbals." He lit another clove and let it dangle at the edge of his lips as the ashes grew and flew.

An impressive line curved around the corner of the concrete building. In attendance, every misfit faction in Sweetville, as well as those without a convenient social group to align themselves. All the freaks had to subscribe to some semblance of solidarity in a town that lacked multiple options. More rampant graffiti decorated the outer walls, making flat statements such as SWEETVILLE SLUTZ ROOLZ or a crude and open to interpretation image of a tiny penis going tinkle.

During the time Mace and Steve had been setting up inside the club, the sun had sunk over downtown Sweetville. The dangerous blanket of night now embraced the patient crowd. A disheveled man huddled next to a nearby dumpster, spooning some unknown slop from a tin can into his filthy pit bull's gaping maw. A prostitute with more rolls than the Michelin Man did her best to blend into the corner of a brick wall. A black Packard Super Eight pulled up to her, the unseen passengers inviting her to join them. A block or two over, glass shattered and a car alarm screamed for assistance it would never see. From even further away came a faint popping sound, a gunshot or a blown tire.

Christopher finally made his fashionably late appearance, his girlfriend Trixie in tow, attached to him with the strength of a suction cup. For reasons unclear to Mace, he was wearing a purple, ankle-length hippie skirt that would have had enough room in it to fit four more of his toothpick legs.

"Interesting choice," Mace said, looking him up and down and whistling like a construction worker. "Circus sideshow's in town next week, though."

"Okay, Mr. Funny Guy," Christopher said, clearly embarrassed with his attempt at making a point, but doing his best to hide it. "Get over it. I just felt like giving people something to gawk at. See how it makes their minds work. Why conform to the gender roles society forces on us anyway? It's just fabric, not a litmus test for my manhood."

"Hey, you know, you might be on to something," Steve said. "Being a spectacle is definitely better than being ignored. Get the kids talking about us even if we suck."

"Steve, the crowd's going to talk about us even *more* if we suck," Mace said. He turned to Trixie and asked, "And what do you think about this cute little outfit? Did you know your boyfriend was a covert cross-dresser?"

Christopher whacked him in the chest. Mace released a muffled grunt but barely acknowledged the interaction otherwise.

Trixie shrugged. "It's cool. I just wish it showed off his sexy hairy legs a little bit more. I did have to coordinate and make sure I wasn't matching his outfit, though. I mean, *that* could have been a real fashion disaster."

"See Chrissie-boy," Mace said, laughing. "She's funny. I like her. A real peach."

"Yeah, I think I'll keep her around," Christopher said, giving Trixie a wink.

"Whatever. Let's go run through a couple of songs before they let these jerks in. I wanna make sure we don't sound like utter shit tonight."

"Oh, wait… Trix, do you still have my marker?"

She dug through the bottomless pit of her purse, first pulling out a mechanical pencil, then a roll of Life Savers and finally Christopher's marker.

"Thanks." Without hesitation, he drew a fat *X* on the back of each of his hands.

Mace rolled his eyes and snatched the marker away. "I've got a much better use for this." He stuck the entire felt tip of the Sharpie up his nostril and snorted. "Mmm-mmm, good. Just like Mom used to make." He pulled the marker away, unknowingly leaving a dark smudge above his lip.

"See you in there, Great Dictator," Christopher said, laughing. He retrieved his marker, grabbed Trixie's hand and guided her toward the club.

"What?" Mace turned to Steve. Steve shrugged. "What?"

* * *

Feedback peeled the paint from the walls. Raw noise excavated into the unprotected ears of the crowd. Moisture oozed from the ceiling's pores.

"All right, you dickwads," Mace said into the mic. "We're Civilized Cannibals. This first pretty little ditty is dedicated to all of those

Operation Rescue assholes. An abortion isn't murder, it's a woman's right to make her own decisions about her body. This song's called 'Rescued from Choice'."

A shirtless Steve began the song with an up-tempo tribal beat on his toms. Christopher soon joined in on the bass, his back to the audience as usual, the veins in his neck already bulging from the aggression of his strumming. He rocked back and forth from one foot to the other. Beads of sweat pushed through his brow. He dropped his pick almost immediately and found it impossible to locate on the dimly lit stage. His fingers tore at the thick strings as if trying to obliterate them. The crescendo increased as Mace crunched his strings, making them squeal. Then a four count on the hi-hat and the song's tempo went into warp speed.

The crowd erupted into a choreographed warzone. Elbows were flung higher than heads, an endless circular march of work boots and Chuck Taylor high tops created a dusty whirlwind. A sole brave diver launched his body from the stage, though the crowd had shifted before he found the comfort of human cushions. Christopher stole a glance at the crowd and noticed a handful of guys from their circle of friends up front singing along. Naturally, they were the only ones who would know the words. A bandana flew into the air and floated down like a feather. Bottles crashed to the ground. Every acceptable bodily fluid made an appearance on the stage, and possibly a few that were suspect. Someone slipped from the imperfect circle and knocked into the microphone stand, which sent the mic smashing into Mace's face. He stopped playing briefly to make sure he hadn't chipped a tooth, wiped blood from his lip with his hand, then lunged almost flawlessly back into the song.

The set continued for a modest fifteen minutes, the energy rarely dwindling. Their final song began with a drawn out, raw and noisy guitar intro. Whoever was operating the lighting was becoming way too generous with the strobe. The song exploded with a vengeance. Their instruments could barely match the speed of their limbs. Mace's voice was a raw, impassioned growl, equal parts melodic and discordant.

Christopher took a moment away from facing his amp and looked stage left. Trixie was hiding in a safe spot behind a side-fill monitor, bobbing her head up and down, grinning with the sort of biased pride that could only come from a significant other. She had likely been in that spot all along, and Christopher had almost forgotten to acknowledge her presence in the midst of his musical haze. He found her actions endearing, since he suspected she didn't really care much for the music. He shot her a goofy expression, sticking his tongue out, then turned to face the crowd and leapt into the air, twisting the neck of his bass so it faced the ceiling, kicking his left leg out like an amateur Bruce Lee. When he landed, he dropped his pick for the umpteenth time and missed a few strums. A familiar face, one that made his stomach churn, peeked through the sweaty sea.

Cypress Glades. Planted right in front of the pit, making no secret of her unwelcome appearance, her smeared smoky eyes looking up at him with sickening lust.

He tried to look at Cypress without actually looking at her, possibly one of the most difficult physical feats for a man to achieve. The front of her t-shirt was meticulously torn to reveal the curves of her cleavage. In certain flashes of the strobe light, she looked hideously plain. In others, she was lust personified. Bodies lost in the flow of the pit crashed against her back, but she didn't seem to notice. He assumed she was probably enjoying the hell out of the free beating.

Not far behind Cypress stood a statue of a man, his arms linked across his chest like one continuous muscle. Toro, the skinhead security beast. Christopher knew it would be an awful time to make any sort of an offhand gesture to Cypress. Toro was notorious for breaking the bones of those who challenged his neo-Nazi princess. A few other skinheads pummeled through the crowd. Christopher and his bandmates were acquainted with some of the anti-racist SHARP skinheads in town, but, unfortunately, none of them had bothered to show up tonight. The unabashed flaunting of chest tattoos proclaiming BLUE EYED DEVIL and shouting of *Sieg Heil* throughout the crowd made that crystal clear.

Christopher turned around in disgust, even though he admitted Cypress still looked damned good, a sentiment that brought him instant nausea and regret. This made him play harder and faster in a fit of rage, which forced the rest of the band to keep up. Christopher jumped at a pause in the song, felt the stage beneath him again and began to stomp his feet to the beat. Without warning, his right foot crashed through the rickety plywood floor and became lodged beneath. As he tried to free himself, his leg sank deeper and splinters of wood scraped and tore his skin. Trixie gasped from her hiding spot, and he did his best to mask his agony. The song mercifully ended and Christopher dislodged his leg from the hole.

"Okay, fruitcakes," Mace howled into the microphone. "We're done. I'm sure that's just breaking your hearts. If you can make it up to Plain Grove on May 15th, come check us out at the Elks Lodge with 7 Seconds. Hopefully they've quit playing that slowed down we-wish-we-were-U2 crap. Doubt it, though." A few scattered people yelled out some half-assed heckles.

"Oh yeah," Mace continued. "No. Fucking. Boneheads. Invited." He spat on the stage and stared unflinchingly into the crowd. Ready to fight if need be, an impenetrable fortress of fists.

Once again, the omnipresent voice of the sound guy vibrated through the room. "Just so you know, the stage repairs are coming out of your door money."

Mace broke the world's record for the amount of times motherfucker could be spat out in the span of thirty seconds.

Christopher darted his head around, dreading he would see Cypress again, but he was relieved to find she had vanished from her spot. The other skinheads had dispersed as well. He hoped she had somewhere more important to be.

Mace turned in Christopher's direction, beaming with idiot glee. He offered him a thumbs up. "Good set, yeah?"

* * *

In the single-stall restroom, Christopher winced, his foot propped up on the toilet lid, soaking up blood along both his shin and calf with cheap toilet paper that crumbled in his hands and stuck to his injured leg. The wound could have been worse. He'd had more than his fair share of brutal skateboarding scrapes, but it still felt like a few angry fingernails had clawed away a complete layer of skin. At least Civilized Cannibals' first appearance at Club Club had been a decent enough success otherwise. With Trixie's pretty face manning the merch table, he figured they'd have a good chance of selling the rest of their demo tapes, stickers and patches. From outside the restroom, he could hear recorded music blasting through the club's speakers, somehow louder than the live music it was sandwiched between. Beneath it Christopher could hear The Loogs tuning up.

The door creaked open, then quickly closed.

Christopher could have sworn he had locked it after entering.

He looked into the mirror, full of deep scratches and esoteric carvings. It reflected the smeared image of a pale specter.

"Hey! Occupied!" He spun around to see Cypress, her hands behind her back, masterfully locking the door behind her. He audibly groaned.

"Killer set tonight," she said. "You guys are really starting to get your shit together. Gotta say, seeing you up there brought back some old memories. H-O-T."

"Get the fuck out of here, Cypress. I've got nothing to say to you." Christopher brought his leg down from the toilet and made his best effort at appearing tough and indifferent.

"Geez. No 'long time, no see?' How rude." Without warning, Cypress was inches away, though he could not recall her even beginning to approach. It was as if those few milliseconds of his life had escaped him. His nostrils tingled with the familiar faint scent of berries coming from her skin. She scraped and curved her slender finger down the front of his chest. It felt incredible in the most conflicting way possible, and there was no way for Christopher to rid himself of that sensation.

The lone fluorescent bulb flickered and, for a second, her finger appeared twice as long as it should have been. He was frozen in sexual frustration. "Who said I wanted to talk anyway? I'm here to blow the band. Can't turn that down, can ya?" Her tongue flicked out, and Christopher briefly thought it looked forked, but then it was normal again. The loss of blood must have been getting to his head.

He was cornered, trying to think of a way of escaping this awkward situation without resorting to hitting a woman, if Cypress was even deserving of such a title. The light flickered again and Cypress's skin seemed to turn paler, her breasts threatening to burst from her shirt and prove they were autonomous beings. Her lips more full and pincushion pouty, her emerald eyes more alluring, more carnally charismatic. This was the same bullshit that had gotten him mixed up with her in the first place, something he could never control or understand, something that went against all of his political principles, something far beyond just average male hormones running the show.

Each time the light came alive, Cypress's face changed shades and could have belonged to almost anyone else. She took a moment to primp in the mirror, then pressed her perfect body up against his chest. He felt little Christopher stirring below and tried to think of skateboards, videotapes, superheroes and Gramma in a muumuu, anything but impending nudity. He shoved her back, creating a much-needed buffer zone.

A light rapping at the door.

"I already told you the last time I saw you," Christopher said. "I'm with someone else now, and I'm happy."

Cypress released a boisterous, witchy laugh. She might as well have been stirring a cauldron of boiling oil.

More knocking, the volume just a bit louder.

"Just let me through, okay?" he said. "I need to get back to her."

Cypress licked her lips in what seemed like slow motion. Her tongue was a serpent offering forbidden fruit. "Don't make me beg, lover. It won't be pretty."

Interview with Civilized Cannibals
reprinted from Suburban Subversion Fanzine
Issue 3, August 1992

CIVILIZED CANNIBALS

Civilized Cannibals are a new local band that recently released a promising demo tape called Feast Like Animals. Their songs thrash and ravage with a dark and driving sound that keeps one foot firmly planted in 80s hardcore, the other facing toward the future. Their lyrics are fiercely political with an unforeseen earnestness, though they are not without sarcastic humor. I thought they deserved some space in Suburban Subversion, so here's a quick little chat I had with the guys a couple months back.

SUBURBAN SUBVERSION: Who's in the band and what do you play?

CHRISTOPHER: I'm Christopher Faith and I play the bass.

STEVE: Steve London. Drums.

MACE: Mace Akers. Resident guitarist, vocalist, lothario and poet.

SS: What compelled the three of you to form Civilized Cannibals?

M: What the hell else are we supposed to do? Boredom leads to boss riffage. Seriously, though, I think it's just a matter of needing to release our negative aggression and somehow manage to twist it. Channel it into something.

S: Mace and I were in a shitty band a couple of years ago called The Candy Fiends. It went nowhere and we really wanted to chill out on the Sweet Candy so we could focus on a project that mattered. Not that we don't still

dabble a bit, but we're not, like, addicts.

M: The bassist for The Candy Fiends was a loser and a thief. If you're reading this Greg Nichols, fuck you! You'd better sleep with one eye open because we know where you live.

S: I think he moved though, Mace.

M: Whatever. We met Chris at an SNFU show about six months ago and hit it off. Figured he'd be a good bassist. Figured wrong on that one. **(Laughter)**

C: And you can fuck right off, Mace. Yeah I had never really played full-time in a band before. Too many flakes in this town. I was hoping to start up something with the potential to provoke thought. Punk should be a

medium for challenging all of the shit shoveled in front of you on a daily basis. If even one person is impacted by our music and lyrics to make a change, then we've done our job.

SS: Have you guys played a lot of shows so far?

M: Mostly some house parties around town, and we're going to go play up in Doomston in a couple of months. Should be a blast and a half.

C: We're trying to get a show at Club Club so people might actually show up for once. I'm not really psyched on the fact that it wouldn't be all ages, but unfortunately Sweetville doesn't really have a lot of venue options.

SS: How has the response been to your demo?

M: Well, Maximumrocknroll gave us kind of a shitty review.

S: That was a shitty review?

M: What part of "If imitation is the sincerest form of flattery, then these guys have their noses deep in the rectum of the early 80s" didn't you understand?

SS: Tell us about the band's name and the lyrics to "Choose Your Flesh."

M: Basically, the first few lines of the song sum up the general sentiment:
Feed on the destitute
False ascension, true disgrace
Lives lost to the opportunistic
Subject to the tastes of the master race.
If you're paying any attention to the fucked-up shit going on in our world lately, you'll be able to figure out that the song's about

Eaters and Taste Subjects. The pigs ignore the problem and the government is just resting on its haunches all due to the convenient loophole that it involves contracted consent, so this sick relationship is just going to continue. A select few with delusions of grandeur feel they have the right to take advantage of poor families and street urchins they think no one will miss. Eaters prey on desperation. It's the behavior of scum.

S: Yeah, it's like some sort of backwards Eucharist/Communion ceremony. Like any other fascist religious practice, it reeks of hypocrisy.

SS: So are you guys all vegetarian, too?

C: Just me. That song's not exactly addressing the issue of whether or not to eat meat, though, even if that element does factor into it. I think it's okay to infer some thoughts about the needless slaughter of animals into the lyrics, but an inference is all it would be. Eaters and Taste Subjects, that's an issue of power. Human above human and how one man can control another into doing the unthinkable.

M: I tried to stop eating meat for a while. Didn't work out too well. I pretty much subsist off fried chicken. Sue me.

SS: Favorite bands?

M: Black Flag, Discharge, Articles of Faith, Cro-Mags.

C: Hmm...I'd say Born Against, Chain of Strength, Swiz, Drive Like Jehu, Uniform Choice, Amenity, Inside Out, really I could go on and on all day.

S: I dunno...I really love the Misfits and Samhain, I guess.

M: Someone's got a boner for the Evil Elvis.

SS: Craziest show you've ever been to or attended?

S: The storm drain show.

M: Yeah. Definitely. This was way back in the Candy Fiends days, and we played this total guerilla show with some other locals. We had to drag our gear through these tiny tunnels and, in case you hadn't noticed, I'm not exactly the smallest guy.

S: We thought we were gonna have to smear him in butter to get him through.

M: Can I please tell the fucking story?

S: Sorry. Excuse me for existing.

M: Anyway, we set up in this big cave of a room. There were puddles of muck just a little too close to the equipment for comfort. My buddy Al stepped in broken glass and dug right through his shoe. Poor guy had to leave before the show even started.

Complete chaos ensued the second we hit our first chord. The echoes were bouncing off the walls and making it sound like every note was delayed by a few seconds. People were losing their minds. Some chick who was wasted out of her gourd got down to her bra and panties and started rolling around in the sewer muck. She was dripping with thick brown scum and started trying to hug people in the crowd. Fuck, man. That was just some nasty business.

SS: Any last words?

S: Why are there so many fat cops?

SS: Why?

S: I donut know. **(Laughter)**

M: We still have a few copies of our six-song demo tape available. If you want one, they're only two bucks postpaid. Send well-concealed cash to: Civilized Cannibals, 138 Legacy Street, Sweetvill

SATURDAY SEPTEMBER 26th AT THE SK8 HOUSE 525 DATE STREET

FROM SAN DIEGO
UNBROKEN

ALSO FROM SAN DIEGO
STRUGGLE.

FROM SEATTLE
UNDERTOW

PLAIN GROVE PUNKS
DAV
(DISABLED AMERICAN VETERINARIANS)

SWEETVILLE
LOCAL HARDCORE
CIVILIZED CANNIBALS

OZYMANDIAS
SHOW HERE →
FIRST
COLLEGE
DATE

PLEASE BRING $5.00 FOR THE TOURING BANDS

CHAPTER FIFTEEN

THE MAIN HALL OF CLUB CLUB became a hollowed-out husk between bands. The majority of the crowd shoved its way outside to grab a smoke, partake in meaningful conversation or have a fuck behind the dumpster. Samuel Haines chose to remain inside for the moment, attempting comfortable rest on a ratty couch wedged in the corner of the club. Cypress Glades hovered in front of him, doing her best to use both her words and body as soft butter. She was balancing a beer bottle between her fingers, gripping it like it had earned a cheap hand job.

"Why do you always expect me to just give you my spare Candy?" Samuel asked. His mohawk was absurdly blue tonight, as if he had blended a Smurf smoothie and used the juice to dye his hair.

"Why do you expect to ever get to fuck me again?" Cypress squeezed herself onto the couch and pressed her breast against his arm.

"The prospect of sex is barely enough motivation to get up in the morning."

"Oh, come on. Let me have just one. I'm gonna try and find Christopher and get him naked or something."

"Sounds to me like you don't need any chemical assistance."

"I've got some new tricks up my sleeve, and I can't wait to try them out on him."

"I can only imagine."

"*Please*, Sammy." Cypress kneeled on the couch cushion and offered him a hug that might have appeared tender to any passersby, but the pressure was closer to an anaconda's embrace. She gyrated her body and her nipple rubbed against his ear. It felt like an aggressive dog lapping him with its tongue.

"Promise to never call me Sammy ever again and you can have two pills if you want. No need to wiggle your vagina in my face right now."

Cypress pulled away and turned down the flame on her carnal kettle. The pheromones she was always going on about must have worked their magic. Samuel felt angry with himself, enraged that he so easily succumbed to her otherworldly charisma, but he got over it in a snap. He looked at Cypress with slight curiosity, his expression altering for the first time since he arrived at the show. He pulled a greasy sock from his front pocket, unraveled it, removed a plastic sandwich baggie and placed two pink hearts into her palm. Smears of color painted her fingers as he pulled his away.

"What do you want with that bore-fest anyway?" he asked. "I thought you were finished with him a long time ago."

Cypress popped both heart-shaped pills into her mouth and chewed them like precious delicacies. Portions of the chewy center became wedged between her teeth, so she took a swig of beer and swished the liquid around to loosen the goodies. "Oh, I couldn't care less about getting back together with him. Fuck that. Stacey said he's got some new girlfriend or whatever. I just want to ruin the relationship. Only seems fair."

"If you say so. Do what you must." Samuel was already disinterested.

"Okay. Catch ya later, Sammy." Cypress winked, smooched him on the cheek, lunged from the couch and headed out on her ex-boyfriend hunt.

Samuel released his practiced sneer and watched Cypress move through the club. She was a walking contradiction, skipping away like a virginal youth in a field of daisies, her ass swaying in predatory rhythm. He peeled himself from the couch and crept around the edges of the club before sneaking out the back door. Outside was where the real party was, and Samuel would sniff out its wallflowers.

He slinked around the building, surveying the crowd for someone who might be a match for his nutritional needs. His requirements for the ideal candidate were, first, that they must be desperate for companionship—no friends, no convenient family, no options. He had to make them believe no one else would be there for them in their hour of need.

Second, they had to abstain from excessive questionable activity. Moderation is metaphysical. Disease is antithetical to the divine.

And finally, they had to be discreet about the transaction. A feeding ground is precious and must be utilized for as long as possible.

Samuel had not been fortunate enough to secure many proper Taste Subjects in recent months. The punk scene was looking to be less fruitful than he had hoped, and he was worried he might need to move on to where the livestock was more attainable. It was time to be proactive. Persuasive. There had thankfully been a select few—gutter punks squatting in the abandoned Sweet and Sourdough Factory—who had allowed him small samples in the meantime, though that approach used up far too much of his Sweet Candy stash, and most of them were about as mouth-watering as a cold, discarded, half-eaten burger from the garbage. What he needed was to find someone alone after tonight's show, someone vulnerable and possessed by intoxication, someone hoping it wasn't too late to catch the final bus home. This was more difficult than it sounded, since many of the young men and women in the crowd tended to group or pair together for social safety. Not many were willing to go the loner route.

With positive patience, he knew his next meal would come soon. It had to. His potential wings were wilting. The nubs were beginning to resemble pitiful tumors rather than sprouting the angelic, elegant feathers he deserved after serving his cause for so many years. Worse, they were starting to smell like Limburger cheese.

There were few potential Taste Subjects to choose from, and most, if not all, were suspect. A girl whose attire seemed to have more holes than actual material. She was the size of a throw pillow and likely not old enough to legally be at the club without a chaperone. Barely enough meat to last him a month. An easy target, for certain, but the pink barnacles peppered along her inner arm were an obvious red flag, forcing

Samuel to halt his initial approach. He had learned his lesson the hard way years ago with that Junkie Creep Sara.

Next he spotted a pudgy boy stretching the seams of his shirt, his hair in that terrible middle stage of growth before it could reach a head-banger's respectable length. His enormous white sneakers were marshmallows gleaming in the moonlight's flames. He was somewhat out of place among the staunch punks and likely did not have many direct ties to this crowd. Though Samuel was still partial to female flesh, he could see much potential in the folds of this young lad. So much girth that he would have to shift the inner architecture of his freezer to make room for the leftovers.

He visualized gutting the boy once they reached Layer Three of their relationship, if he even bothered with the Layers. Though he was diligently attempting to build the trust of his new group of Eaters, he was far above the established law at this point. He was also beyond famished. Skipping the Layers might be akin to eschewing grace before dinner—frowned upon in certain circles, but ultimately not impacting the value of the meal. Though traditional sustenance was enough for him to subsist on a base level, he would never be able to thrive without Consumption Enlightenment. But a body needed basic nourishment in order to think. Only then could Samuel adhere himself more rigidly to his religious rituals.

He could already envision sitting down to dine. He would remove the blubber from the boy's body, fry it on medium heat with olive oil, garlic and scallions. Press it between two pieces of sourdough, garnish it with two slices of provolone and a sweet pickle. He would share it with no one. It would be his special sandwich. For an appetizer or, perhaps, a midnight snack, he would take the first two layers of meat from the buttocks, cut them into squares, wrap and twist them around artichoke hearts, cream cheese or spiced potato. Fried into oblivion, they would make for a side dish of delectable dumplings. But his dream was shattered. A fellow metal-head with a far more impressive mane joined the boy, slapping him on the back with brotherly affection. Tonight would not be the night for this particular taste. But he would keep his eyes on this one for future endeavors.

Samuel shuffled toward the front of the club, his feet never completely leaving the ground. His dilapidated steel-toe boots crashed against the concrete, creating fresh damage in the soles, which was just what he intended. Though he had purchased the boots brand new, he went to great measures to ensure they looked lived in, poking them with steak knives, tossing them off of second story roofs, dipping the buckles in water to bring about the early stages of rust and leaving them in the middle of the street for buses to drive over.

With no other candidates for consumption catching his eye, he re-entered, showing the stamp on his wrist to the skinhead goon running the door. He did not make eye contact. Did not care to. He passed through the constricting entryway and came to a row of plastic folding tables where the bands were peddling their wares. There he spied a young, relatively attractive girl selling tapes for Christopher Faith's band. Perhaps she was this new girlfriend Cypress had been alluding to.

Or, better still, perhaps she would be the next lucky lost soul that The Angelghoul could process through his intestinal tract. He knew this one would have obvious attachments at this show, but he couldn't help but fantasize a little. Hunger pangs karate-chopped within his belly. It felt like he was on a deserted island in an old cartoon, and this girl was the giant turkey leg taunting him. He approached her table, subconsciously licking his lips raw.

* * *

Out of the corner of her eye, Trixie saw what looked to be a giant blue peacock with a man attached to the bottom of it coming toward her. As the gaunt punk perused the prices of the merchandise, she thought she recognized his face—cheeks that looked like they had been scooped away with a spoon, obsidian eyes stripped of all soul. But she couldn't quite pinpoint the memory. The hairstyle and fashion were drastically different, but there was no mistaking that devilish face. After moments of obvious stalling, he introduced himself and extended his hand. She took it limply, quickly.

"Yeah, I think we might have met before," Trixie said. "Haven't we?"

Samuel offered her a look that was a mix of surprise and worry. He leaned closer to her and whispered, "Is that so?" His breath was a thick garlic paste that nearly spelled the words out in front of her.

She struggled to balance her truth and lies. "Oh. I mean, it's just that…did I maybe buy Candy from you a couple times, like a few years ago or something?"

"I suppose that's possible."

"I'm pretty good with faces."

"I'm sorry. I'm quite the opposite. Faces tend to go right in and out. So many customers that it's difficult to keep up with them all. Can you refresh my memory? What's your name again?"

Despite her best judgment, Trixie was polite enough to offer up her name. She figured that should be safe since she knew she would never have given him a name other than Ariel in the past.

"Trixie? Like from *Speed Racer*?" Samuel asked.

Trixie didn't get the reference. She peered around his head to see if Christopher was returning from the restroom yet.

"Samuel's not exactly a typical name for someone who looks the way you do, either. Probably should have given yourself a cooler name. Sammy Shitstain or something like that." She fought to keep her eyes from meeting his again, hoping he would get the point and leave her alone.

Samuel leaned his head back and studied the ceiling, his jaw creaking open like a drawbridge. "You know," he said. "I could just eat you up with a side of fries. Interested in getting out of here or maybe meeting up later?"

"No thanks. Taken. *Very* taken."

"Heard that line before. Ignored it. Ended up making two people very happy, one of which happened to be myself. Naturally."

"You really don't seem like you fit in with this scene. I mean, despite your looks and all. You talk funny, you know?"

Samuel stood up straight, then slouched more. He cleared his throat. He broke what remained of his eye contact with Trixie, and she could tell he found this situation disconcerting.

"Well, that's exactly why you should consider giving me a chance. I'm different."

Trixie raised her eyebrow. "You're confident," she said. "I'll give you that. Now can you please leave me alone? My boyfriend will be back any minute." She glanced in the direction of the restroom again, wishing Christopher would appear.

"I can see you need time to think about this. I'll be back later." Samuel chuckled lightly through his nostrils and turned away in reluctant defeat.

Only a few steps into his retreat he stopped, as if he had run into an invisible wall. Then he practically pirouetted around and approached the table once again. His eyes sparkled.

"Now that I think of it," he said, "I believe maybe I *do* remember you. You went to Sweetville East a few years ago, didn't you?"

"Nope. Sorry. I went to high school up in Doomston." Trixie's lying prowess was working to her advantage. Quick as instant coffee.

"No, I'm quite sure of it now. I watched other students bully you and call you names. Cruel names, really, even if some of them were creative. You might not remember, though. I wasn't a fellow student." He held his fists close to his chest and swayed them back and forth in a mopping motion. His eyes never left hers. A grin formed on his lips.

Trixie stuck to her best poker face and realized that she *did* remember. All it took was mentally scribbling a beard and longer hair onto his face and she realized who she was dealing with. This was *him*, that creepy janitor who got fired after everyone assumed he was a child molester. She did not respond to his comments.

"It *has* been a while," Samuel continued, "and you've certainly...developed, but it's starting to come back now. I also remember you more recently for less respectable reasons. You did buy Candy from me. More than once. You used to run around with a—*ahem*—girl named Gwen, didn't you?"

Trixie stifled a gulp. She paused, her brain not yet figuring out how to react. Samuel had figured her out. She needed to get the hell out of there. Not now. Yesterday.

"I'm right, aren't I?"

"No," Trixie replied, acting as if she were responding to a question that was all business. Her face was serene, her lips slightly parted. "I don't know anyone by that name."

"Fifth and Quail. Ring any bells?"

Sweat beaded at her temples. The weight of it like a vice grip.

"What, Bertoberto's? Good place for some late night greasy goods. They make awesome quesadillas there. I'm not going to dinner with you anyway, so what does it matter?"

"You've got parts you don't want. Parts I've never tried. Parts I can wrap in a tortilla and deep fry until crispy and brown." He licked his lips and leered down at Trixie's crotch, his eyes focused and hungry.

"Ew. What the hell are you talking about?" But Trixie knew. Everything made sense. The devil was a carnivore and this was his local butcher.

This was not just the janitor. Not just some random dealer she had bought Sweet Candy from. This was the man who hid in the shadows. This was the mysterious Angelghoul.

Trixie had been unaware until recently that The Angelghoul was anything more than a street name for her former Candy supplier, but she had read some sparse news coverage on the Eaters and had become somewhat familiar with their covert cause. She always assumed she had never seen one of them in real life, but then The Angelghoul moniker had been mentioned, and it had activated her gooseflesh. She remembered then as she remembered now.

"You know just what I mean."

"Get out of here, you fucking disgusting creep!"

The corners of Samuel's lips curled into a jester's smile. "You're not fooling anyone."

Before she could find the right retort, Mace forced his way between them.

"Hey there, Trixie," he said with his mountainous back to her. All Trixie could see at first was a giant patch safety-pinned to the back of Mace's army jacket: a black cross with the red prohibition symbol around it. "This creep bothering you?"

Trixie moved from behind the table to stand at his side. His stone glare did not stray from Samuel's face, which betrayed no fear. His thick body was an impenetrable side of beef.

Trixie nodded and pursed her lips, then realized Mace wasn't paying attention to her well-timed damsel in distress face. He was focused on pure intimidation. "Yeah, kinda," she said. "Would you mind watching the table for a little bit? I need to go find Chris and see how he's doing."

"Sure thing. Won't let this little weasel out of my sight until he promises to behave." He placed his hand on Samuel's shoulder and squeezed. Knots in Samuel's muscles cracked under the pressure. "Nobody fucks with my friends, bucko. You're lucky I'm in a good mood tonight. I promise not to hurt you...too badly."

Trixie waved a silent thank you to Mace and headed toward the restroom. She weaved through the maze of various punks and freaks and tried not to focus on how dangerously close she had just come to The Truth being revealed or how close that possibility still was. She had to forget about that and focus on convincing Christopher to leave Club Club as soon as possible. She'd fake a stomach ache or something similar. That would have to be sufficient for the time being. She would handle the real problem later. Much later.

When she reached the restroom, she found there was only one door with stick figure images of both a man and a woman drawn on the outside in Magic Marker. She briefly wondered if this made her more comfortable or more confused.

She reached for the doorknob and found it locked, then she knocked lightly. Her body vibrated uncontrollably.

"Christopher? You okay in there?" She knocked again, heard a female's voice cackle, then Christopher's saying, "Just let me through, okay? I need to get back to her."

The door swung open, almost smacking Trixie in the face, and Christopher stepped out. Trailing behind him was a girl who might have been a contender for *Playboy* had it not been for the funny looking haircut that Trixie would never have been caught dead experimenting with. She wondered how someone could be so beautiful and, simultaneously, so butch.

Christopher saw the stunned look in Trixie's eyes. "Hey,'" he said. "*Hey*. Before you have a chance to jump to any conclusions, this is Cypress. She wasn't invited. To the show or to the bathroom. She was just leaving."

Trixie's jaw went limp. It took her a second to place the name, but she soon realized that this was the old girlfriend Christopher almost never mentioned, and for good reason. How was she supposed to compete with this sexpot?

"Well, well, well," Cypress said. She approached Trixie with her chest puffed. The henhouse was about to be covered in a flurry of feathers. "This must be the new squeeze. I'm the old squeeze. You know, the one he still thinks of when he's in bed with you."

Trixie tensed up, her fingers balled into fists, her eyelids stretched wider than nature intended, and Christopher silently shook his head at her. *Not worth it*, he seemed to be saying.

"I just wanted to see what my ex was up to," Cypress continued. "See if he was up for one more fling. I felt pretty confident that he was, if you catch my drift, but no. You had to go and interrupt us. Kind of rude if you ask me."

"Bitch." Trixie's lips leaked with venom.

"Not true! Nothing happened!" Christopher barely got to shout before Trixie lunged at Cypress, her purple claws bared. She managed to get in one good sucker punch to Cypress's gut and a scratch on her bare shoulder.

Christopher wedged his body in between them just as Cypress resorted to hair pulling, which would have given her an unfair advantage, for obvious reasons. Under other circumstances, this could have made for one hell of an erotic dream for him, but in the real world it looked like it just plain hurt.

Cypress was already in berserker mode, beating at his chest. Trixie was worried she'd be snapped in two if Cypress was given the opportunity, but Christopher was holding her back. His fingers dug into her collarbone like he was gripping a motorcycle's handlebars.

"Get out of here, Cypress," he said. "Stay the hell away from us."

"Oh, so *now* you want to touch me. Nice to know you remember I like it rough."

"I'm fucking serious. Leave. Now."

"Yeah," Trixie said, "before I have a chance to rip out the rest of your hair, you bald eagle slut!"

This sent Cypress into another rage. She shrieked and lunged at Trixie. Christopher grabbed Cypress's arms and shoved her against the wall. Her face softened into a near cherubic state.

"Whatever," she said, slapping his arms away. "I'm so over this shit. By the looks of that schnoz, she's probably a kike anyway, so that's worse punishment than I could ever dish out." She spat red saliva at the ground in front of Trixie's feet and disappeared into the crowd.

Christopher turned to Trixie, hoping to calm her. She unconsciously pawed at the middle of her face. A few bystanders who had gleefully observed the scene now acted as if nothing had transpired and wandered away toward the stage. The Loogs began their first song, and the raw sound washed over them.

"I'm so, so sorry about that," he yelled over the music.

Trixie just stared at him, her jaw agape with an expression that seemed to say, *What the hell just happened here?* She waved him away, leaned back against the wall and squeezed her eyes shut. She felt Christopher's lips against her hair. His hands linked into hers, but his touch felt like a ghost tickling her from the other side of reality. Trixie opened her eyes and turned her gaze toward the exit door. Any other time she would have been reveling in Christopher's affection, but she had more crucial things to be concerned with.

Things had gone from pretty damned awful to full-blown shit storm. Cypress was now screaming at Samuel, at The Angelghoul, waving her angry hands in the air like she was trying to fly. She pointed in Trixie and Christopher's direction, and Samuel glanced over, his grin somehow stretching even wider than earlier. Samuel let his stare linger a moment longer before Cypress dragged him through the exit. Trixie's eyes glazed over, her stomach weakened. At least she would not have to lie about a stomach ache anymore.

This was bad. Code Red bad.

The secret was no longer safe.

CHAPTER SIXTEEN

Hello?

"Hey, you fucking loser. It's Cypress."

Hello?

"Hello? Can you hear me?"

Who is this?

"Cypress!"

I'm sorry. Who exactly are you trying to reach?

"Goddammit, Chris. It's *me*. Quit fucking ar—"

Ha, ha, ha. Fooled you, sucker. You're talking to a machine. A simulation of a human. A simple mimic. Technology is slowly but surely taking over our culture. Big Brother is watching your every move. Soon we will all be nothing more than automatons. Question reality on a daily basis. You never know when you're going to get blindsided. You've reached the residence of Christopher Faith. Leave a coded message at the beep, so the Feds can't trace us.

Beep.

"Ugh, you are such a serious asshole. I was *almost* having second thoughts about telling you this, but after that stupid bullshit I think you deserve to be humiliated. No more Ms. Nice Girl. Just remember, at least I'm not being a complete bitch and doing this in public. I'm not that heartless. It's about your, uh, *girl*friend, if you really want to call her that. Get it? Figure out what I'm trying to get through your skull yet, you lamebrain? No? Well let me spell it out for y—."

Beep.

Click.

"Goddammit!"

Redial.

Message repeat.

"Fucking piece of shit machine. So, like I was saying, this guy I know told me something *very* interesting at your show the other night, about your current little bed buddy. Wake the hell up. Call me. Now. I'd rather tell you than your stupid machine anyway. I'm dying to hear your reaction. Fucking priceless. It'll make all of the bullshit between us *so* worth it. And let me go ahead and get this out of the way ahead of time. No, I am *not* making this shit up."

Click.

Dial tone.

January 27, 1992

Friday might have been one of the scariest, most potentially dangerous nights I've ever had, which I guess is saying a lot considering some of the craziness I've encountered over the years.

I mean, this is my life? Really? Who do I need to talk to so I can get a refund? You're supposed to know the answers to these things, Miss Diary. Not like anyone else is offering.

One of my co-workers, a basketball player-sized African-American queen who goes by the name Karma L. Apple, confided in me a couple of nights ago. We were at work and she invited me outside for a smoke break. I think cigarettes taste like a stale fireplace, so I declined that portion of her invite but joined her for the talk anyway because I'm polite like that. It was nice to be acknowledged by someone other than Jesi for once. Not to take away from Jesi, but sometimes we don't work the same nights, and it gets a little lonely when some of the other queens are being bitchy and probably gossiping about me. Am I just being paranoid?

I think Karma must have heard me one night when I was complaining to Jesi about the size of my boobs, or maybe she sniffed me out some other way, but the fact of the matter is she figured out I was trans. Turned out it didn't matter much because Karma said she thinks she might be too and wanted to pick my brain about it. She more or less lives as a guy outside of work right now, but she's been starting to realize something isn't right. She's pushing thirty, too. Girl, what took you so long? Makes me feel fortunate I figured everything out and started transitioning so young. Maybe the only real blessing in my life at this point.

Karma said she wanted to at least get her lips done soon if nothing else and asked if I wanted to come with her to a silicone pumping party. I didn't know what the hell she was talking about. Sounded kinda funky, but she said if I had a couple hundred bucks saved up, maybe I could do something about my itty bitty titty problem. Her words, not mine. Grrr. Or I could just come with her for moral support. Events that are only spread by word of mouth always weird me out, but I figured safety in numbers would be a reasonable approach.

I still brought some money, though. Just in case. Better to be prepared, right? Do you think less of me, Diary?

I was already pretty sure this whole deal was not on the up and up before we got there. Lo and behold, we show up and immediately the first red flag is flying proudly. The party's in the shittiest part of shitty downtown, in some ultra grody apartment that would make a corpse gag. Right outside the front door it smelled like seaweed that had been thrown in a bonfire and left to rot. Inside there were hints of bleach. Let's just say my nostrils were itching like a motherfucker. The hostess seemed friendly enough, but she wasn't exactly easy on the eyes. Her face was rubbery and droopy, like the Cowardly Lion from *The Wizard of Oz* had gotten frisky with some Silly Putty. I was so ready to get the hell out of that place the minute we arrived, but Karma needed me.

The seating in the living room was kind of random. A few plastic folding chairs, a deflated love seat and a giant beanbag with a tear that was letting some of the stuffing pellets escape anytime the girl sitting on it moved. The other guests looked nervous as hell. There was a thick, quiet tension floating in the room. It was kind of like looking into a mirror. Not literally. Duh. I just mean that these other girls had pretty much the same needs and desires that I do, and they were doing something about it. I've felt that desperation to make sure my mind and body match, that yearning to realize, at any cost, my potential as a woman. I just think this was a terrible way of going about it. If nothing else, I gained a heaping pile of street smarts from the nights I was forced to sell my body. No way in hell my hard earned money was leaving my purse that night. This pumping party was bad news, so I begged Karma to take us home. She was still convinced it was a good idea and wanted to move forward. Hell, she wanted to be first in line.

Cowardly Lion started talking about how the rest of the night would go down, but I couldn't really understand her. It sounded like she had a mouth full of saltines. I feigned boredom and started glancing around the room, counting the peeling spots on the walls and the blotchy stains on the carpet. It probably would have been quicker to count the clean sections. Underneath one of the folding chairs I noticed a paper with some random notes and instructions scribbled on it. Part of it said: *Industrial silicone mixed with paraffin wax and peanut butter. Pumped directly into the body rather than implanted under* the skin in sealed sacs. Cost effective and no license necessary. I stuffed it in my pocket and took it home with me. You really think I could remember all of that, Diary?

Next thing I knew, Karma was lying on some sort of make-shift operating table. Hell, I think it was actually a fucking coffee table, for Chrissakes. Cowardly Lion was hunched over her, and she wasn't even wearing gloves, much less anything else that could be considered medically appropriate. The minute I saw that needle approaching Karma's lips, I started to feel sick and got myself the hell out of there. I tried not to make a scene, just tiptoed out and closed the front door as quietly as I could.

God, I'm a terrible friend.

Sucks that I had to take a cab home, but I know almost every nook and cranny of those streets and just how dangerous they can be at that time of night. No way would I want to walk them alone, and it was way too late to call Jesi and bother her for a ride. Times like this I miss the Zanes and the protection they offered. Well, not really.

Now it's Monday, and Karma still hasn't come back to work. No calls or anything. She pretty much always works weekends. I keep thinking I should go to the police, but I know it would be a waste of time. They're not going to care much about girls like us disappearing. Probably just fine with ridding the world of another freak.

I hope she's okay.

Do I even believe there's a chance of that at this point?

CHAPTER SEVENTEEN

A TINY CLANG WITHIN THE FRONT POCKET of Christopher's shorts, a sound too inaudible to be heard against the blaring chatter of bar patrons across the street and the growling of engines hovering for precious parking spots. A small pendant he had just found lying near the stairs leading to Trixie's apartment building now blending comfortably with his loose change and keys. He couldn't figure out how he'd even noticed it with only a dim streetlight to guide his eyes. A death's head—a skull and crossbones painted hot pink. The opposite of a lucky rabbit's foot. He recognized it immediately. There was no mistaking its former owner.

He wondered why the hell Cypress had been here. What she might have been planning. Did she even know Trixie lived here, or was this just a conveniently weird coincidence? No, the latter had to be a far-fetched hope. The death's head was just a casualty of Cypress's war.

Christopher ascended the stairs like a death row inmate about to meet his maker. He couldn't stop thinking about everything Cypress had told him. Maybe she had been bluffing. Maybe he and Trixie would have a big laugh about it later.

But maybes were promises that could never be kept. Deep down he felt certain this was no bluff. Cypress may have made hemorrhoids seem like a soothing alternative, but she wasn't known for being a liar.

Yesterday after reluctantly returning Cypress's call and dealing with the hell that some called her voice, he had run through every little detail of his relationship with Trixie, and the reveal just plain made sense. All the jigsaw pieces so desperately trying to force themselves to fit elsewhere had now found their proper place. With each step, he contemplated how he should approach the situation. Slow, hesitant steps.

Christopher passed through the lobby doors and reached the inner staircase only to find four Junkie Creeps sprawled across the steps. Their deadened eyes stared through him like he was a speedball specter. The sleeves of their blue jumpsuits were rolled up, the infected holes in their arms puckered and ready for a precious needle kiss. He swallowed in disgust and approached the stairs slowly.

"Excuse me," he whispered. The Junkie Creeps did not react, save one who grinned with what was left of his bottom teeth, jagged shards caked with tar. Sweat glued his matted hair to the side of his face. Christopher made exaggerated steps around each of their bodies to avoid touching them. Even sharing the same airspace didn't seem safe. As he reached the landing between floors, he swore he felt a tickle at his ankle. He made a mental note to consider wearing socks sometime. Muffled laughter bounced below him. He ignored it and moved on. One more flight to face the real problem. He knew that Trixie knew that he knew. She had to.

Soon it wouldn't matter. Soon he could force himself to stop caring.

He arrived at Trixie's door and knocked, a soft, noncommittal rap. He contemplated bailing from the scene, but once he heard light footsteps from the other side of the door, he understood it was too late to back out. She opened the door and raised one of her freshly plucked eyebrows, offering him her signature awkward smile, the bottom edges of her incisors barely grazing her lower lip. This time the awkwardness was accompanied by something else. A knowing? A wary understanding? Fear, sadness, perhaps a mix of the two?

Trixie smelled fresh and familiar, like berries and vanilla bean. Her body was mummified within a giant, purple towel, her soaked hair hidden beneath a tightly wrapped matching turban. Christopher could have stepped out of a shower onto her body and dried his feet thoroughly. This was the real Trixie. Sans makeup, dress and styled locks. Nothing to hide who she really was. Just a face. Smooth and beautiful, one that could belong only to a young woman. One that could only belong to the woman he had fallen for.

"What are you doing, you weirdo?" Trixie asked, her performance already worthy of an Oscar. Christopher was impressed with her chosen character, the Everything's Normal Girlfriend. She linked her long fingers into his stringy hair and tightened them like a barrette, then pecked him near his ear. His pores felt the sensation, but his brain did not register any of it. It was as if his entire body from head to toe had tuckered out and taken a big nap. "You know I always leave the door unlocked for you. I guess that's not safe, though. Maybe I should just suck it up and give you my duplicate key. If I can trust anyone, it's you."

Christopher did not respond beyond a half nod. He wandered into the apartment without having a clue as to where his legs were leading him. Federico was lapping at a bowl of milk, blissfully ignorant to the realities of romantic mishaps. New Order's "Bizarre Love Triangle" kept a quiet beat in the background. Christopher was surprised he even recognized the sounds as being music.

"Geez, you sure are talkative tonight," she said, grabbing his clammy hand. "Here, come with me, babe. I need to dry my hair." She pulled him along like a stubborn child, grabbed her blow dryer, plugged it in and faced her cracked full-length mirror. She removed the towel from her head, let it drop to the floor and began the buzz of the blow dryer. The physical candor she presented, so vulnerable and so near nude beneath the high wattage lighting, was a sign offering the comfort of a long-time spouse. Christopher sat on the toilet behind her, his lips numb and limp.

He pulled the death's head pendant out of his pocket and rubbed the anti-talisman between his fingers, wishing these motions were able to make this moment disappear. He held it near his face, analyzing it like an ancient artifact from a far off land. Maybe if he thought about it hard enough, he would discover it had time traveling capabilities. He could travel back to that late night at Audrey's when he and Trixie had first met and never offer her his number. Or maybe he could figure out a way to enter this relationship knowing The Truth from the start and see if his feelings would develop as organically as they had in reality. But there was no way to know if either of those alternatives would have turned out any better. He needed to stop fantasizing about the what-ifs and the could-have-beens. He knew he had to deal with this situation based on reality, the way everything legitimately went down.

"What's that you're playing with?" Trixie asked, her voice now raised to battle the blow dryer. Christopher popped with surprise. He had forgotten she could see every move he made, thanks to the mirror.

"Oh, nothing," he replied. "Just some crap I found. Stupid toy or something." He placed the pendant back into his pocket, made a mental note to toss it when he got home. Forget all about it.

"You're such a pack rat." She paused the blow dryer, brushed out the length of her damp hair and started drying a new section. She showed him her cutest grin, the one that he absolutely couldn't—but absolutely had to—resist. "I can relate, though."

Christopher let the dead weight of his arms hang to his sides. Federico crept from around the corner and began aggressively nudging his head against Christopher's fingers. He pulled his hand away and Federico me-owed as if offended. Trixie had seen the entire exchange and released a tiny, uncomfortable giggle.

Christopher stood up, framed himself within the doorjamb and toyed with different positions. He turned and faced away from Trixie. Each time he turned back around and caught her glance she looked like a frightened fox in a hunter's scope. The blow dryer sounded like a 747 about to crash into the apartment. Perishing in that carnage might have been preferable to what Christopher was going to have to put her through.

"So I was thinking," Trixie said, "maybe tonight we should—"

"Trix?"

"Mm-hmm?"

"I think we need to talk."

"What, hon? Can't hear you."

"Would you mind shutting that off for a sec? Please?"

The blow dryer halted its hurricane. The room became a silent vacuum. Trixie did not turn to face him.

"Come again?" she asked.

"We need to talk. About us."

Their eyes met in the mirror, Trixie's hovering right at one of the cracks. It made that side of her face look like an insect's. Christopher wondered if a connection via reflection could be considered real, or if a person's expression did not count if it was not met head on.

"What...what do you mean, Chris?" Cracks were forming in her act. Within seconds it would be completely demolished.

"I know."

"You know what?" Her last chance to stall. Her time had run out.

"I know The Truth."

Nothing more needed to be said.

An enormous bang echoed through the bathroom. Shards of plastic from the blow dryer skidded across the floor like crapshoot dice.

CHAPTER EIGHTEEN

THE MOVIE POSTERS POSITIONED IN the front windows of Video Drones were faded. *Galaxy of Terror. Private Resort. Scream, Blacula, Scream. Just One of the Guys.* The tape keeping the arguably iconic images held askew to the windows was retiring and coming loose, the creases down each poster's center yellowing and cracking like chronic cheilitis. A jingly little electronic bell rang as Christopher passed through the doorway, the sound fizzling away at the end like it was begging for a fresh battery. A man wearing a plaid sweater vest, pleated khaki shorts, and brown, buckled sandals strutted by him. Then Christopher was suddenly seeing double. Another man, identical to the first in both flesh and fashion, strolled by. The twins nodded politely. Their grinning teeth sparkled like freshly polished china, their hair groomed for a gel advertisement. He wasn't completely sure, but he thought he might have seen these faces before on some late night infomercial wedged between *Columbo* and an Elvira double feature.

One of them paused and turned to face Christopher. He sniffed the air like a bloodhound feeling out the scent of the hunt, then turned back to his brother. The twins locked arms and headed toward the door.

"Is it possible? Do you think he knows..." one of them said, barely breathing the words.

"Yes, we'll have to look into…" the other replied, mimicking his brother's volume and tone perfectly.

Christopher walked backward for a few steps, giving the twins a dirty look that they would never notice. He bumped into the front counter.

Adam Faith stood behind the register, popping his knuckles. Christopher tried to keep his expression blank so his older brother would not know he was beyond distraught. But he knew Adam would figure it out. Christopher had felt this way many times before: when their parents first announced their divorce, when Doyle—his pet chinchilla—had passed away, and when he had received his rejection letter from the American Film Institute. Christopher was terrible at hiding grief.

"Those guys," Adam said. He filed away a yellow slip stamped with the names G. & O. ZANE and added the two returned documentary tapes to his overflowed rewind box. *Pumping Iron II: The Women* and *Corpse Fucking Art.* "Sometimes I think I'd go out of business without them. Sometimes I think I wouldn't mind that option so much."

"Yeah," Christopher said. "Can't say I blame you. Fuckin' weirdos."

"So what's happening, little bro? You look like someone just stole your tricycle."

Adam was a lanky, ungraceful man, a baby giraffe trapped in a human body. A pair of bargain-basement Buddy Holly glasses clung to the bridge of his nose, and a too short t-shirt with Alfred E. Neuman proclaiming WHAT, ME WORRY? exposed a few centimeters of taut, thin skin above his belt. Towers of videocassettes were erected on the counter like a city under construction. A colorful sign above his head, written in perfect penmanship, read: E.T. OR MAC AND ME: YOU DECIDE.

"You sure you want to know?" Christopher looked up at Adam with zombified eyes. A cowlick that wouldn't quit sprouted from the back of his head. Sleep had not been working out too well for him in recent days.

"Yeah I got time. This is like my slow hour. Or couple of hours. But you know that already."

It was true. There was not a single customer in the store. In fact, Christopher could hardly remember there ever being many customers when he visited.

"I may not be Lucy van Pelt," Adam said, "but I'll do my best."

Christopher took him up on the offer. He grabbed a can of iced tea out of the beverage cooler typically used for retail purposes, pulled up a metal stool next to the counter and began to tell his brother all about The Truth.

* * *

After it was exposed, the two brothers were silent for a few moments. Christopher couldn't take the stress of the wait any longer and decided to continue the conversation.

"So what do you think this means? I'm starting to wonder, did I really know this deep down all along, like in my subconscious, and just conveniently ignored it? Am I gay, or what? I mean, I don't think I am. I haven't switched teams, as far as I know. No. No way. But is that just something your brain automatically fills you in on? Like 'Hey, buddy, guess what? You're totally gay.' Something like that?"

Adam considered this for a few moments longer, as if to torture him. Christopher knew his brother was not a cruel soul. He was, however, required by Older Brother Law to fulfill the duty of making his younger sibling squirm every now and then. Adam placed a tape into his rewinder and let it roll. It sounded like a remote control race car.

"Well, of course you're not a sausage seeker, man," Adam said, his arms outstretched like a sideshow barker. "Don't get me wrong, I wouldn't care one way or the other, but you were into her because she's a cute chick, right? No shame in that."

"Yeah, I suppose so." Christopher dug his fingernail into the corner of a sticker attached to the cash register and tried to peel it away.

"I mean, I met her a couple of times. I had no idea. Hell, I wouldn't kick her out of bed for a box of crackers. I could probably ignore some minor appendages if need be. Might take a drink or two, but still..."

Christopher shot him a cold glare.

"Hey, don't take that the wrong way," Adam continued, his hands now held up in defense. "I'm just sayin'. And it's not like it's just a matter of physicality. You care about what's up here, too." He jabbed his finger into his temple a few times. Christopher nodded in reluctant agreement.

A woman's mind was just as crucial to her identification as her body. More so, even.

"I guess that makes sense," Christopher said. "By the way, it's 'for *eating* crackers'."

"Huh?"

"Never mind."

Adam grunted, shrugged and stuck another tape into his rewind machine.

"Yeah, honestly though," Christopher continued, "she's pretty much perfect for me otherwise. Or was. I don't know. On paper we were like an almost perfect match. This is so fucking screwed up."

"That's putting it lightly."

"And there's the whole trust issue now, too. I'm not sure if I'm more upset about being lied to or the actual lie itself. Shit. I seriously don't have a clue what to do. I feel awful for breaking up with her, but I feel like I didn't really have much of a choice."

Adam carried a stack of tapes to the shelves and began to re-file them. He started in the action section and let his advisory mojo flow.

"Have you called her lately?"

"No, but I—"

The bell on the front door jingled. Incessant buzzing followed. Two Withering Wyldes floated into the store, their whispering sounded like the hum of locusts.

"Oh, Christ," Adam said as he returned to the counter. "Not again."

One of the Withering Wyldes approached the register with a clown-like grin on its face. It placed a stack of pamphlets on the counter in front of Adam. They were printed in an array of fluorescent colors, and the scent of fresh ink lingered in the air. The first of the emaciated duo folded its pencil fingers into a pleading position and ran its frosted tongue across plaque-ridden teeth. The Withering Wyldes may have been devoted to their diets, but they were not famous for their hygiene.

Christopher had never before been this close to any of them. He was astonished at how long and almost insectile their heads were. Elongated necks and facial features stretched to an absurd degree, save for eyes the size of watermelon seeds. Shoulders sculpted into bony points.

"No, sorry," Adam said. "I've told you a million times to stay out of here. Did you think I was kidding?"

The first of the Withering Wyldes spun its head almost completely around, as if defying its own anatomy, to face the other. It stretched out its arms and gurgled in confusion. The second one scratched at its temple with a long, curled fingernail. Flakes of dead skin drifted to the ground in a mist.

"Okay, okay," Adam continued, "well, maybe not *you* specifically, but some of your group at least. I really wish you would consider wearing numbers or nametags or something. Just take those flyers back or they're going straight in the trash."

One of the Withering Wyldes made a sound like an airbed deflating. It might have been consternation, perhaps even flatulence.

"See that sign?" Adam said, jabbing his finger in the direction of the front door. "No shoes. No shirt. No pants. No service."

The second Withering Wylde contorted its head at an owlish angle, turned back around perplexed, as if trying to determine the answer to Final Jeopardy. There was no sign where Adam pointed, only a television and a rubber chicken hanging from a noose.

"Okay," he continued, "so there's not actually a sign yet. Consider it a work in progress. But the policy still stands. Take your freaky cult shit out of my store. Now." He pounded on the counter, his fist a gavel.

The Withering Wyldes shifted into a bowlegged stance, their fingers twitching like the legs of a mantis. Christopher got off the stool and gripped the seat, ready to defend Adam if need be. The Withering Wyldes glanced at each other, made noises like sipping soup and popping popcorn, then snatched up their pamphlets and scurried out of Video Drones, leaving behind the scent of freshly baked oatmeal cookies.

"Dammit. I really, really hate those nut jobs," Adam said.

Christopher nodded and reclaimed his seat. "Yeah, that almost didn't go very well."

"You remember my buddy Dave Fisher?"

"He was the one who collected velvet Elvis paintings from Mexico, right?"

"No. That was Kurt Wallace. Dave was the guy who skipped town anytime there was a parade. He was globophobic."

"Okay. Yeah. I think I know who you're talking about. Chubby red-headed dude with a Viking beard?"

"That's the guy." Adam fiddled with a box of Necco Wafers. "Well, Dave eventually got over his phobia, but he ended up becoming so obsessed with the Withering Wyldes' cause that he joined up. Thought it was going to be a great way to lose weight or something. I tried to stop him, even convinced his family to hire a deprogrammer because they were kind of oblivious to what the end result would be. But Dave wasn't having any of it. He sold everything he owned which, granted, wasn't much aside from some T. Rex and Bowie records and some *Love and Rockets* comics. Then he moved into their compound. You know, that huge warehouse over on Tenth and Magpie?"

"Oh yeah. Steve and I have skated there before. There's a great double-sided curb in the parking lot. Waxed so smoothly it's like grinding on butter." Christopher guzzled more of his tea.

"Well, that's the place. I saw him a few days before he did that creepy cocooning thing they do, and he was already barely recognizable. He looked like a skeleton, but not like a real one. Like one of those cardboard Halloween decorations. Nowadays I guarantee I wouldn't be able to pick him out from any of the others. He's gone, man. Fucking sad."

"That's so fucked. I'll never be able to forgive them for William, even if they weren't directly responsible for what happened. Not that I believe that for a second. I went to visit him a month or so ago and it was, well, let's just say the experience was a bit disturbing. More than usual."

"Yeah, don't get me started on that crap. By the way, remind me next time you go to the Happy Hotel so I can come with. It's been too long since I've seen him."

"Yeah. Absolutely."

Adam grabbed a videocassette and took it to the science fiction section. "You know, Chris, the trust thing with Trixie, it's always going to be a problem. You can never truly tell what's going on in someone's mind. Don't put too much stock in trust. One of the key aspects of love is the ability to live with your partner's secrets more than anyone else's. I don't think her lies were designed to hurt you. They probably ate her up inside.

She didn't strike me as the type who got off on others' pain. No way. The bottom line is, do you care about her?"

"Of course I do. That's why this is so fucking confusing."

"Who cares about all the other bullshit, then? It's rare to find someone you really connect with. It doesn't matter what the rest of the world thinks about it. Well, maybe it does a little bit, but only to the people who don't deserve to factor into your life anyway. Shouldn't matter to you or those close to you." Adam grabbed another stack of tapes and moved on to comedy, filing them away in perfect alphabetical order without even a cursory glance.

"Maybe."

"No. Maybe nothing. Remember that girl Molly I dated when I was in high school?"

"The one with the tooth so crooked she used to cut her lip whenever she sneezed?"

"Hey, that tooth was one of the more endearing things about her. Bet you didn't know she had mild schizophrenia." Adam was now in foreign films, his body now obscured by the perpendicular racks. He had to raise his voice a bit to be heard.

"Well, that might explain why she used to call me Cristóbal Colón. I always assumed it was an attempt at a cute nickname."

"The point is, if I can stay with a girl like that for almost a year, then you can certainly give a fair shot to a cool chick who just happened to be born wrong."

The words *born wrong* echoed through Christopher's head. He thought that might be the key to this whole issue. Trixie was meant to be the woman she is now, not the little boy she started out as so long ago. And she had struggled so hard to get where she was. She was right where she needed to be. Almost. If it turned out that God existed, he certainly would have a tough time proving he wasn't a sadistic bastard.

"Why did you end up breaking up with Molly anyway?" Christopher asked.

"She trashed my Nintendo after I beat her at *Super Mario* too many times."

"Hmm."

"Hey, just because I have crappy judgment in my own personal affairs doesn't mean my advice should be null and void."

"I still need to think about it for a while, I guess." Christopher grabbed his drink and headed for the door.

"Where are you going?"

"Band practice."

"Well, the advice is free, but not the tea. Pay the fiddler, little bro."

Christopher turned around, walked backward, dug into his pockets and inverted them as if to show how dirty the color white could get. They flopped to his sides like puppy ears. "Sorry. All tapped out. I'll come cover you for a couple of hours next week if you need to take an extra-long break." Christopher gave Adam a quick wave and kept moving.

The electronic bell buzzed as he passed through the door, but the sound never completely faded. It hummed with quiet, yet persistent annoyance like a jar full of wasps. As he jogged off, he could see Adam through the window, shaking his head and grabbing a screwdriver. A video store owner's work was never done.

and now a word from
OUR SPONSOR

"And that bad little jammer you just heard was, well, it was one of those rap songs about jumping that seems to be so popular these days. Kriss Kross, House of Pain—I can never keep up. I'll let you decide which one it was. As always, thank you to our faithful listeners for tuning in to Kay-Sweet. Here at KSWT, we strive to meet all your sonic needs. This is Bob Roberts signing off. Our graveyard deejay Libby Racine will be with you in just a few moments, so we're going to have a quick commercial break before I hand over the conch."

RADIO STATIC

["Dueling Banjos" attacks the speakers. A confident voice dominates as the music slightly blends into the background.]

"Do you like Deliverance? Well, take a stroll down our action/adventure aisle and you're bound to find not one, but two copies of that classic film waiting to come home with you for a warm and snuggly night.

"Not interested in seeing Ned Beatty get, uh, violated? Well, we've also got one of the best comedy sections in town, always stocked with belly busters. From Monty Python classics to This is Spinal Tap, we've got it all.

"Our foreign film selection's no slouch, either. Sometimes I think the French and Japanese keep us in business.

"Come on down to Video Drones, located at 616 Swallow Street. Open six days a week from noon to seven. Closed on Mondays. We're running a special right now for new customers. Sign up for a year membership and receive one free rental a month plus a movie poster of your choice. Ishtar, Howard the Duck, Leonard Part 6 and Hudson Hawk. Sorry. That's about the best we can do right now. But if you come when we're in the right mood, maybe we'll squeal like a pig for you."

[The volume of the banjos surges, then fades away like a backwoods dream.]

CHAPTER NINETEEN

A SUDDEN VIBRATION. A ringing that initially sounded like a pillow was muffling it now grew more cacophonous. The sound could have easily been a frantic human voice chanting "*Pleasepickuppleasepickuppleasepick-up*" if telephones were capable of conveying the distress of their callers.

"Hello?" Christopher's voice was like gently used sandpaper.

"I need your help."

"Trixie?" Silence for a few seconds, so much so that Christopher thought he could hear the hum of the electric current in the telephone wires. He wondered if he might still be wandering through the dense fog of sleep. He looked over at the red light of his alarm clock, barely defeated the thick film covering his eyes and read the time: 1:13 a.m. "Is that you? What are you… What do you—"

"I don't know who else to call." Her voice sounded desperate. Life or death desperate. "I don't *have* anyone else to call. It's my little Rico. He's really sick, Christopher. He's vomiting all over the place. It's black and bright green. Oh God, it's awful. I'm so freaked right now." She sobbed uncontrollably.

Christopher adjusted to the conversation but still had no idea how to react. He felt torn. He and Trixie had only spoken once in the three weeks since their breakup, a determined plea on her end to try and make things work. Their tight unit had been greased and released.

His little talk with Adam had been helpful, but not necessarily the be-all, end-all solution he had hoped for. Despite what they had been through, or perhaps *because* of it, he loved Trixie. But it was a love that wrestled with an equal level of resentment, an affection that could not be voiced. Even if he could not reconcile his feelings, he knew he had to do the right thing and help her in her time of need. Maybe, at the very least, he could still be a good friend.

"Stay calm, Trix. Let me put on some pants and I'll be right over."

* * *

A reticent drive along mostly vacant streets. Christopher and Trixie were the only ones on the road save for a few cars manned by drivers probably not coherent enough to be operating them. Christopher faced forward, unlike just weeks ago when he would have risked running his Beetle off the road for a chance to steal a glance at Trixie's profile. It was a sentiment from what felt like a much older life. "What Difference Does It Make" by The Smiths hummed quietly on the car stereo.

Trixie held Federico in her lap and gently stroked behind his ear. Federico did not purr. His breathing was sparse and heavy, the rhythm slightly off from the cranky snarl of the car's engine, but almost as loud. She waved his favorite plush mouse in front of his face, but his sickly stare remained unchanged. Trixie let the toy drop to the floorboard.

Now, as they sat in the emergency vet's waiting room, Christopher allowed his demeanor to soften. He held Trixie's hand. Her skin was clammy. Tufts of Federico's fur clung to her sweatshirt. Christopher felt like the biggest asshole for not being able to figure out the right words of comfort. Was there even anything to say that might come close to soothing her pain? He stared at a bright poster on the wall—a prepubescent boy plastered with an expression of unabashed joy, frolicking in the grass with his Golden Retriever puppy. Brand new companions with their whole lives ahead of them. The text on the poster read: WANTED:

LOVE, LIFELONG COMPANIONSHIP AND FURRY FUN TIMES! ADOPT A NEW FAMILY MEMBER TODAY!

"Thank you so much for bringing me," Trixie whispered. "For being there for me. I don't know what I would have done without…" She abandoned all awkwardness between them and leaned her head into his shoulder. He removed his hand from hers and draped his arm around her. Her body's warmth pulsed against his side. He felt guilty for enjoying it, but it felt natural. Right. Like they had never quit.

Only they had, hadn't they?

"It's okay, Trix. I'm glad you called me."

She looked up at him and he caught a tiny smile in her eyes.

The veterinarian appeared in front of them like an apparition. Her expression was cautious, wary of revealing her cards just yet. Trixie sat up straight and grabbed Christopher's hand again, this time much tighter. She wiped the tears from her eyes only to have fresh ones appear. Christopher wished there was a valve he could twist to shut them off.

"Do you know what's wrong with my kitty?"

"We're going to run some blood and urine tests, but I already have some suspicions." The vet's hair was disheveled after a long night on the graveyard shift. The edges of her upper lip showed the hint of unfortunate facial hair. "I've seen this reaction before. I'm fairly certain at this point that your little friend has ingested antifreeze."

"What's going to happen to him? What should we be concerned about?" Christopher caught the "we" in Trixie's question. Were they a "we" again? Was an official reunion that simple? Did they need a witness? Was there a guarantee in "we"?

The doctor's voice was emotionless. "That will depend on how much was ingested, if any. We'll know more after we run the tests. At this point I'm most concerned about kidney failure, but try not to let yourself get too worked up yet. We're going to do everything we can to help her and get her back to—"

"Him," Trixie said, a barely audible squeak.

"Pardon?" The vet resisted raising her eyebrow, but Christopher noticed her face muscles shifting.

"I said 'him.' Federico. That's a boy's name. He's a boy cat."

Clearly embarrassed, but not willing to admit it, the vet continued, "It's going to take a few hours before we've got more information. We'll need to keep a close eye on her—*him* here. Would you like to go home for a little while, and we can give you a call once we know more?"

"No. I'd rather wait."

"Trixie," Christopher said. "I think sitting in here is going to drive both of us nuts. Vladimir's is right down the street. I'm pretty sure they're open twenty-four hours. Why don't we go get a cup of coffee, catch up a bit, get our minds off all the stress? Or try to, at least. We'll come back in a couple hours and check up on him."

Trixie smiled as best she could in her current state. It was tragically pretty. "I think I'd like that."

Without another word, the doctor vanished back into the catacombs of the pet hospital. Christopher and Trixie left the building and entered the chilled night air, huddling together as if they were stranded in the Andes and their body warmth was crucial to survival. He could feel her pressing closer and closer, like she wanted to curl up and fit inside him. To merge.

To disappear.

* * *

Trixie made a beeline to the ladies room as soon as they entered Vladimir's, likely to dry her eyes in private. Christopher noticed that the coffee crowd was especially peppy for this time of night. A man with intense googly eyes and caterpillar brows sat in a corner, his only companion a rusty typewriter that spoke back to him in rapid-fire tapping tongues whenever he seemed to come up with a thought worthy of committing to paper. Two Withering Wyldes played chess, contemplating their next moves. Their bodies swayed back and forth as if they were in the path of a wind gust. Moments after Trixie had made her temporary escape, a strange little man exited the men's room. Christopher thought he looked like a tumorous potato with legs. He was dapperly dressed, though perhaps overdoing it a bit with the hand jewelry. The man waddled to the table where the Withering Wyldes sat in concentration, grabbed a pea coat, which he draped around his shoulders like a cape, and tipped his hat to them. They barely acknowledged him as he exited the cafe. A group of goth children out well past their curfew huddled together at another table, immersed in their game of *Vampire: The Masquerade*, rolling dice like their lives depended upon it. The Birthday Party's "Release the Bats" pulsed from the jukebox, hiding behind the random chatter of Vladimir's patrons. A sign above Christopher's table read: BLACK COFFEE FOR BLACK SOULS.

Trixie returned from the restroom and her drink was already waiting for her. She looked refreshed, revitalized. She sipped from a colossal ceramic mug that might as well have been completely filled with whipped cream. A cloud of cream licked at the top of her lip. Christopher chuckled and took a napkin to it. Her face went pink.

"Thanks for the coffee," she said. They inspected each other's eyes for a few seconds. "For everything. I know I deserve every bit of hostility you're probably harboring, but God, I feel so awful about how things went down. I'm a horrible… I wanted so badly to tell—"

"Trixie, don't worry about that. It doesn't matter." Christopher paused and looked up at the chalkboard menu, squinting to see if the solution to ending their misery was scribbled somewhere between the caffé lattes and the blueberry scones. "Well, that's not exactly true. It definitely *does* matter, but the upside is I'm willing to talk this out. Being with you, the feelings I had for you…"

"Had?" Trixie looked preciously pitiful.

Christopher almost threw caution to the wind and pressed his lips to hers right then and there. He smiled and realized he had been working toward that motion ever since he picked her up.

"I never stopped caring, Trix. Look, the point is, I don't know or understand what it's like to be with a girl like you. Hell, I don't know that I understand what it's like to be with *any* girl. I'm no expert, and you know as well as anyone that my choices have always been suspect." His grin widened.

Trixie's playful pout revealed that she had caught his slight sarcasm. One of the chess-playing Withering Wyldes squealed and threw one of its bishops at its partner. Everyone in Vladimir's, including Christopher and Trixie, glared at them as if they had just committed a cardinal sin.

"All I know," Christopher continued, "is that I sank my teeth into your heart and I liked what I tasted. I've thought about this so much the last few weeks. Every relationship is different. There's always going to be roadblocks and strange things that need to be accepted, right? Why should this situation be any different?"

"You don't need to accept me. Just love me." Trixie's eyes were once again filled with tears, negating her earlier trip to the restroom. She seemed to have temporarily forgotten about Federico, and Christopher thought her tears were now directed along a positive path.

Christopher had no clue how to respond. He simply smiled and stared. He felt the words and had certainly said the words in the past, but stating them now would be ripe with dangerous possibilities. He motioned to her cup.

"You want a refill?"

* * *

Caffeine kept both of them wired as they once again took up residence in the emergency waiting room. Trixie sprawled her body out along the row of chairs, tried to avoid the various sharp slashes in the vinyl cushions and laid her head in Christopher's lap. He combed through her hair, twirled it between his fingers. An elderly man sat alone in the next row of chairs, cracking his knuckles. Christopher felt ill when he saw the man's lost expression. Could this poor soul be on the verge of losing his only friend in the world? The man chewed on the side of his hand to maintain his composure. The veterinarian returned moments later, her expression still stoic, her hair somehow even more electrified than it had been earlier.

The news was the worst it could possibly be.

Christopher took the information in small doses. He was too busy trying to keep Trixie's convulsing body from erupting like a bottle of well-shaken champagne. There was no cheerful spin he could put on the words spilling from the veterinarian's mouth.

"Antifreeze poisoning confirmed…only takes half a tablespoon to be lethal…this was at least three times that amount…peculiarly large… suffering immensely…recommend you have him put to sleep…do apologize…nothing we can do." After that last statement, Trixie's cork finally

243

popped. She buried herself in Christopher's chest. He could feel moisture soaking through the collar of his t-shirt.

They were led down a narrow hall lined with ominous pale walls. A muscular, hairy assistant steered an ancient Cocker Spaniel past them, returning the dog to his equally fossilized human father in the waiting room. The Spaniel had seen better days, but he was alive and beaming with stupid affection.

In the cold, dark room of merciful death, from which many animal souls had likely traveled to greener pastures, Trixie kneeled in front of Federico's face, gripping the edge of the surgical table. The cat's eyes met hers and he seemed to recognize his human mother. Trixie's eyes dampened again. Her well had yet to empty.

"You gave him a good life, Trix," Christopher said, gently massaging her shoulders. "Better than a lot of animals come even close to." This statement burst the dam within her wide open. Her face twisted into a demented mask of agony. Under different circumstances, her expression might have been comical. She could barely form words, but she had to because they would be the last sounds Federico would ever hear. Maybe the cat understood, maybe not, but it didn't matter. The words, the tone, every breath had to count.

"I wish I had a can of tuna for you, Rico. Two cans. I'd give you as much as you want." Federico's tongue protruded a few centimeters and weakly brushed Trixie's nose. The smell of rot wafted up to Christopher's nose. Trixie stroked Federico's front paws. "I'll see you again, baby cat. I promise. I won't ever forget about you. Never."

Sedation. Pressure on the vein. A thin pinprick. Chemical combination with the intent of painless and quick results. Involuntary twitches and spasms. Deep, low gasps. Termination of nerve transmission and complete muscle relaxation. Expulsion, slight defecation. No thought, sensation, movement. Gone.

* * *

They passed through Trixie's apartment door like voodoo victims, trudged past the recently cleaned litter box that would never need to be emptied again, dragged their drained bodies to the bedroom, pulled the dark curtains tight to battle the impending first moments of sunlight, turned on the stereo to help them forget, kicked off their shoes and removed other unwanted articles of clothing, spread themselves into bed, and became one embracing being. They huddled and hugged and stroked and Trixie bawled, hyperventilated and quivered. Mazzy Star's "Into Dust" cast a ghostly sonic aura about the room, beautiful like a Reaper's kiss. Their fingers needed, flesh kneaded. Claims of *I love you, I'll never leave you* and *I'll always trust you we must stick together* were spat out with unabashed eros as lips became locked and less and less clothing became necessary—or even useful—until there was nothing left but the skin attached to their bones, which they would have been more than willing to remove if they thought it might help them squeeze even closer.

Then, like a statue that had been defaced, there dangled a part of Trixie that Christopher had never before seen, didn't believe really existed until his own eyes witnessed it, a penile piece that didn't fit her puzzle. He averted and squinted, using a curtain of eyelashes to obscure the meat. He wanted to erase it or invert it or find a way not to care, all of which were impossible. But through respect or mature acceptance or perhaps sheer dumb lust he accomplished a satisfactory level of indifference. He clutched at her chest and nibbled her navel and mumbled passionate prayers. She caressed him below his waist and realized he was committed to his words at that exact moment, and so she did not hesitate, reaching into her drawer for the conveniently located lubricant and prophylactic. The lovers applied these items, she turned to her side, they spooned, he mauled her small breasts tenderly. Their bodies grinded and chafed and merged, and he entered her where Leviticus condemns. It was tight and warm and perfect, and he gyrated and pumped and never wanted to be anywhere else but this moment, this place right here right now and then he climaxed and it felt like a thousand tingling insects skittering through his urethra, a sensation that he hoped would never end.

March 4, 1992

Big bummer news for you today, Diary. Got the official word that MOXY is closing up. Rumors for a few weeks, and a couple of the full-time employees got laid off during that time, so things weren't looking too good. Should have known the end was nigh, but now Nico's officially spilled the beans. We've got about a week left, tops, before the doors stay locked and we need to start looking for other jobs. A couple of the girls already bailed. This is so terrifying. I don't know what to do.

What makes it worse is that Jesi told me she's leaving for New York in two weeks. That's so like her to be super organized and have some sort of contingency plan. I guess she knows a couple of other big-time queens out there, so she shouldn't have any problem connecting into a new job, a bigger and better drag scene. She asked me to come with her. Part of me is tempted, and I know it's flat out stupid for me to refuse the offer, but I don't think I can make the leap. Not yet anyway.

Somehow, leaving Sweetville might be even scarier than trying to fight for a decent life within its city limits. It's all I know.

Yes, Miss Diary, I'm well aware that "all I know" hasn't exactly been working out too well for me, but I feel like I need to stay. Any sane person would say there's nothing for me here any-more. But it's my home. And New York feels like it's a totally different universe, one I'm probably not cut out for. It's proba-bly like Sweetville times one thousand in a city that huge. Jesi's been so amazing for me, but she knows she can't force me to go with her. And she's too damned proud to beg. Not that it would help. But she said that the offer remains open, so I suppose if I end up changing my mind somewhere down the line I can try to summon some bravery.

I've got a tiny bit of money saved up. Enough to start a new life, I guess, or at least enough to carry me over for a little bit while I continue this shitty one. Maybe I just need time. Some perspective. If it takes me too long to find another job I might have to. I can't revert back to the streets. That's absolutely *not* an option. You're my witness, Diary. You need to hold me to my word.

May 11, 1992

Sorry I haven't written in you lately, Diary, but I've been busy. This time I actually have a good excuse, though.

I can't believe my luck. About time, right? Well, it's more than just luck, I guess. I shouldn't downplay the fact that my hard work paid off. I think my fingers are permanently inky from hunting through the Help Wanted ads on a daily basis. Unemployment checks kept a roof over my head, but I sure as hell didn't like having to live back in the Friendship Motel again. Had to force myself to diet a little more than I had grown accustomed to while living with Jesi's greasy culinary skills—*God*, I miss her homemade *chile relleno*—but I probably needed it anyway. No need to look like I'm preggers. I shoplifted some extra goods from Graves Park Groceries a few times, only when I really needed to. I feel totally awful about that, but I didn't have much choice. Felt like the old days when I used to steal from Mom's purse or shoplift my clothes from Modyrn Gyrlz. Geez, that was forever ago, wasn't it? Way to regress, huh?

But yeah, get to the point, Trixie! Duh! I managed to score a new job! It's kinda on the outskirts of town at this 24-hour diner called Audrey's. Working from ten at night to six in the morning might seem like it's tough to get used to, but I definitely have some familiarity with that sort of a schedule. But you already know that, Miss Diary. Sucks that it feels like it takes a full week for the bus ride up there every night, but whatever. It's steady pay and so far removed from my past that I really do feel like it's a fresh start.

I just moved into a new apartment, too. Can you believe it? I'm not doused in adult responsibility repellent after all. The apartment's nothing fancy, but I couldn't have expected something posh when I haven't exactly been blessed with steady employment. It's an okay size and feels like it's mine, like it could be some semblance of a home. It's on the third floor and there's no elevator, which kinda blows, but I guess it'll keep me in shape.

Oh! And there's this totally cute little calico kitty cat that hangs out on my fire escape. Doesn't have a collar or anything, so I don't think he has a home. I've been putting some tuna fish out there for him and he loves it, natch. Maybe I'll start leaving the window open and see if he'll come in. Ooh, maybe this means I get to think of a cute name for him, too! I'll scribble down some choices in you, Diary, so maybe you can help me decide. I sure do need a friend right now, so even a furry one will suffice. Did I mention he's super, super cute?

So yeah, Audrey is a sweet older woman. Not just because she gave me the job. She really feels like a caring grandparent or something. Her hairdo looks like a hive of bees co-opted a cotton candy machine. I love her cat-eye glasses, though. I can't even imagine being that old, but if and when my eyesight goes bad I'm definitely getting some cool frames like those.

Obviously I've had waitressing experience, but I was really worried that there might be some judgment about where it had taken place. As luck would have it once again, Audrey had never even heard of MOXY, so I just played it off like it was any regular old restaurant. Since Nico skipped town and there aren't any real remnants of MOXY left—someone even stole the huge sparkly sign that used to hang in the front window—there was no way it could be verified.

Only problem was, I had to buy *another* fake ID, this time one that didn't have my old boy name and gender on it. Ugh. So glad to be rid of that gross thing. Didn't matter much at MOXY, but I needed to make sure I totally passed for this job. Good thing I kept the number for that guy Jesi hooked me up with before. He sure is getting a lot of my money. One of these days I'm just going to have to get my name legally changed. Seems only fair.

Audrey took a leap of faith hiring me without any sort of legit reference, and I've been busting my butt to prove myself these first few days. She seems happy with me so far. I'd like to think my attempts at needy puppy-dog face helped a little, too.

What's really amazing is how well I pass here. No one knows a thing about my past and no one needs to. I'm just another pretty face working the graveyard shift. The truckers and assorted weirdos that come in occasionally flirt with me, and I just pretend to be flattered. Sometimes it results in a better tip, but not as much as I wish.

Maybe this is far from wonderful, but it's definitely one more step toward erasing my past.

Now If I could just score a boyfriend with little to no baggage, I'd be living pretty large as far as I'm concerned. Got any tips, Diary?

CHAPTER TWENTY

CHRISTOPHER WAS NORMALLY A HEAVY SLEEPER. A nuclear holocaust might even have a tough time waking him up on any other morning. But the events of the last few hours—events of death, sex and promises that could not be kept—had left him struggling with slumber. Still naked under the partial protection of Trixie's threadbare sheets, he looked over at her. Her back was to him, the covers pulled over her body like a cotton tumulus. She looked peaceful, and Christopher hoped her dreams were absent of thoughts of Federico.

The cause of the poor cat's death had got him thinking. There was still one worm burrowing into his skull that he couldn't quite remove. Cypress.

He rolled over, found his shorts crumpled on the floor just barely within arm's reach and fiddled with his pockets, searching for the hot-pink death's head pendant. He stopped after a few seconds when he remembered he had tossed it in a dumpster the day after he found it outside of Trixie's apartment building. The day after they had broken up.

Over and over the possibilities had run through Christopher's head like an infomercial repeating ad nauseam on a late night channel, but his discovery of the death's head was beginning to make sense. He had strong suspicions why Cypress had been in the neighborhood, suspicions that would confirm Cypress could sink lower than the Titanic. He knew what his ex was capable of, was well aware of her sick penchant for revenge, and questioned if he could stomach telling Trixie his theory. He couldn't help but dwell on thoughts of poor Federico, how he hadn't deserved to go out the way he had. There was no easy way to share his theories with Trixie. With zero proof it would result in failed comfort. It would only add to her stress. It would only make things worse.

Besides, they had other things they needed to talk about.

Christopher wondered if he had been dreaming since they had returned to her apartment, that maybe her extra appendage had been just a trick of the eye, a cruel prank, a test of his devotion. Or perhaps the power of Cypress's words had gotten the best of him and this was all just a big misunderstanding. He wanted to drop this whole deal and shove his tongue down Trixie's throat, squeeze her sides, make insane love to her again until they were both parched and panting.

But he knew he could only trick his mind so much.

A sun-drenched room led to a more lucid situation. No more darkness to keep the facts comfortably in the shadows. Neither Trixie's unfortunate birth body, nor her current feminine figure, was an illusion. They were both true. Coexisting. Trixie had blossomed into an all-encompassing human being, a chimerical wonder that somehow beat the odds and had found her balance of self.

In theory, Christopher had come to terms with this, even appreciated it on some level. Last night—or this morning, technically—had been driven by a mixture of love and hormones, but the aftermath had left his stomach feeling like a pot of over-stirred stew. He wanted to perform the part of the open-minded young man he always believed himself to be, but he was beginning to feel the effects of a battle between a passionate heart and a rational mind.

Sure, it might be fine for now. Maybe even fun. Things could be like they were before. At least somewhat. He might be able to continue averting his eyes from The Truth. Hell, he might even get used to it. But he knew the sensation didn't have a fighting chance. Could he honestly see himself in for the long haul, knowing his girlfriend had equipment that matched his own? He was still young, a whole future of relationship mistakes to make. He didn't think it was fair to limit his possibilities when this wasn't what he had planned for his life.

More importantly, it wasn't fair to Trixie.

The bed was a mixture of safety and danger. Dehydration forced him to get up and face the day, as confusing and unwelcoming as it might be. He slid out of the bed and oozed into his shorts like a gelatinous mass. It took him a few toddler steps before he achieved basic balance and was able to waddle into the kitchen. He removed a clean glass from the cupboard and turned on the faucet. The liquid that dripped into the glass resembled water in the same way urine resembles lemonade. Small particles of indeterminate origin floated in the glass like baby Sea-Monkeys beginning their colony. Christopher poured the contents into the sink, placed the glass upside down above the drain in hopes that the strange germs would find something else to infect and reached into the refrigerator. The first beverages he found were wine coolers, which he ignored. The only other option was a six-pack of generic diet cola. He was not a major fan of aspartame, but it was the only available non-alcoholic, bacteria-free option for quenching his thirst, so he begrudgingly took one. He popped the tab and it sounded like an exhaust pipe backfiring in the otherwise silent apartment.

The first few sips of chilled carbonation jarred him. His nose wrinkled, his head vibrated. He noticed photographs taped to the front of the refrigerator that had not registered upon his initial glance. Trixie and himself snuggled together like an ideal couple, taken on the night they had double-dated with Adam and some random blonde girl his brother had never seen again. Trixie was shoving a plastic straw partway up her nose and sticking her tongue out, while Christopher barely recognized his own face burying into her shoulder. Next to that photo, a shot of Federico. Wide-eyed, batting his paw at a feather on a string. Frozen in a perfect moment, alive despite impending cremation. Even though Christopher had not been particularly close to Federico, was moderately allergic to felines, he felt somehow responsible for the cat's death and for Trixie's pain. He was certain his theory about Cypress's involvement was closer to indisputable fact. Guilt wrestled in his chest, scratched along his ribcage. So much had gone wrong so quickly. Was it out of his hands now? He wanted to forget all of the drama, rewind the tape and edit out the scenes that had gone sour.

If only it were that simple.

"Hi."

He almost dropped the soda. He set it down on the counter and turned around slowly, like his bones might shatter if he moved too quickly. Trixie had sneaked up behind him, her slippers barely making a patter against the carpet. She was wrapped in a bathrobe with the hood pulled over her head, making her look like an extremely tired wizard. Her eyes smiled, but Christopher could tell those almond marbles were working hard, saving their tears for solitude. Without another word she embraced him, leaned into him as if she might collapse.

The silence continued before Trixie finally broke it. "Please stay."

"What makes you think I'm leaving?" Christopher squeezed a handful of her robe like the scruff of a dog's neck.

"I'm not stupid, you know."

A horn blared from the street, sucking them both out of their private vortex.

"I don't know if… I don't think I can."

"You were so good to me. We were amazing together, weren't we?"

More commotion outside. Shouting and arguments over turn signals, parking, intersections, right-of-ways.

"Well, yeah, I mean, I was starting to think, before all of this…" he said.

"I'll do anything. Please. Things don't have to change just because I—"

"Things already *did* change, Trixie. No matter what happens from here, it's just… It's just different."

Trixie lifted her head and tried to meet his gaze, but he kept sending his askew. A mewling chorus crescendoed from the fire escape across the alleyway. Christopher peeked through the tiny kitchen window and watched a loose assembly of feral cats—all shapes, colors and sizes—joining in for an off-key funeral dirge.

"But I love you," Trixie said.

Christopher felt nausea having a party in his belly. He turned away from the cats outside and made an effort to face Trixie head-on.

"I know. I do… I care about you so much, Trix. Honestly. It's just that I'm so goddamned confused right now. I thought I was ready, that everything could go back to normal with us. But I was wrong. I need some time to think. To see if I can even deal with…everything and be good enough for you. Right now I don't think I—"

"Right *now* you don't? What about last night? What about this morning? Didn't any of that actually happen, or are you just choosing to block it out?" Trixie's bruised expression turned to fire-red ire. Christopher had never her seen her like this before. It gave the moment a slap of reality. He pulled away from her. Gentle, quiet motions.

"Maybe we shouldn't have." Christopher's eyes continued to avoid Trixie's vehement stare. He was a dog that had left a huge steaming turd on the freshly cleaned floor. He didn't want to face the punishment he knew he deserved.

"Great. Just fucking convenient, Chris. It all comes down to one damned thing, doesn't it? I've been hiding it my whole life, but screw it. It's public knowledge now, isn't it? Yeah, I have a penis! So fucking what?"

Christopher cringed from this statement and internally kicked himself for reacting that way. He tried to make his brain tell his arm to reach for her, but it was superglued to his side. His other hand unconsciously lifted the soda to his lips.

Trixie grabbed the soda can from him and hurled it across the room. It exploded and splattered across the kitchen floor. The liquid fizzled and popped like the last few seconds of a once-raging fire.

"If you love me," Trixie continued, "then you shouldn't give a shit. None of this should matter."

"It's not that simple."

"You made an exception for that stupid Nazi slut. Why not me? I'm twice the woman she is. She's pure goddamned evil. I'm not. I'll always be good to you. I prom—"

"Don't you think I know that? It doesn't mean I can even comprehend what *this* is." Christopher motioned between them, gripping the air as if their relationship were something tangible. A concrete slab. A sturdy brick wall.

"But what if—" Trixie closed the gap between them again. Christopher could feel the tension in her body, tight like a ball made of too many rubber bands.

"I'm sorry, but I just can't." He unglued himself from her. "My promises are shit right now." He kissed her forehead and returned to the bedroom to retrieve the remainder of his clothing.

* * *

Trixie stared dead ahead, a zombie unsure of which direction her body should move. She wandered to the junk drawer next to the stove and opened it, her hands hunting between the Chinese takeout menus, paper clips, coupons and batteries, hoping to find the recycled mint tin where she kept her current stash of Sweet Candy. Her fingers found the special mix tape that Christopher had made for her after their first date, simply titled TRIXIE TUNES. She hovered over it for a few seconds, then reached to the back of the drawer, found the tin, opened it with desperate determination.

Empty.

She licked the inside of the tin, knowing full well that any tiny remnants of Candy dust hiding within would not come close to accomplishing a high. No opportunity for a vivid, happy trip.

No escape from reality.

She grabbed a dishtowel and began to mop up the spilled soda. She refused to turn around. She did not flinch at the creaking of the front door as it opened or steal a glance when the latch clicked closed. Nor did she give chase after hearing what were likely her final memories of her lover's footsteps, fading away down the filthy hallway.

**Evangelical Tract
Found on the Corner of Third and Raven
in Downtown Sweetville**

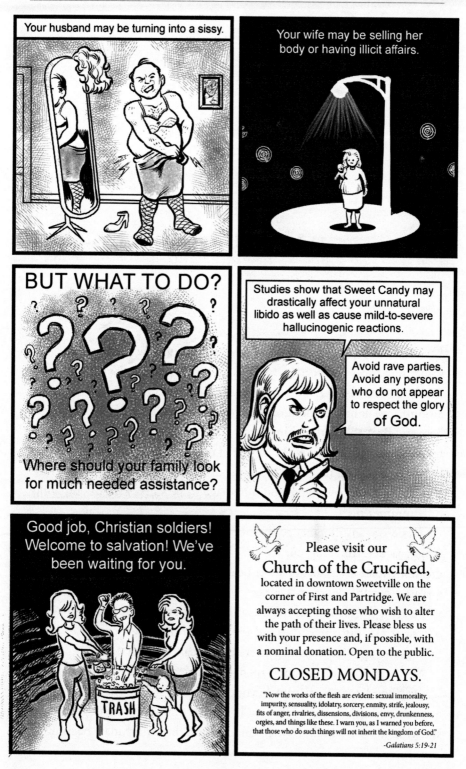

CHAPTER TWENTY-ONE

DUSK HAD SETTLED IN A BIT, the tired day now ready to slip into something more comfortable, as Trixie rapped her knuckles on Samuel's front door. Across the street in Graves Park, two homeless men huddled around a weak fire. Undernourished trees surrounded them like scabrous beggars. Broken bottles shimmered across the balding grass. A child's tennis shoe was wedged within a row of crispy brown bushes, protruding from the dirt. The neighborhood was otherwise deserted, at least to the naked eye. Only Sweetville could manage to be so backwards and chilly on a summer night.

Trixie was insufferably cold. She wished she had remembered at least a light jacket. The crop-cut tee that hugged her body had not been the greatest choice after all. A pair of headphones caressed her neck, sending a plastic tendril down to connect with her Walkman. Insulated music was a great distraction on the bus ride over, but did not make for much of a scarf. At least she had found the sense to wear a warm pair of jeans, though the open-toed sandals more or less cancelled that out.

She waited a few seconds then knocked again, this time more assertive. Loud footsteps from beyond the door, a thump, a mild crash and something breaking, followed by a bout of muffled cursing. A small, stocky man with a bulbous maroon nose and the unfortunate beginnings of male-pattern baldness answered the door. He could have been any age, from any era. A nobody set to blend in to the world unnoticed. The generic, almost pleasant scent of alcohol crept through his teeth, seeped from his lips. Once that effect had worn off, the overpowering stench of seafood and tooth rot came out to party. Trixie started to second-guess her desire to confront The Angelghoul. Even without the halitosis force field, the presence of a chain lock prevented her from shoving her way in.

"Yeah, what d'ya want?" Bulbous Nose sneered at her. He looked like he had been practicing a few intimidation tactics of his own but hadn't quite gotten the hang of them.

Trixie felt he was more of a jerk-off than a threat. This guy had a lot of work to do before he would be capable of scaring her away. After all, she had nothing left to lose anymore.

She leaned back to double check the apartment number. "Do I have the right place?" she asked.

"Dunno. Depends on what you're looking for."

Trixie wrinkled her face into the toughest expression she could manage. "I need to see The Angelghoul."

Without breaking eye contact, Bulbous Nose squirted a stream of dark spittle through the crack in the door. The salivary slug landed centimeters from Trixie's feet. Her toes curled as if it were about to sprout legs and start inching its way toward her. "Can't," he said, picking at his teeth with a long, grimy pinky nail. "S'busy."

"I'm not a cop or anything."

He chortled. A string of goo trickled from his nose like a snot stalactite.

"Wasn't really worried about that, honey pie. Pigs don't usually bother making their way down to this side of town." His eyes wandered, swallowing her body. His failed attempt at a subtle glance at her breasts caused an eruption of gooseflesh on her exposed arms. "Even when they do, they don't usually look like you."

"Well, I still need to see him. It's important. I don't need any Candy or anything. I just need to talk to him. It shouldn't take more than a few minutes."

Bulbous Nose snorted up a fresh patch of mucous and swallowed it like precious sustenance. He stared at her for a moment, successfully creating the effect commonly known as awkward silence. Then, "Maybe later. Come back…Thursday. Yeah." The door slammed. The sound rippled along the street like it was following an invisible bouncing ball.

"Shit!" Trixie plopped down onto the steps. She paused before realizing that *today* was Thursday. Had he meant *next* Thursday? It had taken her far too much trouble to track down The Angelghoul's home. Revisiting old haunts and crevices of the city that were best avoided. Speaking with sketchy souls that controlled the keys to crucial information. Encounters with people she hadn't seen in years. Encounters that left her owing far too many favors, ones she would never be willing to repay. She couldn't give up so easily.

The chill of the concrete seeped through the fabric of her jeans, but she decided to wait for a moment regardless, try to think of a way she could convince that ugly toad to let her see Samuel. She had to get in, had to confront that bastard for triggering her relationship's end. He wasn't worthy of wielding that power. It was meant to be her truth to tell, and it would have been told.

Eventually.

She had almost been ready, the moment almost ripe, but The Angelghoul had ruined everything.

And Cypress. That Wonder Bread whore would need to be confronted next, with no interruptions. Claws out, the rules of a fair fight torn to shreds and burned. Maybe she was even here now. That would be perfect. A twofer. Trixie wondered what Christopher had ever seen in a girl like Cypress, but then she remembered that Christopher was, after all, a guy.

She pulled her headphones back over her ears and immersed herself in music for a few minutes while contemplating her next move. Lush's "Bitter" vibrated with beautiful rage. She took out the tape mid-song and switched it with another. Christopher's mix tape. A priceless artifact made with great care. She could not ignore it and let it waste away in her junk drawer any longer.

Though Trixie had not been initially enthralled by most of the music, she had memorized every note and lyric she could discern over the following weeks, treating each song like a sacred mantra. She knew the music meant the world to Christopher, so she had found her own path to loving it as well. Some of it wasn't so bad. A few songs were even a decent listen. Quicksand's "Dine Alone" ended side A as the song cut off when the tape ran out. It was like a sexual act nearing climax that had suddenly been robbed of its orgasm.

She glanced over to Graves Park. The homeless men had left to find another desolate spot. Their hopeless fire had been doused, but not to Smokey the Bear's standards. The frostbitten wind applied enough pressure to the trees that they seemed to dance a woodland jig. Dead leaves drifted and scattered, covering the ground in a patchwork quilt. Trixie thought about that brief period back in high school when her "secret" boyfriend Aron had brought her here, deep into the forested area, where the chances of another soul occupying the same space would have been highly unlikely. Armed with a few blankets and pillows, a six-pack of lukewarm beer, a condom and some smooth talk, Aron had taken her virginity, robbing her blind of any innocence she might have had left. That relationship had been only the first in a long line of stupid decisions. She chastised herself for a lifetime of repeat offenses.

Suddenly one of the trees in the park moved from its root, which Trixie initially shrugged off as her imagination getting away from her. The tree looked even shorter and skinnier than most of the other neglected plant life in the park. She got up from the staircase and took baby steps across the street to get a better look. Used condoms decorated the sidewalk like snails crushed during a rainstorm. Trixie felt another shock from her past and quickly shook it away.

After a few seconds, the tree moved closer, stepping into the beam cast by a failing streetlight. Trixie realized it wasn't a tree after all. It was one of the Withering Wyldes, coming toward her whether she liked it or not.

It appeared to be dancing. A horrible, idiotic skipping-to-my-Lou that should have been relegated to a sparsely attended traveling sideshow. She strangely could not recall ever seeing one of them alone before, a deviation that seemed dangerous, similar to a rabid raccoon wandering suburbia in the daylight. She wondered if it felt the same about her, or if it even understood that it was, at least partially, still human.

The Withering Wylde—*is it even okay to refer to just one?* Trixie wondered—crept up to her on its tippy toes, its fingers held limp in

Chad Stroup

front of it. It looked her up and down as if attempting to absorb her entire history in one glance. A small stack of pamphlets sprouted from a fanny pack clipped around its waist. It cocked its head at her, passed her a pamphlet, pulled a stapler from the fanny pack, attached another to a nearby utility pole without even so much as glancing at it and headed toward Samuel's apartment.

Trixie did not like to litter but realized rampant rubbish was part of this neighborhood's décor. She let the pamphlet slip from her fingers and quietly followed the Withering Wylde back to the stairs. It turned around as it reached the door and hissed at her, mumbling something in its indiscernible language. When Trixie showed no fear or intent of leaving, it ignored her and knocked. Its rubbery flesh against the wood sounded like a squid being beaten with a Louisville Slugger.

She patted her pockets for weapons that were not packed. Of course, as usual, she had nothing to protect herself. No shivs, no shanks, not even any trusty pepper spray. So stupid.

Bulbous Nose answered the knock. Without a word he released the chain lock and opened the door wide for his guest. The Withering Wylde glided in as if the ground beneath its feet was merely a formality.

Trixie took her chance and dashed past Bulbous Nose, elbowing him in the gut before he realized what had happened. She darted straight for the hallway and heard a shrill whistle behind her, Bulbous Nose doing his best attempt at an alert. But she was in, and she would damn well have her say.

The apartment was cramped, loaded with frayed and filthy furniture that you couldn't pay someone to take away and donate to Goodwill. Barely acceptable enough for bonfire fodder. Trixie had seen closets that were bigger than the living room space—the Zane Brothers' multiple walk-in wardrobes didn't count, though. That would just be unfair. A man was sprawled on the floor near a dilapidated love seat, the stains beneath him like a chalk outline formed from sweat and other bodily fluids. Trixie wasn't sure if the man was a corpse or just in a junked-out funk. The flies that circled his body didn't help matters much.

A rickety staircase sat a few steps from the front door. Trixie took advantage of her long legs and sprinted up the stairs two at a time. The wood screamed beneath her feet, begging her to stop. At the top was a

266

hallway blanketed in a dull haze that seemed to grow darker the farther she looked. She entered the first room to her right and slammed the door behind her.

She was not expecting to end up in an abattoir's toolshed.

Every sharp utensil and instrument of slaughter imaginable hung from the ceiling and walls like deadly decorations. From marrow spoons to meat hooks, some gleamed so brightly that Trixie could have done her makeup in their reflections. Others were old, dull and rusty—at least she hoped it was rust. The effluvia in the room was like a mix of loose change, barbecue residue and disinfectants. A table sat in the far corner. It looked as though someone had spilled a bowl of fruit punch on both its surface and the surrounding walls. White plastic buckets filled with a strange, clear gel were labeled with marker and masking tape as NUMBING AGENT.

Without looking, Trixie grabbed the tool nearest to her and left the room as quickly as her body allowed. She could hear Bulbous Nose oafishly ascending the stairs. She could barely see two feet in front of her, but she needed to keep moving. There was only one direction to go: down the hallway into darkness.

She felt against the wall until her fingers found another door. She flung it open. The light inside was shockingly bright. A small bedroom with no furniture and a kitchenette off to the side. A woman in a pantsuit, her hair pulled tightly back, turned around and glared at her. She held a butcher knife, wet with visceral juices.

"Can I help you?" the woman asked. She stared at Trixie with cold, dead, fishlike eyes. Trixie caught a glimpse of her cutting board on the counter. Shining, jiggling organs. Something that looked like, but couldn't possibly have been, a navel. Without a word, Trixie slammed the door.

A few steps further into the darkness of the hallway and she tripped on something. A crack, a bunched up rug, her own feet—she couldn't be certain. She threw out her hands to catch herself and unwittingly dropped the weapon she had earlier procured. She heard it bang against the floor twice before it slid off into the black.

At the end of the hallway, a weak light emanated from the open doorway into the last room on the floor. It had to be the one she was looking for.

And it was.

Inside, Samuel Haines sat in a plastic folding chair with a TV tray in front of him. His face was glued to the television set, a small black-and-white machine long past its date of use that offered the only illumination in the room. There was movement somewhere in the faint light behind him.

Samuel's mohawk was deflated. He was hunched over a ceramic plate, savoring small slivers of meat. It looked raw. Smelled fresh. His lips were smeared red with blood. He looked like a child experimenting with his mother's lipstick.

In the time since Trixie's truth had been revealed, during the long, late nights she had searched for Samuel's apartment, she had asked around town to learn more about Eaters, especially The Angelghoul himself. Still, even with this knowledge, the sight of him partaking in his holy supper was repulsive.

Two tumorous knobs protruded from his back. Pus and blood drizzled out of dry cracks. Some of the fluids were fresh, others crusted and in dire need of medical attention. His failed wings. Word on the street was The Angelghoul had contracted the equivalent of an STD from one of his recent Taste Subjects. Judging by the way he looked, Trixie was ready to believe that rumor.

Samuel glared up at her, finally acknowledging her presence, annoyed with the interruption of his sacramental meal. He shook his head at her without lifting his face from the plate of meat and wiped his mouth with a cloth napkin. The effort barely made a difference in the mess on his face.

Bulbous Nose appeared in the doorway, shifting back and forth from left foot to right, ready to bounce Trixie if given the order. He was wheezing heavily from his flight up the stairs. Samuel attempted to wave him away.

"You've got a customer here," Bulbous Nose said. "It's one of *them.*"

"That's fine, Rudy" Samuel said. "They can wait until I'm finished Eating. You should know how to deal with this already. Go make a wheatgrass smoothie for it or something. I don't care."

"But—"

"Do you want to continue to learn the ways of the divine or do you not?"

"Yes, sir. Sorry to have questioned your authority."

Rudy attempted one last sneer at Trixie before leaving. She rolled her eyes and shook her head.

"Pledges. What a headache," Samuel said to himself before turning back to Trixie. "Yes?"

"You know why I'm here."

"I assume it's because you've decided to take me up on my offer. As you can see, though, my meal plan is stable for the time being. But we can reschedule. I'd be more than happy to accommodate." His smile stretched and she could not tell where the deep red of his lips ended and the streaks of blood began.

"I know you're not *that* big of an idiot."

"Would you prefer to speak somewhere more private?"

"Like where? The bathroom? Seems like every room in this place is so tiny you could probably hear a mouse fart in the next room over."

The Angelghoul stood up. Trixie could now see behind him the shape of a man leaning back on a chaise lounge that was ready to collapse at any moment. The man appeared to be breaths away from the end of his days.

"You were foolish to come here alone."

Trixie lunged forward and snagged the steak knife from Samuel's tray. She poked it in his direction.

"Stay the fuck away from me," she said. "Not even one step closer or I swear I'll gut you."

Samuel held his hands in front of him and cringed in faux fear. "You know," he said. "You're a bit outnumbered here."

"Remember that big hunk of man meat back at Club Club who almost kicked your ass into next year?" Trixie noticed the legitimate concern in Samuel's eyes. "Yeah, *that* one. If he doesn't get a phone call from me in thirty minutes, he'll be here to finish what he started that night, and it won't be fucking pretty." It was an off-the-cuff bluff, but effective enough. She wished to God Mace was here backing her up. Even Steve would have been better than nothing.

The Angelghoul sat back down in his folding chair. "Well, go on," he said. "Spit out whatever the hell it is you have to say to me. Can't you see I'm busy?"

Trixie ignored Samuel and met the gaze of the man behind him. There was something familiar about the face peering at her through the darkness, but her rational side refused to acknowledge it. The man on the chaise lounge made a failed attempt at a laugh that came out more like a weak snort.

"You two know each other?" Samuel asked.

"Thomas?" the man mumbled.

The name formed immense hands inside Trixie's mind, grabbed her, shook her and choked her, just like this man's real hands once had.

Five years.

Five years had passed, and it looked as if he had aged a full lifetime and then some. His receding hairline had become a crescent moon of fuzz at the far back of his head. Bags hung under his eyes as if they were designed to catch tears to be transferred to a public well for future consumption. His body had morphed from average build with optional beer gut into a shapeless blob, someone who had given up caring about appearances long ago. Skin bronzed by jaundice. He smelled of urine, garlic and badly aged cheese.

Portions of his flesh had been removed from the fat of his upper arm. The slices formed an almost pitchfork-like pattern. Some of the same clear gel Trixie had seen in the first room coated his wounds.

"Well, oil me up and fuck me with a cucumber. It's really you, isn't it?" the man asked, his voice laced with shrapnel, his expression almost pleased.

The steak knife slipped from Trixie's hand.

"D-dad?"

"Sounds like you two have some catching up to do," Samuel said. "Get Out of Jail Free card for me. We'll talk later." He dabbed the corners of his mouth with the napkin again, stood up and zipped out of the room. After a few seconds of fleeting footsteps, Trixie heard the front door slam. The Angelghoul, that chickenshit little bitch of a man, was suddenly the least of her current concerns.

"What in the hell are you doing here, Hank?"

Her father belched and shifted in the chaise to face her. It appeared to take every ounce of his strength.

"I should ask you the same thing."

"None of your fucking business, really."

Hank chuckled. "Ran out of options, I guess. Life's a bitch that mugs you for your wallet."

For perhaps the first time in Trixie's life, she shared common ground with her father.

Hank looked at her with supreme disappointment. "Don't know how I even managed to recognize you underneath all of this bullshit." He waved his hands at her. "Decided to go full-blown queer, huh?"

Trixie suddenly felt sixteen again and weak all over, remembering why she hated that almost forgotten era of her life. She clenched her fists, ready to battle both the regression and the human cause of it.

"Ah, well. What the hell does it matter anyway? I guess a man can never really forget what his son looks like, even if his son now has titties." Hank attempted to laugh again, but it came out as a barely controllable hack. "God *damn*. What do you think your mother would say about this?"

"Hank, you need to shut the fuck up. Now."

Hank's head bobbled. "Well, look who finally grew a pair. Or did you cut those off? Hows about you let your dear old Dad take a look."

Trixie took a step forward and slapped her father across the face. No hesitation. Hank's color swelled into a dark pink, and he patted his cheek with Play-Doh fingers.

"You know," he said, "if I wasn't so fucking fat and old right now, I'd make mincemeat out of you, you little, ungrateful son of a bitch."

Trixie laughed, releasing fierce bellows like she was auditioning for a sitcom laugh track. "You're a real peach, Hank. A complete joke. Why did I ever think for a minute you were capable of being a parent? Why was I even afraid of you?"

He had no answer.

"You're just a pathetic pile of shit," she continued. "I hope The Angelghoul gets even sicker from eating your rotten flesh, and that you catch something from him, too. I never want to see you again."

"The way things have been going, I don't imagine you will. But hey, there'll be a decent chunk of change left over if Mr. Angeltool convinces me to go all the way with his little Eating project. You might as well come back and try to claim it when he's done. He's an honest businessman…I'll give him that. Not like I've got anyone else to leave it to. Maybe you can buy yourself a brand new collection of porcelain fag dolls."

Trixie had heard whispers about the amount of money The Angelghoul paid his Taste Subjects. If the rumors were truths, the money he was paying Hank could be life changing for her.

"No. Fuck your money. Fuck you. Not that you would, not that you even thought about it after I left home, but don't come looking for me. Ever! Have a beautiful, lonely funeral." Trixie left the room and headed for the front door.

Downstairs, she saw Rudy and the Withering Wylde exchanging cash and small plastic bags of pills. She exited the building in a rush and almost ran chest first into a familiar body.

The olive pea coat, the pork pie hat, the elevator shoes, the gaudy rings.

Kast.

The dwarf looked up at Trixie and smiled, his busted teeth and gingivitis-ridden gums shifting like the jaws of a goblin shark. He placed his rough hand upon hers. Even though it felt like he was wearing gloves made of reptile skin, it was a gentle, almost loving touch.

"Trixie, my dear," he said. "So long since we last met. You're looking so lovely, pet."

"Wh-what… But how did you know—"

Kast squealed with delight. "Don't be silly, my sweet. This is sheer serendipity, is it not? Have you thought about my offer? I've left more messages than I care to count. Surely you've received them, yes? I've been hoping to get a call from you. Why haven't you come to see me yet?"

Sometimes the opportunities one wishes for require years of struggle to achieve. Other times the dominoes fall into place far too easily to be ignored.

Dr. Julius Kast's Personal Instructions and Notes
for the Preparation and Performance of Male-to-Female
Sexual Reassignment Surgery (SRS)

Inspired by Dr. Dorian Wylde's Original Notes
Revised, Expanded and Updated December 1992

PRE-SURGERY

- Contact candidate/potential patient to inquire about interest in SRS. Approach her with caution and concern. Politeness and understanding of her situation is of the utmost importance.
- Make contact with candidate at any cost. You will never have the chance to convince her if you do not command her attention.
- Endear yourself to the patient. Make your best attempt to use appropriate gender pronouns at all times. Write a note on your hand if necessary. Do not forget. She will appreciate your effort.
- ~~Patient must be at least 18 years of age and/or have consent from a parent or legal guardian.~~
- ~~Psychological evaluation is crucial before taking the next steps toward surgery. Ensure patient has met with a professional therapist and obtained written letter of recommendation to proceed with gender reassignment.~~
- Ensure patient has had at least one year of Real Life Experience. OPTIONAL.
- Hormones should be discontinued approximately two weeks before surgery in order to prevent pesky blood clots. This is a guideline, not necessarily a rule.

DAY OF SURGERY

- Make certain a clean gurney, bed and wheelchair are available for the patient. The proper levels of comfort will soothe the patient both pre- and post-operative. Remember, cleanliness is next to godliness. Surgeons are the gods of the corporeal world.
- You are an artist. Prepare to shape the form like clay that will develop into a valuable sculpture.
- A primary incision at the perineum. Delicate, like slicing the petal from a still-blooming flower.
- The right spermatic cord clamped, ligated. A pinch that does not steal the dream.

- Continue up the ventral side of the shaft, share a slice of bratwurst and place it on the grill.
- Develop the anterior flap.
- Dissect the urethra from the shaft. It should now resemble a frill-necked lizard.
- Separate the corpora cavernosa in order to assure a minimal stump.
- Complete the perineal dissection and perforate the anterior flap to position the urethral meatus.
- If necessary, graft skin from the thighs, hips or, less desirably, the colon to assist in creating the lining.
- Suture the skin flaps like a wounded teddy bear. Place them in position in the new vaginal cavity.

POST-SURGERY

- Important! Do not forget to inform patient that use of a suitably sized vaginal dilator to preserve the cavity is crucial. Advise patient to insert and remove as needed.
- Check patient's eyes to ensure she is in an appropriate Demerol haze.
- Provide the option of a complimentary snack. Be sure to inquire about any allergies she might have.
- Inform patient that she is now set to begin enjoying her magical journey into true womanhood!

September 10, 1992

There's this sort of recurring dream that's been haunting me lately, Miss Diary. Maybe recurring isn't really the right word. It's more like a soap opera serial that picks up where it left off the previous night, or week or month or whatever. I swear, sleep is such a strange thing. I look forward to it for the rest and the escape I suppose, but sometimes I dread what might attack me in that world when I have zero control. *A Nightmare on Trixie Street, Part 77 ½*. Have you seen that one, Miss Diary? It sucks.

But this one isn't a nightmare. It's just frustrating, I guess. In this dream, nature didn't screw up my birth—I'm a girl from day one. No confusion about the path I'm supposed to take. My parents don't even have to think about whether or not to accept me for who I am. It's a non-issue. I'm just their daughter, fitting myself into the accepted gender code like the perfect puzzle piece. Then it shifts to my pubescent years and I get my first period. Can I even know what that's supposed to feel like? Do I even want to? So weird. Part of me is glad that I've never had to experience that, but I'd take a little menstruation in a heartbeat over what's been my reality.

So the dream keeps moving on to losing my virginity—*not* with Aron, thank God. The guy in the dream has scruffy facial hair and a few tattoos. I have absolutely no idea what his name is and he's totally not my type. After that I have my pick of various blurry boyfriends all the way up to my current age, where I go away to college, major in Liberal Arts—with a minor in Spanish, go figure—and have this weird experimental lesbian phase. Ew. So not interested in that. I mean, that's cool or whatever, but *so* not for me. Eventually it flashes forward to getting married, working in some office where I'm writing articles for some fitness magazine and having—*gulp*—kids. I'm not even sure if I would have wanted any of that. I always assumed I could just adopt someday if I ever really had the urge for a child, but how can I know that for sure? I wasn't privileged with being born right. My life has been impacted by so many chance factors that I can't understand. Biology, fate, a coin toss, God. Who's in charge here?

I know what you're thinking, Diary. Doesn't seem like such a terrible dream, does it? The problem with dreams, though, is that eventually you have to wake up from them.

I'm an imperfect woman living under the regime of a false binary identity. Born a young boy, a *wrong* boy. I'm the only one who can take action to right the mistakes of nature. It's so unfair that the solution is right there in front of me but still seems so out of reach. Why was I given the shaft? Why was I not granted the easy, normal path? When can I stop thinking about all of this and just be me?

CHAPTER TWENTY-TWO

TRIXIE WONDERS WHAT SHE IS DOING HERE. She is not even completely sure where "here" is. She has already forgotten what it felt like to be on the bus just moments ago. The jerking vibrations, the zombified commuters, the faint scent of watermelon vomit and alcohol-drenched urine are all a distant memory. It took two transfers and one hour to complete the trip. In the time between the first transfer, she almost decided to take the bus that would have returned her home. "Here" would have remained "there." It would be safer and more comforting to be home in her bed, clutching her unwashed sheets that still retain the unmistakable scent of feline.

Now she hovers at the busy intersection of First and Ozymandias, two long blocks from her destination of Sweet Pepper Lane. The streetlight turns green and she glides slowly, avoiding eye contact with the few people bustling about, following the handwritten directions left for her in her mailbox one month ago. She has been informed that the door leading to the Monarch Metamorphosis Syndicate building will not be clearly marked.

She checks the map, double-checks it, then enters a quiet, clean, unassuming alley. Garbage is confined to its proper cans. A blue macaw peers silently at her from inside a tinted apartment window. Two young boys who could have been extracted from a Norman Rockwell painting toss a football back and forth. It may be the only alley in Sweetville devoid of graffiti. She wonders if "here" is even the correct "here."

Trixie reaches a dull white door with a silver knob. A dime-sized sticker with the number ninety-nine is attached to the top corner of the door. She removes a key from her back pocket. The key was also left in her mailbox, attached to the map with a single piece of clear tape. She inserts the tiny key into the lock and turns the chilled knob. The bolt clicks and unlatches with a crisp *tick*. She turns to see if the boys throwing the football are watching her, but they have vanished and returned to their normal, picturesque lives.

A thick darkness resides behind the door. Trixie slices the key through it, expecting that the voluminous black mass will have the texture of pudding left to rot. But it is only air. Stygian, shadowy air.

She enters the unknown.

Stairs, stairs and still more stairs leading down, down, down. It cannot reasonably be more than a handful of flights, but Trixie has been descending them for at least two minutes and has already lost count. Strings of blue Christmas lights now illuminate each level, clinging to the handrails like electric vines. Trixie wonders if there is adequate oxygen this far below the surface, if it is even possible to sustain life this close to the Earth's core.

Trixie has heard whispers, rumors, echoes through the streets over the years, but until this moment, she has never realized that Lower Sweetville takes its namesake so literally.

Trixie reaches the bottom and feels a gush of icy wind as she approaches doorless entry. Powerful, pungent air conditioning. She pauses for a moment before crossing the threshold, considers turning back, then considers she does not want to head back up the endless flights of stairs and back into her past.

She takes the first steps into what appears to be a diminutive underground city. Paved sidewalks, minimal foot traffic. Blinding, creamy lights. A blank, useless brick wall on one side seems to go on for miles, and there are a few spaces reserved for commerce on the other. She squints and thinks she can see a stopping point to this city, then passes a cone-shaped information booth. The person within it is so corpulent, so soft and squishy, that the indicators of his or her gender have been all but erased. A man with a neck goiter the size of a deflated soccer ball rushes by, heading for the exit that was just moments ago her entrance, heading for the precious and natural light of day. A woman with a cotton bandage across her eye, adhered to her face by a melon-colored crust, carrying a plastic bag full of bouncing baby crickets, exits a store called Salamanders of the Underworld. A sign in the window reads: NO NEWTS IS GOOD NEWTS. A teenage girl with Down's syndrome sits on a concrete bench, stroking the head of a black Neapolitan Mastiff. Two Junkie Creeps wearing fresh blue jumpsuits shuffle into a store that appears to sell nothing but blue jumpsuits. This is a meeting place for misfits. Less a city, more a mutant mini-mall.

Trixie faces forward as she walks, only forcing brief glances as she passes each new storefront. She does not want to miss her destination. She does not want to go too far, though she knows she already has. She cannot unsee what has been stamped into her retinas.

It is not long before she mercifully encounters Suite D7. The Monarch Metamorphosis Syndicate building. Unsurprisingly, a gorgeous butterfly is painted across the front window, using every possible color choice from the palette. Less expected, however, is the subtle image of a human face superimposed on the butterfly's head.

She enters the building. It is barely a hospital. Barely a building even. The waiting room constricts and suffocates, seems to grow smaller with each step. It is the size of a two-stall restroom, and does not smell much better. A receptionist's face and torso poke through a large, professionally cut hole in the wall. Her face is perfectly crafted, pin-up beautiful, her lips wet and waxy cushions, her eyes like pools of chocolate fondue. For a brief moment Trixie feels she is back on planet Earth.

Until she notices the receptionist's breasts. There is not a letter in the alphabet for her cup size. Enormous, solid masses that would be suitable for the lead percussion in a tribal drum circle. Nipples poking through the fabric of her shirt, curving like opposable thumbs.

"You must be our two o'clock," the receptionist says. Trixie nods and forces a smile, approaches and tries to fool herself into thinking this is a routine check-up. Maybe just a simple skin tag removal.

"Do I need to sign in or anything?" She is really going through with this.

"No, doll. You're actually our *only* o'clock today. Dr. Kast has been expecting you."

Trixie wonders if she can afford the procedure, if she will owe despicable favors, if she will have to live on ramen and chunky salsa for the next few months, then counters these thoughts by realizing that she cannot afford *not* to have it done. The price of her mental stability is immeasurable.

"Why don't you take a seat and I'll let the doctor know you're here."

"Thanks." Trixie avoids eye contact. She can barely breathe. The oxygen supply in this waiting room feels even less substantial than in the entrance to this underground world. She thinks the room might be shrinking.

The receptionist disappears momentarily, then reappears. Her face shines like it has been brushed with vanilla glaze. "And don't worry," she says, "you're in amazing and talented hands. He'll make an already beautiful girl like you into pure perfection. Trust me. I know from personal experience." She winks and vanishes again.

Trixie backs into a plastic folding chair, the only seating that has a chance of fitting in the room. There are no tables, no decorations on the walls save Kast's framed medical license, which Trixie cannot read as it is written entirely in Siamese. A piece of paper is folded and trapped beneath one of the chair's feet, presumably left and forgotten by a previous patient. She lifts her weight, takes the paper and unfolds it. It is a page torn from some magazine, a portion of an unnamed essay written by Dr. Dorian Wylde. She floats into a sitting position and reads the words:

A technicality: as embryos, we all begin as female. Appearances can be and often *are* deceiving. Perhaps it is more accurate to say that we begin the daunting journey to eventual doom with the absence of any sex between our legs. The playing field is perfectly even from the get go. However, at some point during those critical first few post-fertilization weeks, the indifferent gonads take form.

Either X or Y has ridden the sperm coaster to ovarian heaven. Nature has covered its eyes, plucked down its trusting finger and taken its pick of the white wiggly wonder that has traveled so far in hopes of completing its magical insemination. Soon after the initial weeks, the female Müllerian and male Wolffian ducts begin to develop. Do those names not sound like superior beings from another galaxy?

Gender is alien, foreign.

It may also be fluid, fickle and free. A fetus cannot be expected to hold true to its original blueprint.

Both sexes will form a ureter. One will earn a vas deferens. The other Fallopian tubes, uterus and cervix. Androgens or estrogens soon come forth and determine the future of one's gender identity. Which features will degenerate? Eventual stimuli via clitoris or glans? Ambiguous genitalia? Intersexuality? Complete androgen insensitivity syndrome? How does one explain a man's useless yet still sensitive nipples? Or a woman with a distinct laryngeal prominence?

Being female does not consist of the absence of maleness. It is the presence of a goddess within, a force that will be released no matter what lies between one's legs. However, there is a catch: the goddess and god are often interchangeable. Take the Hindu deity Ardhanarishvara, whose name translates to "the Lord who is half woman." The concepts of androgyny and fluidity of gender are considered a privilege. This angle can also exist for situations that are not bound to religious connotations. Consider Henry Darger's Vivian Girls, a colorful, innocent depiction of arguably ambiguous genitalia that does not match the norm, an unspoken acceptance of these free-spirited deviations.

Are gender identity and the physicality that oftentimes does not correspond with said identity just chance or fallacious miracles? A hormonal crapshoot? Sometimes, nature's magic makes an egregious error. Sometimes, that error is a domino that can impact one's life in unfathomable ways.

Trixie is in a congested, confused haze. She chooses to not read whatever is printed on the other side of the paper. Not yet. She folds it back up and stuffs it in her back pocket. It is not stealing. It is trash turned treasure, a free gift to herself. It may be further words from Dr. Dorian Wylde. It may be a frantic note screaming from the page: GET THE HELL OUT OF THIS MADHOUSE WHILE YOU STILL CAN. It may be coupons. She will save the surprise for later, when she recovers from the surgery.

When she is complete.

* * *

Him.

Her brain struggles to form the letters that spell his name, as if they are encrypted into some foreign cipher with no hope of translation.

She believes that he will finally want her after all the slicing and shifting is over and done with, once the transformation is complete. There is a chance. He cannot help that he has rigid desires. He is a regular guy with regular needs. She simply needs to remove the irregularity. Only then will she be capable of fulfilling these needs. It is possible that he could conveniently forget about the parts of Trixie that were never supposed to exist. Pretend they were fragments of fractured dreams. He will come to his senses and realize the only thing that matters is how they feel about each other, how they face the world together with strong hearts. She knows he will.

He has to.

Except there is no way she can force this to occur. Wishes are just bits of fiction that sometimes manage to cross over into memoir.

Trixie has spoken to him sporadically since he walked out on her back in May. He was kind enough to call her a couple of weeks later to see how she was holding up. They have remained on the cusp of cordiality. A torturous limbo.

Fine, she had said during the call. An outright lie. He knew it, she knew it, but it was the only word she could have spoken. Anything else would have stirred her emotional stew. She called him back soon after, attempting to bridge the gap, left pitiful notes begging for forgiveness at his doorstep. Anything, everything, nothing. He did not budge, and she had single-handedly destroyed her dignity.

She had almost called him again, the day after she had encountered her father wasting away in The Angelghoul's hovel. She had planned out every little detail. She would have offered to meet him at Vladimir's. Neutral ground. She was ready to tell him every pivotal moment of her teenage life. She had needed him then as she needed him now. Who else could she have confided in?

But she realized that none of her efforts would be worth a damn unless their reconciliation was a sure thing. She would read him the unabridged book of her life only when she was certain he would be her devoted listener.

This morning, just hours before her current predicament, she attempted to contact him. Twice. She could not bring herself to leave a message. She hated the way her voice sounded on those stupid machines and had already brought enough embarrassment upon herself. What could she have said that would have made sense anyway? *Oh, hi, ex-babe. In case you're not sick of me calling you yet, I'm finally getting rid of my final link to boyhood. Wanna come with? You can watch if you want. Maybe they'll serve popcorn. If you're too busy, I can ask them to put what's left in a jar with formaldehyde, take it home and show you later. Bet you'd think that was real swell, huh? Call me back! Muah!*

But he was not at home. Not at work. Not available.

Now Trixie wishes he were here by her side, his callused fingers squeezing hers, his hushed voice cracking inappropriate jokes, his wintergreen breath soothing her senses on this most important of days.

Him.

She will never put him through hell again.

She is going through hell just for the chance to prove that.

Maybe she can ask the receptionist to use the phone. Just for a quick call.

285

A harsh cough shatters Trixie's daydream. She runs her tongue across her teeth. She can still taste the faint flavor of grape bubblegum from earlier in the day. She wonders how much time has passed, if there is still daylight outside or if it has shifted into night while she has been entombed within this room.

Trixie lies stiff like a fresh corpse on the arctic operating table, protected by a loose-fitting, gender-neutral hospital gown. She keeps a steady, constant pace to her breathing. Her heartbeat pulses in her head, the pressure like deep-sea narcosis. Mint-green hues dominate the room—set for solace, bound to fail.

Dr. Julius Kast hovers over her, which she feels must be an optical illusion. This sensation is rectified when she glances to her side and notices he is standing on a wooden stepladder. He is smiling, his sparse teeth displayed like forgotten ruins. A surgical face mask hangs below his chin like a wattle.

"Darling," Kast says, lightly patting her hair. "It looks as if you are still awake. That should not last long. I promise you will not regret taking this adventure. My associates and I will take great care of you. Only the utmost professionalism."

Kast nibbles at the end of a red licorice stick and moves his deformed hand to her shoulder. Despite the hand's rough, scaly grain and abnormal weight, the motion is comforting. He smells like an Old Spice factory spill. His violet eyes seem benevolent, which softens the impact of the bizarre scars on his face.

This is the first time Trixie has been able to see them in a fully lit space. Swirls and curls like ocean waves, patterns of forgotten language, offset by intersecting straight lines. The scars are precisely carved, deep and deliberate grooves, likely performed by a talented colleague here in Sweetville's surgical underground. It is like looking at a tic-tac-toe table designed by a sadist.

"I'm scared," Trixie says, her voice barely a coherent mumble. "Why does it have to be this way? Isn't there a...um..."

Though general anesthesia is beginning to take effect, the room is tight enough that her clouded eyes are able to take in most of the sights. Holes decorate the walls like polka dots. Whether placed there by an angry fist or a rat's jagged teeth, Trixie cannot tell. Tiny moats of stagnant water block the two corners of the room that she can see from where she lies. There are strange machines and devices that she cannot comprehend. They look nothing like what she has seen on *Doogie Howser, MD*. These machines bleep and blip like something out of a no-budget science fiction film. Rows of sharpened silver surgical tools with very specific duties are strewn across another table, organized by size, shape and sting. Trixie has to trust in their sterility. All of Kast's excessive hand jewelry is placed nearby in a small wicker basket like the glistening gold of a pirate's precious booty.

His two Withering Wylde assistants are dressed for duty, swaying like supermodels in questionable fashion, waiting for their turn on the runway. Elongated arms extend from their white lab coats, fuzzy tendrils floating in empty space. Their face masks do not prevent them from giving Trixie the terror shivers, but instead create an image even more fearsome than usual. They are beanstalks with souls. She is under their spell. The masks make them appear as if they have no mouths, and so Trixie wonders what devious thoughts might be dying to escape their infernal maws.

She thinks she can hear them whispering, presumably to each other, though they are both looking in her direction. The hushed tones crawl across the walls and wiggle their way into her ears. She wishes William Ekkert were here. He would know how to translate, how to whisper into her ear and tell her just what the Withering Wyldes were saying. Even if it was a comforting lie. A lie repeated in rhyme.

"Did you think it was going to be magic, my dear?" Kast asks. He does his best to stifle a laugh, but tact has never been in his nature.

His claims of professionalism are clearly a façade. Trixie questions if it is too late for her to back out of the agreement, if this is possibly a terrible decision. But the anesthesia forces that thought to take a hike before it has a chance to fully gestate. She can only pray that his craft trumps his etiquette, that his artistry excels despite his physical limitations.

"I assumed by now you were well aware that I'm far from your fairy godmother," Kast says. "There will be no waving of wands or 'Bibbidi-Bobbidi-Boo' occurring in this room. Sorry, love. As skilled as I am, there are some things even I can't accomplish. I won't lie. This will hurt, but you will not feel a thing. At least not *during* the procedure. Recovery is a reliable lover. Does all of this make sense to you? I will take care of you, and you will be satisfied with the end result. That much I *can* promise."

Trixie whimpers. She is a helpless infant. She can feel the Withering Wyldes fiddling with the bottom of her gown. Terrible tufts of fur tickling her toes. Fidgeting fingers sliding across her shins like a swarm of centipedes.

"Dream, my sweet pupa," Kast continues, "and wake up as you were always meant to. A beautiful woman."

"No...but...wait...what about..." Trixie drifts off to the Land of Nod. Not terribly different from any relaxing night at home, drifting into a deep sleep while watching late night reruns of *The Newlywed Game* or *Win, Lose, or Draw.* Her dreams are strange, occasionally bland. Shopping at Modyrn Gyrlz with a rotund girl in pigtails who she has never met, stuffing absurd amounts of bras and underwear into her pockets as a freckled sales associate flirts with a man made solely of muscle. Making spaghetti with mushroom sauce and cheesy garlic bread for Christopher—she drinking a glass of flat red wine and he a can of ginger ale. The garlic bread is burnt and, for some reason, gives off an indeterminate citrus flavor. Her mother, in perfect health, life surging through her eyes, a Barbie doll vibrating in her hands like it has Parkinson's. Wearing a fuzzy pink snowsuit, trapped beneath an impervious block of blue ice, beating at it until her fists are numb and raw, her father nowhere in sight. Federico dragging a dead baby possum across the living room floor, staining the carpet with puddles of blood that will never be cleaned. The corner of Fifth and Quail at an undisclosed hour—except now Trixie is the one steering a vehicle through the sullen streets, struggling to make her difficult decision at the manly meat market. The men on display are plentiful and nude. Their enormous exposed appendages swing back and forth like vines awaiting Tarzan's grip. Or maybe Jane is the one acting like the human monkey this time. Who knows?

Upon recovery, Trixie will not recall these illusions. They are lost and buried in memory's tomb. She will one day only remember the distant delusion that she was once a girl who dreamt she was a boy for many years and did not love it. But now the dream is more than dormant—it is dead forever and the true, wonderful woman is finally allowed to awaken.

Reassign, realign, redefine.

ACKNOWLEGEMENTS

First, I'd like to extend my undying gratitude to Tony Rivera and Sharon Lawson for believing in this project. (You're obviously very disturbed individuals and should be ashamed of yourselves). I couldn't have asked for a better home or finer hosts.

To Mel Freilicher, who saw something special in the short story that sowed the seeds of this book.

To Stephen-Paul Martin, who mentored me while developing the novel and helped get it into publishable shape.

To Randall Lahrman, Tone Milazzo, Kevin Cullen, Evan Post and Richard Carr, for every small and large thing that needed tinkering in early drafts.

To Rick Blair, Nicholas Friesen and Adam Rusch for the ripping tunes (and Rob Logic for the recording).

To Valerie, for all the nights I've been locked away, thank you for being patient.

And to you, the reader, for being brave and open.

ABOUT THE AUTHOR

Chad Stroup's dark short stories and poetry have been featured in various publications. *Secrets of the Weird* is his first novel.

Stroup received his MFA in Fiction from San Diego State University. He is a member of the Horror Writers Association and the San Diego Horror Professionals, and he dearly misses playing music.

Visit his blog at subvertbia.blogspot.com, or drop by his Facebook page at facebook.com/ChadStroupWriter.

MORE DARK FICTION FROM
GREY MATTER PRESS

"Grey Matter Press has managed to establish itself as one of the premiere purveyors of horror fiction currently in existence via both a series of killer anthologies — *SPLATTERLANDS, OMINOUS REALITIES, EQUILIBRIUM OVERTURNED* — and John F.D. Taff's harrowing novella collection *THE END IN ALL BEGINNINGS.*"

- FANGORIA Magazine

GREY MATTER
P R E S S

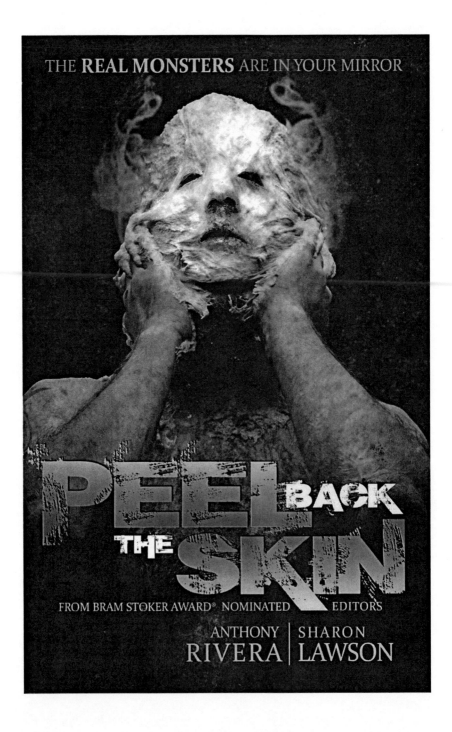

THE **REAL MONSTERS** ARE IN YOUR MIRROR

PEEL BACK THE SKIN

FROM BRAM STOKER AWARD® NOMINATED EDITORS

ANTHONY **RIVERA** | SHARON **LAWSON**

PEEL BACK THE SKIN
ANTHOLOGY OF HORROR

They are among us.

They live down the street. In the apartment next door. And even in our own homes.

They're the real monsters. And they stare back at us from our bathroom mirrors.

Peel Back the Skin is a powerhouse new anthology of terror that strips away the mask from the real monsters of our time – mankind.

Featuring all-new fiction from a star-studded cast of award-winning authors from the horror, dark fantasy, speculative, transgressive, extreme horror and thriller genres, *Peel Back the Skin* is the next game-changing release from Bram Stoker Award-nominated editors Anthony Rivera and Sharon Lawson.

FEATURING:

Jonathan Maberry	James Lowder
Ray Garton	Lucy Taylor
Tim Lebbon	Joe McKinney
Ed Kurtz	Erik Williams
William Meikle	Charles Austin Muir
Yvonne Navarro	John McCallum Swain
Durand Sheng Welsh	Nancy A. Collins

Graham Masterton

GREY MATTER
P R E S S

greymatterpress.com

DREAD

a head full of bad dreams

JONATHAN MABERRY
BRACKEN MACLEOD
WILLIAM MEIKLE
JOHN C. FOSTER
JOHN F.D. TAFF
MICHAEL LAIMO
TIM WAGGONER
RAY GARTON
JG FAHERTY
JOHN EVERSON
TRENT ZELAZNY
AND MANY MORE

from editors
ANTHONY RIVERA
SHARON LAWSON

THE BEST OF GREY MATTER PRESS VOLUME ONE

DREAD
A HEAD FULL OF BAD DREAMS

There are some nightmares from which you can never wake.

Dread: A Head Full of Bad Dreams is a terrifying volume of the darkest hallucinatory revelations from the minds of some of the most accomplished award-winning authors of our time. Travel dark passageways and experience the alarming visions of twenty masters from the horror, fantasy, science fiction, thriller, transgressive and speculative fiction genres as they bare their souls and fill your head with a lifetime of bad dreams.

Dread is the first-ever reader curated volume of horror from Grey Matter Press. The twenty short stories in this book were chosen solely by fans of dark fiction. *Dread* includes a special Introduction from Bram Stoker Award-nominated editor Anthony Rivera who says:

> "Readers who embrace darkness are souls of conscience with hearts of passion and voices that deserve to be heard. It's from this group of passionate voices that the nightmares in *Dread: A Head Full of Bad Dreams* were born.
> "Turning over the reins of editorial curation for this volume to the readers who matter most may well have been the best decision I've ever made. This book that you've created embodies your passion for dark fiction and serves as your own head of bad dreams come to life."

FEATURING:

Ray Garton	Jonathan Maberry
John F.D. Taff	JG Faherty
William Meikle	John Everson
Rose Blackthorn	Michael Laimo
Bracken MacLeod	John C. Foster
Tim Waggoner	Jane Brooks
Chad McKee	Peter Whitley
T. Fox Dunham	J. Daniel Stone
Edward Morris	Jonathan Balog
Trent Zelazny	Martin Rose

GREY MATTER
P R E S S

greymatterpress.com

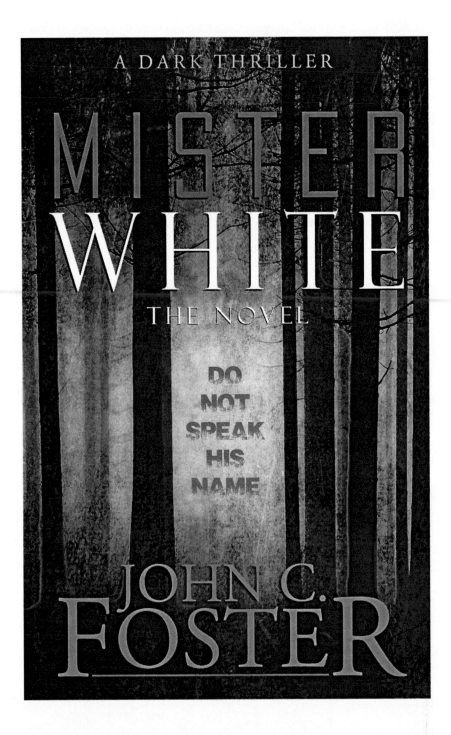

A DARK THRILLER

MISTER WHITE

THE NOVEL

DO
NOT
SPEAK
HIS
NAME

JOHN C.
FOSTER

MISTER WHITE
BY JOHN C. FOSTER

In the shadowy world of international espionage and governmental black ops, when a group of American spies go bad and inadvertently unleash an ancient malevolent force that feeds on the fears of mankind, a young family finds themselves in the crosshairs of a frantic supernatural mystery of global proportions with only one man to turn to for their salvation.

Combine the intricate, plot-driven stylings of suspense masters Tom Clancy and Robert Ludlum, add a healthy dose of Clive Barker's dark and brooding occult horror themes, and you get a glimpse into the supernatural world of international espionage that the chilling new horror novel *Mister White* is about to reveal.

John C. Foster's *Mister White* is a terrifying genre-busting suspense shocker that, once and for all, answer the question you dare not ask: "Who is Mister White?"

"*Mister White* is a potent and hypnotic brew that blends horror, espionage and mystery. Foster has written the kind of book that keeps the genre fresh and alive and will make fans cheer. Books like this are the reason I love horror fiction." – RAY GARTON, Grand Master of Horror and Bram Stoker Award®-nominated author of *Live Girls* and *Scissors*.

"*Mister White* is like Stephen King's *The Stand* meets Ian Fleming's James Bond with Graham Masterton's *The Manitou* thrown in for good measure. It's frenetically paced, spectacularly gory and eerie as hell. Highly recommended!" – JOHN F.D. TAFF, Bram Stoker Award®-nominated author of *The End in All Beginnings*

GREY MATTER
P R E S S

greymatterpress.com

THE END IN ALL BEGINNINGS
BY JOHN F.D. TAFF

The Bram Stoker Award-nominated *The End in All Beginnings* is a tour de force through the emotional pain and anguish of the human condition. Hailed as one of the best volumes of heartfelt and gut-wrenching horror in recent history, *The End in All Beginnings* is a disturbing trip through the ages exploring the painful tragedies of life, love and loss.

Exploring complex themes that run the gamut from loss of childhood innocence, to the dreadful reality of survival after everything we hold dear is gone, to some of the most profound aspects of human tragedy, author John F.D. Taff takes readers on a skillfully balanced emotional journey through everyday terrors that are uncomfortably real over the course of the human lifetime. Taff's highly nuanced writing style is at times darkly comedic, often deeply poetic and always devastatingly accurate in the most terrifying of ways.

Evoking the literary styles of horror legends Mary Shelley, Edgar Allen Poe and Bram Stoker, *The End in All Beginnings* pays homage to modern masters Stephen King, Ramsey Campbell, Ray Bradbury and Clive Barker.

"*The End in All Beginnings* is accomplished stuff, complex and heartfelt. It's one of the best novella collections I've read in years!" – JACK KETCHUM, Bram Stoker Award®-winning author of *The Box, Closing Time* and *Peaceable Kingdom*

"Taff brings the pain in five damaged and disturbing tales of love gone horribly wrong. This collection is like a knife in the heart. Highly recommended!" – JONATHAN MABERRY, *New York Times* bestselling author of *Code Zero* and *Fall of Night*

GREY MATTER
P R E S S

greymatterpress.com

COMING SOON
FROM GREY MATTER PRESS

Before by Paul Kane

Little Black Spots by John F.D. Taff

Little Deaths: 5th Anniversary Edition by John F.D. Taff

The Madness of Crowds: The Ladies Bristol Occult Adventures #2 by Rhoads Brazos

MORE TITLES
FROM GREY MATTER PRESS

The Devil's Trill: The Ladies Bristol Occult Adventures #1 by Rhoads Brazos

Dark Visions: A Collection of Modern Horror - Volume One

Dark Visions: A Collection of Modern Horror - Volume Two

Death's Realm: The Anthology

Dread: The Best of Grey Matter Press - Volume One

The End in All Beginnings by John F.D. Taff

Equilibrium Overturned: A Volume of Apocalyptic Horrors

I Can Taste the Blood

Mister White: The Novel by John C. Foster

The Night Marchers and Other Strange Tales by Daniel Braum

Ominous Realities

Peel Back the Skin: Anthology of Horror

Savage Beasts

Secrets of the Weird by Chad Stroup

Seeing Double by Karen Runge

Splatterlands

RETURNING IN 2017
FROM GREY MATTER PRESS

The Bell Witch by John F.D. Taff

Kill/ Off by John F.D. Taff

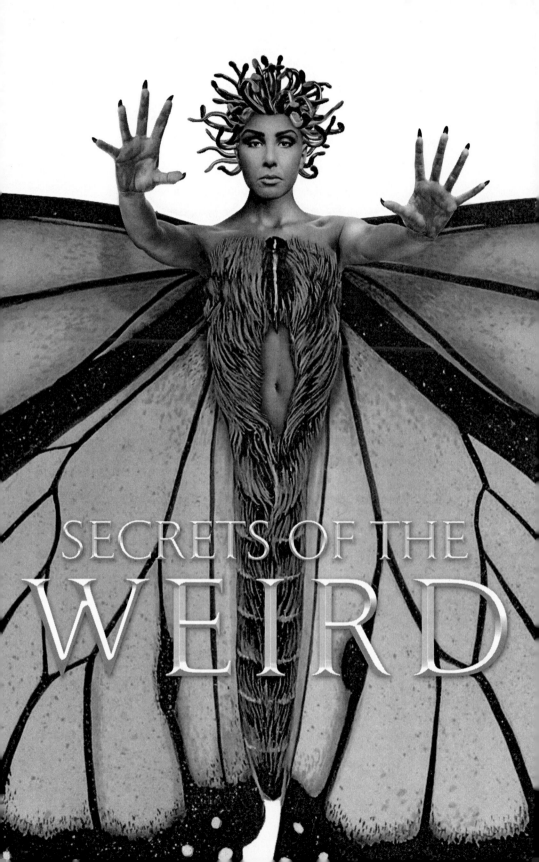